BEACH
WEDDING

BEACH WEDDING

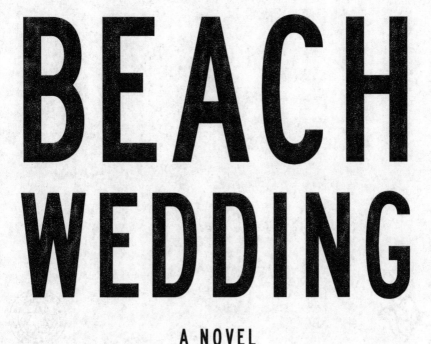

A NOVEL

MICHAEL LEDWIDGE

HANOVER
SQUARE
PRESS

HANOVER
SQUARE
PRESS™

Recycling programs
for this product may
not exist in your area.

ISBN-13: 978-1-335-42575-1

Beach Wedding

This edition published by arrangement with Harlequin Books S.A.

Hanover Square Press
22 Adelaide St. West, 41st Floor
Toronto, Ontario M5H 4E3, Canada
HanoverSqPress.com
BookClubbish.com

Printed in U.S.A.

BEACH
WEDDING

PROLOGUE

DREAM HOUSE

1

A gull circling in the sea breeze banked into a clumsy slide, then settled gently on the tallest of the beach mansion's brick chimneys like it wanted to be the weather vane.

At the far end of the back lawn where the sod became beach grass, I stood with my brother Tom, looking up at the massive castle-like structure, taking it all in.

At least trying to.

Tom, playing tour guide, had just explained that the Southampton summer dream house he'd rented was a proper traditional two-wing manor, built in the French Renaissance Revival style after a famous house of landed gentry outside of London. Past the sun terrace we'd just walked across, you could see the pool peeking out around the side of the thirty-thousand-square-foot house like a giant block of sapphire wrapped in travertine.

To say that Tom was a tour guide wasn't even an exaggeration, as the place was literally about the size of a museum.

"So?" Tom said. "What do you think?"

I turned away from the white elephant of a house and took a sip of my drink, studying the private staircase of weathered teak that dropped down the windy bluff at our back. I looked south to where the wood slat fence wound along the dunes, and beyond it, the Atlantic's infinite slate blue waves rose and curled and broke and crashed with a soft hiss as they washed up onto the private beach thirty steps below us.

Being from the poor man's Hamptons, Hampton Bays across the Shinnecock Inlet, Tom and I had been more of the to-the-split-level-born class. The only exclusive club we'd ever been members of was that of the hustling townie contingent. Up until now, the only times I'd ever gotten within spitting distance of these Southampton eight-figure beach castles was by working events as a busboy or a bartender or a valet. I'd never even dreamed of actually staying in one.

"What do I think of this beer?" I finally said, holding up my bottle. "Exceptional, Tom, really. What is it? Craft stuff? Head and shoulders above the cans of Miller Genuine Draft in my beer drawer back in Philly."

"Ha ha, dummy," Tom said, elbowing me. "C'mon, really. What do you think?"

I turned, studying my brother. Tom usually looked pretty pale and stressed from his 24/7 Wall Street pressure-cooker managerial duties at Emerald Crown Capital Partners, the hedge fund that he had started. But he'd already been out here for a couple of days, and it had done him a ton of good, I saw. My dark-haired brother looked actually sort of relaxed for once, tan and handsome and happy in his preppy red shorts and half-unbuttoned cream-colored linen shirt.

"What do I think?" I finally said. "What do you think I think? It's impossible, Tom. That's not a house. It looks like a Park Avenue apartment building. I mean, where is Zeus staying now that you rented his house? Summering in the South of France? No, wait. Visiting Poseidon?"

Tom slowly put an arm around my shoulders.

"Zeus is right here, Terry," he said, winking at me with a wide grin. "I am Zeus, come down to stand here with you stupid mortals. Right here before your very eyes."

"Yeah, right," I said, shouldering him away. "I remember all those times Zeus clipped his divine toenails into my Captain Crunch at the kitchen table like it was yesterday. And all the birthday punches. With one for good luck, too. Every time. The gods are so benevolent."

As my brother cracked up, I smiled and took another sip of my beer.

Because I felt happy, too, then. Or maybe *suddenly at ease* was a better way to describe it. Truth be told, I'd been a little reluctant to make the trip up from Philly and all the way back home after all these years.

Actually, more than a little.

Even with the fact that my oldest brother was finally tying the knot.

There are reasons why some people leave the place they were born and raised and never come back. Usually, they're very good reasons.

But maybe, I thought as I took in Tom and the billion-dollar scenery some more.

Maybe this wasn't such a big deal after all. Time had passed. Quite a bit of it. And didn't they say that time heals all wounds?

At least it wasn't a big deal as far as Tom was concerned, I realized.

Despite his new ginormous pockets, Tom was still just Tom. Tom, who used to let me ride back home on the handlebars of his ten-speed from Little League practice when I was a kid. Tom, who let me read his comic books as long as I kept them neatly in the plastic covers. Tom, who hit a kid who was bullying me in the head with a basketball from half-court in the schoolyard that time.

Just Tom, I thought, looking at him as the summer wind scattered some more expensive sand across the back of my pale neck and knees.

Only with a couple of specks of white in his black Irish hair now and more than a couple of extra zeros in his bank account.

"Okay, I'll bite," I said then. "Only because I know you're dying for me to ask. How much is it running you?"

"What? You mean with the staff and everything?" Tom said, comically wrinkling his brow.

Tom had already mentioned the chefs and the maids and the gardeners, and even the chauffeur and limo that the rental came with to heighten the full modern money-be-damned *Great Gatsby* experience.

"Yes, the whole kit and caboodle. Out with it, moneybags. How much?"

"Five," Tom said, staring at me calmly.

"Five? What do you mean? Five what?"

He looked at me again silently for a beat before I got it. If I hadn't already just swallowed my beer, I probably would have spit it all over him.

"That's impossible! Five hundred grand? Half a million dollars for the season?" I said in shock.

"Oh, no," my brother said, chuckling softly as he shook his head.

He gave me another wink as he brought his own beer to his lips.

"That's just for July, Terry," he said. "Just July."

2

"Just for July?" my wife, Vivian, said.

It was half an hour later, and we were upstairs in one of the mansion's dozen huge white-on-white Ralph Lauren photo shoot bedrooms.

It seemed like everything in the interior of the massive beach house was a blazing brilliant white. I'm talking everything. The ceilings, the walls, the couches, the intricate millwork, the slender Euro chairs.

And just when all the blazing whiteness wasn't done with you, your mind had to try to wrap itself around the size of the rooms. Because it just didn't compute. Even upstairs, the ceilings had to be fifteen feet high.

If the house were a museum, it was as if we now had the Egyptian section all to ourselves.

"Just for July?" Viv said for the second time.

"That's what the man said," I told her from where I was lazing back shirtless and barefoot in the center of a huge bed that had perhaps once belonged to Henry VIII or maybe Genghis Khan.

"But that's like—"

"Sixteen thousand one hundred and twenty-nine dollars," I said, having already done the math on my phone. "A day."

"Oh, my goodness! How? How, Terry?" Viv said in a frantic whisper as she carefully closed the top drawer of the priceless-looking white bureau she was unpacking our stuff into.

I smiled over at my wife. Just out of the Carrara marble cave of the shower, she was in a fluffy bathrobe, her golden blond hair up in a towel. She was six months pregnant with our second kid, and the bathrobe in the front was having its work cut out for it.

"Tom's this rich?" she said, waving around some electric hair wand thing at our soaring royal slumber chamber. "But this is like billionaire rich, right? I mean, is he on the *Forbes* list now? Wouldn't your mom have told us? She sends us the link every time he's on CNBC."

"Hey, who knows?" I said, leaning even farther back into the posh wilderness of throw pillows with a yawn. "Maybe it's business or something. Maybe he needs to impress his Wall Street buddies and clients. How many people are going to be at this wedding? What did my sister say? Three hundred?"

"Four hundred and fifty," Viv said, biting at a nail.

"Four hundred and fifty? That's not a wedding, that's a college graduation ceremony! We had what?"

"Fifty-four maybe?" my wife said with a shrug.

"Exactly! A human amount of people. My goodness. Four hundred and fifty. I told you Tom is crazy. But I guess he knows what he's doing. At least I hope so. In the meantime, I have no problem playing along. Pass the champagne and lobster, lovey darling, would you?"

"We're out of champagne, my liege, but will this do?" my

wife said, removing a bottle of the superb craft beer Tom had introduced me to upon our arrival from a mini fridge beside the writing desk in the corner.

Tom really had thought of everything, I realized as I settled the cold soothing glass over my belly button.

"Do you think the car is parked okay where it is?" Viv said, frowning toward the sliding doors of the suite's ocean-view terrace.

"It's fine, Viv. I'm sure the staff buried our Honda CR-V *real* deep," I said as I cracked open the beer with the opener Viv handed me.

"I'm sure they've been around the block a time or two," I said after a cold sip. "They must know that sometimes the have-nots arrive from the lower classes. I'm sure these frightfully embarrassing things happen from time to time."

I laughed as Viv stuck her pretty little tongue out at me.

What was really funny was that right at that moment as I lay there, I actually was quite content with my life. I had a great, beautiful wife of five years. We had the world's cutest three-year-old daughter, Angelina, sleeping in the adjoining room, along with another kid (that I was hoping hard was a boy) on the way.

As the lead sergeant of the Philly police department's busiest street crime squad, I even had a challenging, exciting, meaningful day job.

I was thirty-nine, happy and healthy, with good hard-charging work to do and several drop-dead cute someones to love. I mean, what the heck else in the world was there?

But I understood where Viv was coming from. I, too, being one of those mere mortals with a less than seven-figure-a-year salary, had thought I might feel envious or competitive or at least somewhat insecure about Tom's Southampton wedding extravaganza.

But as I sat way back on the California king-size bed, handcrafted probably from some special species of thousand-year-old endangered wood, I was suddenly oddly cool with it.

19

This was Tom's life, I decided, lazing there like an extra in an overpriced perfume commercial. We were just visiting. There was beer and sunshine. It was fine.

I was just going to roll with it, I decided, sipping some more beer to help in the flowing of the power of now.

"Wait. When are the others getting here? This afternoon, right? Your mother, too?" Vivian said a moment later, insisting on ruining my chi.

For his wedding, Tom had invited everyone in my sprawling Irish-American family to stay here together for a Rourke family reunion. And I mean all of us. Three generations were going to be playing millionaire beach house together for the next several out-of-control roller-coaster weeks.

"Yeah, my mom texted when you were in the shower," I said. "They're coming around four. Stop worrying. By the way, how's Miss Snuggle Bunny Princess? Did you check on her? You need to. If she gets out of her room and starts wandering around the halls of Hogwarts here, we may never find her again."

"Don't worry. She's still sleeping. She's wiped out after that crawl up 95. You have to see her in her bed, like the princess and the pea. It's so awesome that Tom gave us this jack-and-jill setup."

"Exactly. It's all awesome. Now you're getting it. Stop worrying."

"I'm worrying!" my wife cried, letting slip a little of the South Philly Italian moxie that occasionally soundtracked our whirlwind romance. "What about you?"

I patted at the bed beside me.

"Come on, would you?" I said. "Stop making sense and come up here, Jill. Jack needs you up here on the hill."

3

"Look, Daddy! Mermaids!" my daughter, Angelina, shrieked later that afternoon as we were outside at the pool.

And what a pool. Like the over-the-top house, the marble man-made lake was something out of old pre-income-tax Hollywood. There were two diving boards and art deco sea-blue tiles. Even the pool house way down on the other end from where we were sitting was white marble with Doric columns and Greek temple steps. I stared out at it, waiting for Clark Gable to emerge onto the stairs whipping at Katharine Hepburn with a beach towel.

When Clark didn't show, I repositioned myself down another travertine step in the pool and exchanged a smile with Viv, who was sitting behind me on a chaise reading a paperback. Then I sidled over a little next to my daughter as she stuck her goggled face back into the water to get another look at the mosaic-tiled mermaids that lined the massive walls.

"Mermaids!" she cried again when she came up for air.

"You keep saying that. Wait a second. I know! You must be a mermaid, too!" I yelled.

Angelina stared at me wide-eyed through her goggles, then leaned in close to my ear.

"Yes," she whispered. "I am."

"I knew it," I whispered back. "Are the mermaids on the wall pictures of you?"

Again, she gave me her wide imagination-filled eyes.

"I'll go see," she said, sticking her face back under.

"Well?" I said when she came back up.

She shook her head.

"No? Not you? Then who are they?" I said.

"They're...my little sisters!" she said, splashing at the water.

"Sisters, huh?" I said, frowning over at Viv, who looked up from her book with a grin and a nod of superiority.

"What about brothers?" I said hopefully. "Do mermaids have any handsome and helpful little brothers that they like to swim with?"

"Yuck, Daddy. Don't you know anything? Boys can't be mermaids," she said as Viv chuckled.

"Laugh it up, Viv," I said. "While you can. I'm betting that we're going to be evening up the odds around here very soon."

My wife and I were still exchanging eye rolls when I spotted Tom coming toward us down the courthouse-like steps of the mansion's side entrance. As he started across the gargantuan green plain of the lawn, I could see he had changed out of his play clothes and was wearing a pin-striped navy suit, his dark hair slicked back now, his easy smile very white against his tan.

Speaking of Clark Gable, I thought.

"Well, I'm off to the city for a little while, so you'll have the

22

run of the place," he said as he waved at Angelina from the pool's ornate wrought-iron gate.

"No, you're leaving?" I said as I hopped out of the water and came across the glowing limestone.

"That stinks, Tom. Do you have to?" Vivian said as she got into the pool next to Angelina.

"Something came up at the office. Can't be helped." He shrugged.

I didn't even want to know what that meant. I'd been to Tom's Midtown office once before, and his desktop looked like his own personal Pentagon war room with three blinking screens that he stared at all day. The dizzying array of constantly changing multicolored graphs looked like some kind of impossibly advanced mathematics video game.

I didn't know how the hell he did it. Whatever it was that he actually did.

"I'll be back by dinner. At least hopefully," he said, checking his fancy steel wristwatch that probably cost more than my hatchback.

"Hey, I'll walk you up," I said, opening the pool's heavy gate with a creak.

The Yankee Stadium outfield of just-watered meticulously cut grass that we walked across was pleasantly cool under my bare feet after the sun-warmed pool stone.

There was an elaborate coffered arch built through the bottom of the house's north wing, and as we arrived on the other side, a shining black Mercedes was coming to a stop in the circular drive.

Was it an SUV? A limo? A bit of both? Whatever it was, when it stopped, a uniformed chauffeur quickly got out and opened its back door.

"Exactly what movie are we in right now?" I said to my brother with a laugh. "Is it *Trading Places*, or no, it's *Wall Street*, right? Greed is good?"

"Very funny, bro. Listen up now," Tom said, putting a hand on my shoulder. "I hate to bug you, but you know everybody is coming this afternoon. Mom and all the rest of them. So, could you meet and greet and get everybody to their rooms for me? If I'm running late, make sure Robin, the house manager, and the rest of the staff take care of all of you for dinner."

"Oh, I see," I said. "I'm supposed to explain all this Palace of Versailles stuff to Mom and somehow keep her from hyperventilating? Are you really sure you have to go to work?"

"Shut up, dummy, and listen," he said. "I already spoke to the chef, Freddy. This dude's ridiculous. From Per Se or French Laundry or one of those places. He's going to hook us up big-time. So, make sure you get everybody in their Sunday best, okay? Robin is also a sommelier and knows the massive wine cellar, so you have at it. Mom especially might need a glass or two. I'll try to get back before the first course."

"Tom," I said, suddenly unable to stifle my laughter as I gestured at the elaborate mansion and chauffeur, "I knew you were rich, bro, but really? You're like *this* rich? Scrooge McDuck rich?"

Tom smiled at me as we stood along the edge of the crushed seashell driveway. He shot his cuffs and looked like he was about to pinch my cheek but then stopped himself.

"Let's see," he said, taking out his phone and glancing at it. "Am I this rich? Well, it's not like it's nothing, but I wanted it to be a special occasion, Terry. I mean, how many times am I going to get married? Wait. Forget I said that. Don't answer."

I pretended to zip my mouth shut.

"Ha ha. Besides, how many times am I going to get to stick it to old you-know-who a few houses up the road here?" Tom said, jerking a thumb to the north up the beach with a sudden crazy twinkle in his eye.

I slowly looked over at him, stunned. Then took a step back.

"What? Don't tell me you're surprised," Tom said.

I stood there mute, the seashells under my feet suddenly sharp, like little bits of broken glass.

His own smile vanished as he stared me right in the eye.

"Terry, honestly," he said. "You out of everyone I thought would figure it out. Did you think I picked Meadow Lane out of a hat?"

4

I stood there in the July heat looking at my brother.

In some unfortunate Irish families, there are sons who are referred to as holy terrors. Overflowing with impulsive energy and a fly-by-the-seat-of-your-pants mischievousness that borders on performance art, like most natural-born pirates, they often end up dead, in jail, or rich. Tom was the Rourke family's holy terror, but we'd thought that Wall Street could contain his bottomless energy.

Maybe we were wrong, I thought as all my dread of coming home instantly landed like an uppercut to the jaw.

Because I knew it then. What this was *really* about. Why we were here. Why this house. Why his wedding was on Southampton's most expensive beach road.

The Rourke family actually had a history with Meadow Lane.

And it wasn't a happy one.

Quite the opposite.

"Are we really going there, Tom?" I finally said. "After all this time?"

"Oh, we're going there, Terry," he whispered as he reached over and grabbed the back of my head, pulling me closer to him.

As our foreheads met, I caught a whiff of his expensive cologne, a masculine perfume of mint and lemons and spiced wood and fresh money. Up close, I could see the twinkle was even brighter now. It looked like it was about to shoot out of his left eye like a spark from a spitting road flare.

"For twenty years, I've slaved forty hours a day for this, Terry," he said, "and we're going there big-time for the rest of the month with barrel bombs of white phosphorus and flaming napalm."

"Now, Tom, listen. Be reasonable, man," I said calmly. "What do you have planned?"

"Oh, you know," he said with a shrug as he slipped his phone back into the pink silk that lined his glove-fit Savile Row suit jacket. "The usual. A fireworks barge. Helicopters. A couple of marching bands. Then there's the horses, of course."

"What!" I cried.

He winked again.

Was he serious?

I shook my head as I scanned his tanned poker face. There was no way to tell.

"Terry, I'm going to do anything and everything I can think of to block up traffic and to piss off every one of these rotten bastards up and down this little sandbar. I'm going to let them know, especially old you-know-who, that we lowly Rourkes can get knocked down, but my oh my, can we get back up again."

"But, Tom," I said, peering at him. "What about the consequences? You know, the authorities? Cops, lawyers, injunctions from the town, getting sued? All that kind of stuff?"

"Hey, that's where you come in, little brother. We've got a boy in blue right here in the family. Keep that badge handy."

I squinted at him.

"Right, like my tin badge from Philly is going to fly in the billionaire Village of Southampton? Are you feeling okay? Tom, listen, we're grown up now. Please, I have a kid. Don't bring on the dancing horses, Tom. Don't be nuts. Just this one time. For me. I'm begging you."

"Ah, no worries, Terry," Tom said, his unhinged pirate grin suddenly ear to ear as he headed for his limo. "Revenge, er, I mean, fun, will be had by all."

5

I didn't know how the house staff managed to get the entire twenty-strong Rourke clan at one outdoor table that night, but somehow, they pulled it off.

Beside me and Viv and Angelina on one side of the long table were my sister, Erin, and her husband, Nick Murray, with their three grade-schoolers, Kevin and Billy and Megan.

Facing on the other side were my brother Mickey and his wife, Jo, and their four kids, Caitlin and Patrick and Dermot and Geraldine, who ranged in age from four to eleven.

Beside Mickey was my other brother Finn, along with his wife, Stephanie, and their two kids, Scott, who was nine, and Evelyn, who was seven.

My seventy-year-old mom, Rosemarie, sat at the end of the table, and at the head sat the man of the hour, the groom-to-be, Tom Rourke himself, who had managed to get back from the office just in time.

So far, so good, I thought, wiping my face with my napkin and placing it down beside the stripped remains of the most tender and delicious rack of lamb my mouth had ever had the good fortune to encounter.

I swirled my just-topped-off purply black glass of Bordeaux and had another sip. As I closed my eyes, the complex hints and notes of all the wonderful things the house manager and sommelier, Robin, had told me earlier to be on the lookout for (but I had immediately forgotten) tingled along taste buds I didn't even know I possessed until that very moment.

Yes, I thought, opening my eyes as I leaned back. I looked around at my family, at the mansion behind them lit up like a temple in a dream against the night.

All things considered, even after Tom's troubling revelation, so far Rourke Reunion Arrival Day was coming off pretty sweet.

"Excuse me, everyone! Excuse me! I'd like to propose a toast," Tom said, suddenly standing, as the last of the dinner plates was expertly whisked away by the white-jacketed house staff.

Everybody was still laughing and talking and hardly heard him until our mom, Rosemarie, rang a crystal glass with some silver.

"Mickey and Finn, would you close your mouths or do I have to come down there with my slipper?" she said in her Northern Irish brogue.

We all laughed at that, remembering the road trips to East Durham in the Catskills, where one of Mom's crazy brothers ran a ramshackle resort. In the era before stun guns, Mom had quieted the back-seat brawls of her four hooligan boys with the prodigious use of a slipper she kept handy in her lap for smacking us back to our senses.

"Why, thank you, Mother," Tom said, laughing. "I had actually hoped you'd packed that slipper. We may very well need it before all of this is said and done. All joking aside, first I'd like to thank all of you for arranging your schedules to come out to celebrate my upcoming wedding."

"What wedding? There's no bride," Finn said. "Is this all a hoax?"

"Exactly," Erin said. "When do we get to finally meet her?"

"Soon. I promise. Very soon," Tom said, smiling. "Introducing her to the likes of you is a very delicate operation that requires perfect timing. I've waited quite some time to tie the knot, so I don't want to mess things up at the last moment. The trap is set. I can't blow it now."

High-spirited laughter and Bronx cheers abounded until Rosemarie gonged at the Waterford crystal again.

"Seriously, though, I love you guys," Tom said, as he looked down the table. "I really do. Every last one of you. I can't describe how happy it makes me feel after all this time to see us all at the same table again."

We all actually did quiet down at that.

Because we knew how much it came from his heart.

After our dad died, Tom pretty much took his place. When he wasn't working roofing or restaurant jobs, he was going to night school to get his MBA. Gave every one of his paychecks to Mom. Never complained about it. Not once. Wasn't in him. People talk about manning up. Tom did it. Without a peep.

"That's why I rented this place for us," Tom continued. "I wanted to bring you all back here together to share in the good fortune God has shared with me. I wanted us to come back here to this place where we lived and worked and grew up together. I did it so we could put all our worries aside—if only for a few weeks—to look back and to truly realize what a wonderful and beautiful place Mom and Dad raised us in."

"That's so sweet, Tom," said my sister, Erin, in the silence.

"No. Honestly. That's why I did this. If I'm sorry about anything, it's that Dad isn't here with us," Tom said. "He would have gotten a kick out of this, I think. I wish he was here to see that, well, I really did listen to him. That I absorbed everything he taught me. I wish he had known that. I know at times I worried him."

"Tom," my mother said, her eyes near tears. "Please. Don't be so hard on yourself. He knew."

A moment later, we turned as Robin came out onto the deck with two waiters carrying drinks on a tray.

I noticed the wineglasses weren't filled with wine but beer. Even before one was set down before me, I knew which kind.

It was Pabst Blue Ribbon, our dad's favorite.

"So, if you guys would stand and raise a glass with me," Tom said as he turned and faced the ocean.

We all stood and followed his lead with glasses of our father's signature drink raised out toward the sea. The table was completely silent now. The only sounds were the wind and the waves beyond in the dark.

I looked around the table at the candlelight flickering off the tear-filled faces of my brothers and sister and my mom.

"Thank you, Dad. We love you," Tom called out to the dark, softly rushing water. "Rest in peace, Dad. I got this. We all got this now. You really can rest in peace."

"Amen," I whispered in the dark as Viv squeezed my other hand.

6

We woke up the next morning and headed out early for bagels in the village. There was, of course, a huge breakfast buffet set up at the house, but this morning, I had something important to do.

"Where are we now, Mommy?" Angelina called out from her car seat behind me as we pulled onto the Montauk Highway.

"We're going to see where Daddy grew up," Viv said.

"This is so boring," my daughter whispered around the straw of her juice pack, and we laughed.

Ten minutes later, I pulled over five blocks in from Shinnecock Bay on a quiet narrow street in the Hampton Bays.

And puffed out a long nervous breath.

I put the transmission in Park and sat looking at 167 Donellan

Street. Its bay window, my mom's favorite cherry blossom trees still there in the front yard. To the left was the strike-zone panel on the garage door that we threw things at all childhood long. Tennis balls, Spaldings, Wiffle balls. I couldn't believe how tiny the split-level looked.

It was the first time I'd been back to my old house since high school. After my dad died, I went to Villanova on a track scholarship and majored in journalism, and basically stayed there. After freshman year, I didn't come home for Thanksgiving or even for Christmas, and I spent summers working and living at school.

I'd meet my mom and family in Manhattan from time to time, but for whatever reason, I couldn't come all the way back.

But that wasn't really true.

I actually *did* know the reason.

My dad's death when I was seventeen had hurt too much, and I just couldn't face it, face my mom, all that pain, that loss.

And I used that excuse for all it was worth.

I spent the summer of my junior year interning as a crime reporter doing ride-alongs with the Philly PD. Once I graduated, I decided why report on crime when I could actually fight it? And one cop test later, that was all she wrote.

"Okay, we saw it, Daddy. Now it's beach time, right?" Angelina said.

I looked back at her, smiling. She was geared up to go swimming again, already in her bathing suit and matching pink star-shaped sunglasses.

"Soon," Viv said. "Did you eat your bagel?"

"Well," she said. "Most of it."

"What about Tina?" I said, referring to Angelina's imaginary friend who had decided to come on vacation with us. "Did Tina eat hers?"

"She has a little bit left, Daddy. Tina, finish up now, please," Angelina whispered.

34

I exchanged a smile with Viv.

During last night's feast, I'd been planning to mention to her the unsettling conversation I'd had with my brother, but as the amazing courses and wine flowed, I hadn't gotten around to it.

I looked back at my old house.

Probably because I was still attempting to process it myself.

"So, this is it. Where it all began," Viv said, taking off her own sunglasses.

"Picture if you will, Viv, four crazy little freckled boys in increasing size and one crazy little freckle-faced girl, slapping hockey pucks at each other, climbing trees, playing football, and daring each other to do wheelies up and down this driveway and street here.

"Then further picture the sudden screams and many hurried trips to the hospital for broken fingers, ankles, and stitches in our trusty brown Buick Electra station wagon, piloted at panicked speed by the intrepid Rosemarie Rourke."

As we sat there, I remembered the roaring sound of Dad's little rattletrap MG as he came in from work or shanghaied one of us for a trip to the hardware store.

"Now, please fasten your seat belts and keep all extremities inside the vehicle," I said, trying to keep my voice steady. "Day in the life of a Hamptons townie, location two, coming right up."

7

A silver, streaking LIRR commuter train hammered southbound across the railroad bridge over North Main Street behind us as we arrived before a two-story sun-faded brick building back in Southampton ten minutes later.

"Ladies and gentlegirls, may I have your attention?" I said, gesturing expansively at the building. "Behold, Our Lady of the Hamptons, the old alma mater. This schoolyard here was the site of many Rourke knee-skinnings, bullyings—both as victim and perpetrator—and truly bewildered nuns. This is also the former location and frequent parking spot of the aforementioned brown Buick Electra as our ever-suffering mother, Rosemarie, was called in to try to plead down the latest Rourke act of mischief. As our *D-A-U-G-H-T-E-R* is present, I can't even go into what Tom did there when he was raising the flag on the roof pole one time when he was in eighth grade."

"I can see you in your little red plaid tie from your class picture," Viv said excitedly. "My goodness, were you cute."

"Where were you when I needed you, Viv?" I said, cordially kissing her hand. "As hard as it might be to believe, the nuns, as well as the other girls in my class whom I often terrorized, did not share your most excellent taste."

"Where's your high school? Nearby? Bishop what was it called?"

"Bishop McGann Mercy. No, that's in Riverhead. Let's skip it. I certainly did as often as I could."

"Oh, boy," Viv said as I swung a U-turn back for the train underpass. "Where to now?"

"No, no. It's a surprise. You'll see," I said.

Ten minutes later and six miles to the northeast back in the Bays, the power-line buzz of a cicada started up as I stopped the car and rolled down the window. I folded my arms, smiling out at a patch of faded asphalt parking lot behind the Southampton town police department.

The things we remember, I thought, looking at weeds growing along its edges. The little things that once seemed so important.

I gestured out again at a small utilitarian building beside the police department.

"This, Viv, as you can see by that sign yonder, is the Southampton town justice court, where Dad used to work and where Mom would drive us once a week to make him watch us after school while she went food shopping. Picture epic games of catch out in this parking lot here, and a crazed-looking man in a tie feeding bologna sandwiches to his five hungry plaid-clad kids under that tree there where there used to be a picnic table."

"Probably removed to the Smithsonian for its crazy Long Island suburban family diorama," Viv said.

"See, Viv. Now you're getting it," I said, peeling back out of the lot. "Okay, now for the real juicy part."

A few minutes later, we pulled off Halsey Neck Road back onto Meadow Lane at the beach.

But instead of making a right back toward Tom's beach mansion, I took another nervous breath and hit the left clicker and headed north in the direction of where my brother had gestured the day before.

8

Hedges suddenly appeared on both sides of the sandy road. Big, boxy manicured hedges, high and thick and intensely dark green, separated at generous intervals by tall white wooden gates.

As I drove, I suddenly remembered how my buddies from high school used to call this section of hedge-lined road the Canyon of Zeros. Zeros, not as in losers, but as in the nine you needed in your bank account to afford living in one of its privacy shrub–bordered beach houses.

After about three and a half miles, I slowed and stopped on the right-hand shoulder of the sun-faded blacktop. There was a thin gap in the hedge to our right, and through it, down a hopelessly elegant slope of lawn, one could just make out the hard, razor-sharp roofline of a vast modern glass house against the ocean.

Staring at it, I thought about rolling down the window, but then thought twice and just turned up the AC instead.

The many-winged house, built by some famous architect in the early sixties, looked more like some kind of school or corporate park building, I knew. I had looked it up on Google Maps once, and from the air, the glass box structure on the landmark estate almost looked like a giant question mark.

How ironic, I thought as I lifted my iced coffee and silently peered at the roof's tempered blue glass edge.

Because it was a question all right.

The question was:

Why the hell did I decide to come back home after all this time?

"That's it? That's her house?" Viv said.

"Yep. That's it. They call it *the* Glass House around here. Very famous. And why not? After all, it's where *the* end began. You know the rest, Viv. Okay, end of tour," I said as I dropped the coffee back into the cup holder and went to put the car in Drive again.

"Oh, no. No way," Viv said, grabbing my wrist. "We're here now, Terry. You've been carrying this stuff with you so long you can't even see how it eats at you. Get it out. All of it. Once and for all. I want to hear the story in a straight line. From your own mouth. Right here, right now."

"I've told you a million times," I said.

"Never from beginning to end. And never all of it."

"Come on, Viv. We need to get back."

I saw a hardness enter Viv's pretty caramel-colored eyes.

"Tell it, Terry," she said. "Get it off your chest. Tell it now."

What an idiot I was to dredge all this up, I thought as I looked over at my wife with a quickly building annoyance.

But she only stared back at me steadily.

I looked at the house again through the hedge. Then I looked back at Angelina, who had fallen asleep. I envied her.

That's when it happened.

All of it started coming back.

As I sat there, more than twenty years disappeared, and I started to recall everything.

Why I had gone away to college in Philadelphia. Why I had never come back. Why even now I was reluctant to be here.

"Tell me from the beginning, Terry," my wife said. "Tell me the whole thing."

I looked out at the sunlight starbursting off the glass roof edge of the beach house, off the ocean in the distance.

Then I began to remember it.

The very worst memory of my life.

PART ONE

PARTY LIKE IT'S 1999

9

July 4, 1999, fell on a Sunday, and like every Sunday that summer, I was outside in my driveway drenched in sweat.

It was a little after two thirty in the afternoon as I dribbled the basketball in front of my garage on Donellan Street. The ball was a faded orange Wilson with rib lines all but worn away, and the smashing ring of it off the asphalt only ceased when I turned and leapt up to make it whisper through the rim with a perfect shot.

I was on a roll that muggy afternoon. I drained everything, hook shots from the baseline, impossible three-pointers from the corner.

Sundays in the summer were my one day off from my lifeguarding job at the Beach Point Country Club in Amagansett, and I was still out there in the heat when I heard some music. As it got louder, I turned and then had to fly off to my left into the rhododendrons to avoid the car swinging hard into our driveway.

The car—or boat, as we called it—was a 1979 Cadillac Cabriolet Deville, black with a bloodred interior. Behind its wheel, listening to some vintage Guns N' Roses, was my brother Tom's best friend and my sister Erin's on-again, off-again boyfriend, Nick Murray.

Nick, like Tom, was a bit of a town legend. Always the first to throw a party or a punch, he was a tall and lively and athletic townie who always had some sort of moneymaking scheme going on, restoring cars, painting houses, playing poker. He'd gone for a year on a basketball scholarship to Seton Hall but had come home after he'd punched out one of the assistant coaches.

We'd gotten along pretty well when we were younger, but I still hadn't forgiven him for not so helpfully lifting me up at a high school dance in freshman year in front of a tall girl I was talking to so that, as Nick very unhelpfully put it, "we could talk eye to eye."

So, when he rolled in, I casually dribbled the ball between my legs, doing my best to pretend I didn't notice how amazingly badass he looked in his long black car.

"Hey, where the hell is your damn brother?" Nick said as Slash tore into a solo.

"What's that?" I said and dribbled again, studiously ignoring the obvious urgency on Nick's face. We both watched as the ball hit off my heel and disappeared into the rhododendrons.

"Smooth," Nick said as I retrieved the ball.

I suddenly noticed what Nick was wearing. He was in a white shirt and black pants complete with a black tie. Since Nick's wardrobe usually consisted of AC/DC and Metallica and Slayer concert T-shirts that showed off his extremely jacked arms, the getup was definitely a switch for him.

"You feeling okay, idiot? Hello? Wake up. Your brother.

Where is he?" Nick said as he jumped out of the music-blasting ragtop without opening the door.

"Oh, Tom? Yeah, I heard he went down to the Jersey Shore last night with some girl he met at the Boardy Barn. Something like that. That's what Mickey said."

Nick threw up his hands.

"The Jersey Shore! That jackass. He promised me! I'm going to be so screwed."

"What's up?" I said.

10

"What's up is Tom said he would help me out with something," Nick said with his hands now clapped to his head. "I promised Denny I would come through for him and now what? He's going to kick my ass."

Denny was Denny Milton, a shady guy who was probably the biggest crook in the Hampton Bays. Even I knew he was a bookie. One who owned several delis and three liquor stores and a rowdy bayside bar. Some people said Denny was a loan shark and coke dealer, too, which sounded very believable.

"Where's Finn or Mickey?" Nick asked.

"Gone, too, dude. They went fishing with Dad and Uncle Jack early this morning. Blues are biting."

"Things are biting all right," Nick said.

I actually felt a little sorry for him. No way anyone wanted to be on the bad side of Denny Milton, who stood about six foot three or four and easily weighed three hundred pounds.

"Everybody, and I mean everybody, is gone. What am I going to do?" he said to himself, shaking his head.

Then he finally looked at me with a quizzical look on his face.

"Hey, wait. How old are you now?" he said.

"Gonna be eighteen. Next week," I said.

My birthday was actually in five months, but who was counting.

"Seventeen," he said, peering at me.

He finally began to nod.

"No choice. Screw it," he said. "Okay, punk. How would you like to make, oh, four or five hundred bucks?"

"What?" I said, smiling, suddenly forgetting to act tough. Five hundred bucks was what I made in two weeks. Then I frowned when I thought of Denny Milton.

"What do I have to do?" I said.

"Everything I tell you. I have a very intense catering gig, and I need somebody with arms and legs to bar back for me."

Bar backing! I'd actually done it once at an Italian place in Southampton Village where I used to wash dishes. It was fun as hell. Bars meant sneaking beers and, even better, tipsy hot older chicks everywhere.

Nick looked at his watch.

"You have exactly five minutes to shower and get your ass back out here in black pants, black shoes, and a white dress shirt."

I ran for the door.

"And grab Tom's black tie!" Nick yelled. "I bought him one last time, and he still hasn't paid me back, the son of a—"

But I was already inside, tearing off my clothes, running toward the shower.

"What are you up to now?" my mother, Rosemarie, called

in her Northern Irish accent from the living room, where she was doing the ironing while watching an old black-and-white war movie.

"Work!" I yelled as I turned on the shower in the hall bathroom. "Nick's outside. Tom was supposed to help him at a catering job. Nick needs my help."

"He's going to take you?" I heard my mom say. "Wow, he must be desperate."

"Gee, Mom, thanks," I said and slammed the door.

In three minutes flat, I was out of the shower and in front of my dresser mirror in my *Reservoir Dogs* outfit, putting a little gel in my cropped sandy hair that I'd gotten cut a few days before.

I looked at my slate blue eyes just like my dad's. I had a kind of stubble thing going on, so I didn't bother shaving.

I can pass for twenty, I thought.

Maybe.

Then I heard the Caddy's horn honk, and I flew out the door.

11

My Sunday has just taken one heck of a turn, I thought with a smile as I sat back in the soft leather passenger seat of Nick's bouncing and gliding black Cadillac.

"So, where we going?" I said just as we got onto the Montauk Highway.

"Shut up," Nick said as he spun the wheel and we pulled into the lot of Beachhouse Liquors and Spirits.

"Hey, isn't this Denny Milton's liquor store?" I said.

"Get the wax out of your ears. Don't you say a damn word, you hear me?" Nick said as he wove the Caddy around back into the loading area.

Denny's store manager, some tall long-haired old pothead

named Alex, was at the low concrete loading dock's back door, waiting for us as Nick pulled to a hard stop.

"Hey, who's the kid? I thought you said Tom was helping you," the hippie said in greeting.

"It's his brother," Nick said as we hopped out.

"No, it isn't. I know his brother, Mickey. I busted him for fake IDs all last summer."

"Hello? Tom's Irish, remember? This is his other brother."

"You've got to be kidding. How old is he?"

"Nineteen," Nick lied.

"Nineteen, my ass," Alex said. "Denny know about this?"

"What the hell do you think?" Nick said in an awed subdued way that suggested he wouldn't dare to breathe without Denny's go-ahead.

"Okay. Whatever," Alex said, handing him a clipboard. "As long as Denny knows."

Nick mounted the concrete steps in a single bound and grabbed a hand truck and then passed me another.

"Yeah, screw Denny," Nick said to me under his breath as we went through a doorway into the hot, dim storage room. "What Denny doesn't know won't hurt him."

Going off the clipboard, we quickly started loading up the Caddy and the liquor store's beat-up delivery van with boxes of booze.

I started to wonder what kind of party this would be as we did four and then five full hand truck runs back and forth from the storage room to the vehicles. In minutes, I was sweating my ass off again.

But even after we humped out about thirty heavy cases, we weren't done. Nick led me back into the storage room's walk-in cooler and we rolled out not one but two ice-cold barrels of fun courtesy of the Heineken company.

After we laboriously got everything up into the van, Alex came back out and carefully double-checked all the boxes off the clipboard to see that we hadn't tossed in a few extra cases on a five-fingered discount.

As Alex finally went back inside and closed the door, Nick looked at me and then at the van and the Caddy, trying to decide.

He finally fished out his Caddy keys from his black jeans and reluctantly handed them to me.

"We're heading over to Meadow Lane, okay, moron?" he said. "You follow me. Very, very carefully. Because if you put one little scratch on her—"

12

A minute later, after I slipped on a pair of Ray-Bans I found in the glove box, I was out on the Montauk Highway, rolling in Nick's booze-filled Caddy, looking around for anyone I knew to hopefully see how incredibly cool I suddenly was.

Because of this, I was a tad late to see Nick's brake lights on the liquor van ahead, and the Caddy's brakes shrieked as I slammed a foot down on them just in time.

I smiled sheepishly at Nick staring at me in the van's side-view mirror with a look like he was about to come out swinging.

I got this, I mouthed at him as I gave him a calm thumbs-up.

We got on Halsey Neck Road and then made a left onto Meadow Lane's beach road and began driving by the money-green high hedges. A couple of miles north, we slowed behind a small traffic jam of cars as a truck, a massive 18-wheeler, tried to pull in through one of the narrow hedge gates.

The driver was having some issues. He was going back and forth, trying to figure out how to get his big rig through the hedge wall and down the slope of the seashell drive without flipping the whole thing over.

As we waited, Nick got out of the van and came over.

"Hey, dummy," he said as he took the Ray-Bans off me. "You didn't crack it up. Or at least not yet. Good job."

"What's up with the tractor trailer?" I said as I looked beyond the hedge we were parked beside. "Wait a second. Whose house is this? No! Is this...? No...! *The* Glass House?"

"Yes," Nick said. "Yes, *it* is."

"Noah Sutton's place?" I said. "No way! We're working a fricking Noah Sutton party?"

Nick nodded.

And my jaw dropped.

Because even I knew who Noah Sutton was.

Often called the Kennedys of the tristate area, the Suttons were a very large, rich and powerful, photogenic family who wielded massive amounts of political juice from the Jersey Shore to the Connecticut side of the Sound to the tip of Montauk.

There was a senator from New Jersey, a congressman who represented Greenwich, Connecticut, and two other congress-men from tony Westchester, one of whom was reportedly being groomed to run for president.

And just like their doppelgängers, the Kennedy clan from Boston, the Suttons were often getting into hot water.

Every six months or so in the tabloids, it seemed one of the Suttons was OD'ing or getting divorced or getting their pants sued off for paternity by angry pregnant nannies.

Most recently, I'd seen at the supermarket checkout line that one of the Sutton cousins, a young doctor from Palm Beach,

Florida, who looked like a soap actor, had just beaten a sexual assault charge lodged by one of his patients.

But the house we were waiting to get into belonged to the Hamptons Suttons. There were four of them. Nelson Sutton in Sagaponack, Henry Sutton in Amagansett, Brooke Sutton in Sag Harbor, and Noah Sutton here in Southampton.

The four siblings were the most demure and apparently richest branch of the Sutton clan. The family business was some huge private chemical company called Cold Springs Chemical that their father, Stephen, had acquired in the sixties.

Cold Springs Chemical had something to do with the processing of oil. Or was it medicine? Fertilizer? All three? I wasn't really sure.

Whatever it was, this Hamptons branch of the Sutton family wasn't really involved in politics and never seemed to die on ski slopes or kill other people like their cousins up and down the Eastern Seaboard.

What the Hamptons Suttons were mostly known for around town was shelling out major bucks to local charities and causes. The spring before, they'd donated a whopping ten million to the town to create a new football field and science wing at the high school.

They were also known for throwing the biggest, most spectacular soirees of the summer. Their specialty was extravagant old-money-style affairs like polo matches and yacht races.

Noah especially.

He was the handsomest of all the handsome Suttons. He had blond hair and a bit of a James Dean thing going on, about as cool as you could get for a rich privileged fop. They said he had been begged to run for office by his political cousins repeatedly but refused. Why would he? Why run for office when you were already the world's most interesting man?

Noah was especially popular with all the pretty society people, as well as the Hollywood crowd. The tabloids didn't go by a week during the summer season without Noah being sighted with some A-list celebrity, actor, or director at the beach or at brunch.

The press had gotten really jazzed over him recently because of his surprise wedding to his former real-estate broker, some very attractive dark-haired number from the city who looked like a petite Cindy Crawford.

As I quickly remembered all this, I sat there dazzle-eyed as I imagined Noah and his wife coming over to the bar for a drink.

You seem like a real cool guy, Terry, I pictured Noah saying as he shot the cuffs of his white tux. *Why don't you put down that bar rag and come to the after-party. I'd like to introduce you to a few people. Like my wife's little sister. She's a model, too.*

I grinned from ear to ear at the thought. I couldn't believe this was actually happening. Five seconds ago, I was playing driveway b-ball and looking forward to maybe watching an afternoon rerun of *Star Trek.*

But instead I, Terry Rourke, was about to go into *the* Suttons' magical never-neverland of a beach house party!

I snapped out of it as there was a diesel roar of the tractor-trailer guy finally getting his rig through the hedge gate without killing everyone.

Nick gave me back the shades.

"On second thought, leave them on, peach fuzz," he said as he headed back for the van. "Maybe if the security guy squints, he won't notice that you're still in eighth grade."

13

The first thing that tipped me off that I was no longer in the Hampton Bays happened straightaway when I pulled under the *Alice in Wonderland*–type green hedge gate.

Because I'd seen linebacker-sized security guys before.

Just never one wearing Armani.

"Beer's here," I said casually as the stylish hulk wrote something on a clipboard.

The guy mumbled something into his hands-free mike and rolled his eyes as he pointed down the steep slope of the driveway.

As I laid my eyes on a full frontal view of Noah Sutton's house for the first time, I realized they didn't call it *the* Glass House for nothing.

The flat-roofed glass building looked like a large piece of art.
I didn't know if it was the type of glass it was made out of or
maybe the early evening light reflecting off the multiple pools
that edged all the way around it, but it had a kind of hard and
intense purity to it.

It didn't even look like a house, I thought, gazing at it. It
looked like a pristine iceberg somehow plucked from Antarctica,
shaved into a perfect rectilinear slab and set down on a park of
manicured grass beside the sea.

I tore my eyes off it just long enough to follow Nick in the
van into a huge parking area they'd roped off on the perfect
grass to the south of the house. We drove into the lot's corner
beside the 18-wheeler where a half dozen huge white tents and
a dozen portable generators and porta-potties were arranged in
a semicircle on a Central Park Sheep Meadow–sized lawn facing the ocean.

As we were disembarking, another massive security guy in
Armani appeared and told Nick to set up in the tent closest to
the parking lot. My eyes went wide yet again as we arrived and
saw that there was a bar inside of it, an actual real pinewood bar
with red leather trim and beer taps and a varnished bar top that
was about the length of a bowling alley.

There was a second bar tent adjacent to ours where another
crew was setting up.

"Wait here," Nick said as he went over to talk to them.

When Nick came back, we started bringing in the boxes
from the parking lot. I noticed for the first time that most of
them were filled with the same thing, something called Charles
Heidsieck Rosé.

"Hey, is this stuff any good?" I asked Nick as I bumped four
cases of it on a hand truck over the grass.

"Yeah, you could say that," Nick said.

"How much per bottle?" I said.

"Oh, about seventy-five bucks."

"Seventy-five bucks a bottle! What? That means—"

"Nine hundred bucks a box," Nick said.

"Wait," I said, immediately slowing down. "How many boxes all together?"

"Thirty-three," Nick said.

"No way! We've just delivered like thirty grand in champagne?"

Nick laughed at me.

"Welcome to the bigs, high school," he said.

As we started breaking out the boxes of pink champagne and stacking them in some coolers below the bar, I began to see what the 18-wheeler was all about.

Some scraggly long-haired white guys had arrived from somewhere, and they were taking scaffolding and equipment out of the back of it. In a few minutes, they got a huge tower of a speaker set up, and they started testing one-two-three on it.

"What's up with the roadies?" I said over to Nick, who was lining up champagne glasses on the bar top. "There's going to be a concert or something?"

"What do you think happens on Meadow Lane? Hot dogs and six-packs? Get with it," Nick said.

"Do you know who's going to be playing? Someone big?"

Nick made a shushing gesture.

"Silence, kid. The universe awaits you," he said.

14

By the time we unpacked all the boxes, the huge stage was set up, and the roadies were dropping bass lines so loud it made the glasses chime. After we got the kegs clicked into place beneath the bar, Nick showed me how to open a champagne bottle without taking people's eyes out and how to pour with a little twist on the end to minimize the spillage.

When I looked up from my lesson, I saw some movement on the stage and watched as the roadies set up some huge swings beside the massive speakers. A couple of minutes later, some girls showed up, good-looking blonde girls in jeans and T-shirts, who sat and stood on the swings like they were testing them.

"You should be paying *me* for this," Nick said, watching my eyes, which had grown to the size of bread plates.

The guests started arriving around six. I looked out as down the slope rolled shining BMWs and Mercedes and Range Rovers. It looked like a car show was about to start.

"You've gotta be kidding me," I said to Nick as three Ferraris glided down the slope, one red, one white, one blue.

"It's the Fourth of July, dude," Nick said, smiling. "Have to be patriotic."

The people exiting the cars looked pretty incredible, as well. Out of the shining luxury vehicles stepped tall and serene beautiful people with glowing tans and perfect hair and hard white perfect smiles.

Nick and I stood there watching.

"See, that's the famous director Tony Milo," Nick said as the owners of the globe stopped to air-kiss each other in the golden light of the setting sun.

"And that's his wife, the supermodel Bixenta. There's the gazillionaire investment banker Karl Anselm. And Jeremy Creeve, the abstract impressionist from his studio in Montauk with his little buddy. And next to him is the writer Xavier Kelsey."

"No way! Kelsey?" I said, looking at the bow tie–wearing dandy who'd recently won the Pulitzer. "I just read his book, dude. *Red Diamonds.* He's the best true-crime writer there is."

"He's the best all right."

"What, you read *Red Diamonds*, too?"

"Shit, no," Nick said. "I see him at all these parties. He's a lush, and he tips like crazy."

"Where's the man of the hour? Noah and his hot wife? What's her name?"

"Hailey. I don't see them yet. But don't worry. They'll be around."

15

There was no more time for chitchat or celebrity-spotting as the beautiful crowd converged upon us. Once the tent filled, the pink champagne bottles I'd already opened began to disappear about as quickly as their nose-tickling bubbles.

Nick was a pouring machine, but we almost immediately started getting backed up. After about half an hour of doing nothing but opening bottles, I looked up and saw we were still four-deep at the bar as more and more luxury vehicles just kept coming down the now darkening slope from Meadow Lane.

Nick was running around like a demon, so I made a command decision to help out by pouring and handing, pouring and handing. No more twisting, no time for formalities. We were under siege.

As the sun went down, people started smoking dope right out in the open. The first time I went to use the bathroom, I noticed that the long lines at the porta-potties didn't seem to go any faster despite the fact that often two or three people were going in at the same time.

I was coming back across the sunset-lit grass when the music started.

It was some catchy sort of salsa rhythm that was vaguely familiar, maracas and an African bongo drum. Then when the playful piano melody kicked in, my eyes almost popped out of my head, and the hair actually stood on the back of my neck as I realized what it was and who was playing the party.

The voice started singing, and all of the guests there on the grass beside the sea let out a roar as George Michael himself, the world-famous pop singer, appeared on the stage.

I stood there, gaping at his mirrored aviator shades and leather jacket and frosted blond hair, as he began to belt out his hit "Freedom."

Rooted to the grass in astonishment, I was watching George and his band bop along to the dance beat when I suddenly noticed that the swings were moving.

On them were the young ladies I saw before. But they weren't wearing jeans and T-shirts anymore. They were wearing shiny black leather dresses the size of hand towels, along with spiky silver stilettos, going back and forth on the swings with their long blond hair trailing out behind them like twin tractor-trailer mud flap fantasy girls come to life.

As I finally threaded my way back to the bar, I shot a look over at Nick as two more model types wearing similar dresses got up onto the varnished pine and started dancing like we were all suddenly in an MTV music video.

"How?" I screamed over the music at Nick as I stumbled over to him in awe. "How is this happening?"

"Don't worry," Nick screamed back in my ear as he clapped me on the back and handed me a champagne glass on the sly. "You know me. I'll find a way for you to pay me back."

16

Coming on an hour later, Nick had just left to hit the head when the girl appeared.

I was down behind the bar, opening up yet another box of champagne, and when I straightened up, the most beautiful girl I'd ever seen in my life not in a magazine was staring into my eyes.

She had short black hair and had to be a model. She didn't seem real. She looked like an elf or a Greek goddess or something.

"You look like someone I know," she said as her gaze seared through the back of my skull and soul.

You do, too, I thought, swallowing. *Aphrodite.*

It would have been a great line to actually say, but that had a 0 percent chance of happening. My mouth opened, but no words were available at the moment apparently. Seeing her had thoroughly disconnected my brain from my tongue.

"You *really* look like someone I know," she said again.

I couldn't help but notice she had an accent. English, Australian, something awesome.

"Lucky guy," I finally got out.

"No, I'm serious," the girl said, a smile playing on her pouty lips. "Have you ever been to Birmingham?"

I opened my mouth again, but I couldn't even get a "no" out this time, so I just shook my head.

She tilted her perfect face at me.

"Oh, well. Do you do any tricks?" she asked.

"What?" I said.

"Tricks. You know, like Tom Cruise? Don't all Yank bartenders know tricks?"

I looked at her, then turned and picked up an Absolut vodka bottle from the shelf behind me and flipped it and actually ended up catching it.

"I'm really not allowed to," I said with a wink. "What can I get you?"

"One cosmo," she said, holding up a finger.

A cosmo? I thought.

Cosmo to me was a magazine that my mom wouldn't let my older sister, Erin, bring into the house. But when had being an ignorant fool stopped me? Especially on this incredible evening.

I did the flip thing again and grabbed a tumbler and poured in some of the vodka. Then I went into one of the coolers and added some ice and a few more liqueurs, rum, and a little gin. I saw some red juice next to the gin and put that in there, as well.

I shook the concoction and poured it into a wineglass and added a straw and was about to hand it to her when it happened.

I slipped on the slick swamp grass of spilled beer and champagne behind the bar and went down flat on my ass.

So that's what those rubber mats behind a bar are for, I thought as I got up, my butt and the whole back of my shirt soaked and dripping with booze.

The good news was I was still holding the drink. The bad news was that I was wearing half of its contents like a crime scene all down the front of my white shirt.

I looked at the now giggling girl and was about to open my mouth to say something when I decided to just hand her what was left of the drink.

"If only you'd spilled the whole thing," she said after she took a wincing sip. "That's the single most horrid drink I've ever tasted in my life."

Then she looked at me and burst out laughing.

As she laughed, I saw that she had a little gap in her front teeth that would have made me fall in love with her right then and there. Except that had already happened two minutes before when we first laid eyes on each other.

"Well, at least you're as cute as Tom Cruise," she finally said.

"What was that?" I said.

"You heard me. Give me something to write on."

"Like a piece of paper?"

She flipped over a coaster and pulled the clipboard pen out of my shirt pocket and wrote down something.

"I'm here with someone, but I want you to call me tomorrow. I'm in the city for the summer. You do know where the city is? New York City?"

"It's in Manhattan, isn't it?" I said over the mad beat of my heart.

"Yes, it is in Manhattan," she said.

My breath caught as she leaned in super close and slipped the coaster with her number on it and my pen back into my shirt pocket.

"All the way in," she said in my ear before she pulled back.

"Wait—what's your name?" I said after seeing it was just a number written on the coaster.

But she just turned on her white-sandaled heel and stepped away into the beach shadows beyond the tent and was gone.

17

Maybe an hour later, the entire bar tent was empty.

George Michael was halfway into "I'm Your Man," and we were boxing up the empties when Nick elbowed me in the back so hard, I cried out.

I stood up and turned around.

And saw that the man of the hour had arrived.

"Hey, boys. Working hard or hardly working?" Noah Sutton said as he leaned over and grabbed a bottle of Heidsieck champagne out from beneath the bar.

He was taller than he seemed from the society pages. And just as perfectly and remarkably good-looking. He was wearing all white, I saw, but not a tuxedo. His linen shirt was half-open, and he had on a pair of white jeans.

That he was soaked to the skin didn't seem to faze him. Quite the contrary. He looked like a very happy man.

"Hello, Mr. Sutton. Can I get you a glass?" Nick said politely.

I elbowed Mr. Badass back as he suddenly became Mr. Kiss Ass.

Then we all turned to the mouth of the tent and saw why Noah was so happy. Two women waved at Noah. One was blonde, the other had red hair, and they were both cat-eyed and wearing white high-cut one-piece bathing suits.

"There you are! You can't get away that quick," the redheaded beauty called out to Noah.

Noah waved them in with the champagne bottle.

"Sir?" Nick said as the girls suddenly rushed in, giggling and whispering.

"What's that?" Noah said as the girls swung themselves under his arms.

"Would you like glasses with that?" Nick said.

"Won't be necessary at this juncture," Noah said as he was being dragged away. "But thank you."

"No problem, sir," Nick said.

"Boys!" Noah called over his shoulder without looking at us.

"Yes, sir," we answered in unison.

"You didn't see me." He grinned.

"See who, sir?" Nick said, elbowing me again.

"Now, that," Noah Sutton called as he was pulled off into the darkness, "is what I like to hear!"

18

I opened my eyes the next morning.

It was one of those times when you wake up and everything is different. Where it feels like several hundred million years have passed. Or maybe you've been transported to a new planet.

"A dream," I immediately said to myself as I remembered everything.

Driving Nick's Cadillac, the Armani-suited security guy, the blue glass spaceship Sutton house beside the ocean, the girls on the swings, George Michael. Noah freaking Sutton himself.

"George Michael," I mumbled, laughing. "I mean, that's impossible. It had to be a dream, had to be."

Then I raised my head off my pillow and looked down.

At my red-stained shirt, my crusty black jeans, my disgusting sticky wet black booze-soaked Reeboks still glued to my feet.

It wasn't, I realized with an explosive smile and a fist pump of triumph. It had actually happened. All of it.

Then I saw the money. On my bureau, there was a wad of cash, a massive one, more money than I'd ever come close to seeing in my entire life. I got up and started quickly counting my cut of the tips. There were fives, tens, twenties. Lots and lots of twenties. There was a fifty. And no! A hundred?

"Eight hundred fifty-five bucks!" I cried as I finished counting. *In one single night!*

I went over the blur that was the end of the night, packing up, breaking down the boxes, having a few more sips of pink champagne, the Charlie, as Nick and I started to call it. After a couple of hours, Nick gave me a hilarious ride back home in his Cadillac, singing George Michael the whole way.

What a night, I thought. The greatest night of my life. Heck, anyone's. Man, Nick Murray was the coolest. And my brother as well, for not being around so I could take his place. What a score and a half!

Then it felt like the top of my head exploded as I remembered the very best part.

The English Aphrodite girl!

The real-life fairy princess who had given me her number.

My hand shot to my shirt pocket for the coaster.

My empty pocket.

"It's not there!" I yelled.

I rifled through everything on top of my bureau. Then started panicking.

"Where are you?" I yelled.

I tossed my room, looked in the bathroom.

"I can't believe this! Where the hell is it?"

"Where's what?" Tom said, appearing in the doorway.

I stared at him. I guess he had just come back from the Shore.

"Nothing," I said, shooting past him, still in my grimy outfit from last night.

"What's up with the catering outfit? That better not be my tie! And where are you going?" he said as I opened the door to the garage and jumped on my bike.

I headed straight to Nick's, five blocks to the north. I went around back to his window and saw him sleeping. I knocked on the glass, but he was dead to the world.

"Screw it," I mumbled as I went into his open garage and started combing through the Caddy.

"Please be here," I mumbled as I checked everywhere, between the seats, under the floor mats, in the glove box.

But it wasn't.

I got back on my bike again and retraced the route back to Meadow Lane. Maybe it had fallen out on our way back to the car?

As I reached Meadow Lane and got closer to the beach house, I noticed some cars out front at the Sutton place.

They were cop cars, I suddenly realized. A bunch of them. One of them was a van.

Was it a noise complaint from last night? I thought.

Just as I rolled up to the white gate, it opened and a car pulled out of it.

It was a gray Ford Crown Victoria. As I stood there balancing the bike, the window rolled down, and I found myself face-to-face with a lean, tough-looking guy with blue eyes behind the wheel.

"What the hell are you doing here?" my dad said. "Leave the bike there and get your butt in this car. Now!"

19

"Well?" my dad said as we flew south down Meadow Lane a second later.

Though my dad was actually a very nice guy, he could be really intimidating when he needed to be.

He was pushing fifty and in very good shape, though from all the deep-sea fishing he did, the corners of his eyes and the back of his neck looked cracked and beat-up, like a baseball mitt somebody left on the beach.

We were going at speed now. My dad had the worst lead foot in history. Especially if Mom wasn't in the car. My mom would always say that someone had mistakenly taught Sean Rourke that in order to drive a car, its gas pedal must be kept in contact with the floor.

Despite how fast we were going with the window open, he managed to light up a Marlboro red with his Zippo before he looked over at me again.

"You were there last night. At the party at the Glass House. Catering with that Nick," my father stated, not bothering to ask me if it were true.

"It's okay, Dad. Mom knew about it. I was filling in for Tom."

He looked at me, squinting, his hard blue eyes suddenly hurt.

"Seventeen," he said, shaking his head. "You smell like a brewery. Now I have to worry about you, too, huh? Keeping Tom out of jail isn't bad enough? Why don't you all just get together tonight while I'm sleeping and put me out of my misery with a baseball bat? I'm insured."

"Dad, I'm sorry," I said quickly. "It's not what you think. I wasn't drinking. I was working. It's my sneakers. They're covered in spilled drinks."

"Working! You'll be working all right. You'll be working a bid in Suffolk correctional if you keep hanging out with that Nick and Denny Milton."

He looked at me very closely.

"Now you tell me, and don't you even try to lie. What were you doing on Meadow Lane just now?"

"I was…looking for…a number. Some pretty girl at the party gave me her number. She wrote it on a coaster for me, and I can't find it."

"Is that it?"

"Yes."

We suddenly screeched to a stop on the side of the road in a huge cloud of sand, my seat belt locking painfully against my chest as we went from sixty to zero in about zero point zero seconds.

My father mashed his cigarette into the ashtray. I'd never seen him so worked up. Well, at least not with me.

He stared at me and then looked out at the Shinnecock Bay beside us.

"It's okay, Terry," he finally said after about thirty seconds of dead silence. "I believe you."

He closed his blue eyes then and rolled his leathery neck.

"What is it, Dad? What's up?"

He opened his eyes and looked dead level right at me.

"Noah Sutton is dead," he said.

I shot back in my seat as if I'd been punched.

"What? No! That's impossible!" I said.

My dad nodded his head.

"He's dead. Just seen him with my own eyes."

"Holy shit! Noah Sutton, dead? That's horrible! What happened?"

"Shot in the head," my dad said, lighting up another cigarette. "Twice."

I felt my heart beat faster in my chest. I couldn't believe my ears.

Shot?

"You're saying he was murdered?" I cried.

"It's a distinct possibility," my dad said.

That's when I realized why my dad was involved.

He wasn't just involved either. As the head assistant district attorney of Suffolk County, and the head of the homicide unit, my dad was actually *in charge*.

"Holy shit," I said again, thinking about what was about to happen. "This is gonna be huge, Dad. A guy this famous is murdered at the party of the summer at his own house! The media is gonna go nuts!"

"You got that right, son," my dad said. "You got that right."

"What are you going to do?"

"Drive your grounded ass back home," my dad said as he suddenly screeched back onto the road.

"Then what?" I said as he whipped a U-ey.

"Then I'm going to figure out who killed Noah Sutton, put them in jail, and call it a day."

20

On January 7, 2000, an excessively gloomy day six months after my conversation on Meadow Lane with my dad, I got off a bus in front of the headstone-gray entrance of the Arthur M. Cromarty Criminal Courts Building in Riverhead, Long Island.

I thought I had an idea about what was coming when I'd woken up that cold morning, but as I turned up the lapels of my overcoat and looked through the lightly falling snow at the mob in front of the courthouse, I realized I was dead wrong.

It was like the building was under siege. There had to be at least two hundred media people on the windswept concrete plaza out in front of the ugly modern courthouse. They all stood around the outdoor press conference podium that had a mass of twisting microphone cords on it thick enough to hold up a bridge.

Across from it in the media pen stood a black forest of camera tripods, ladders, and stepladders. After a moment, I realized it was for all the photographers to shoot over and around each other like they were tiered rows of Revolutionary War–era soldiers.

A news van passed me as I was about to cross the street, and as I skirted the courthouse's packed parking lot, I saw that there were about thirty more of them already there. The networks had actually brought in those crisis bus type vehicles you see at NASCAR races.

Gaping at the massive media encampment and the coliseum-like atmosphere, I suddenly realized the full enormity of what was going on, and the tiny butterflies I had in my stomach when I'd gotten out of bed that morning became the size of pterodactyls.

Because the heavy eyes of the entire world were now upon two people, I knew.

Noah Sutton's beautiful widow, Hailey Sutton.

And my dad.

21

One month after Noah Sutton's death, my dad had arrested Hailey Sutton and charged her with second-degree murder.

And nothing had been the same since.

The pundits were already calling it the East Coast equivalent of the OJ trial. For three weeks straight, the "Sutton Slay," as it was referred to now, was the top story of almost every major news outlet. The cable networks especially just couldn't get enough. It seemed like the case was on the cover of the *New York Post* or the *New York Times* every single day.

We never saw my dad. He came home to shower and to sleep. The phone rang off the hook with interview offers from the media. Mickey had opened the door one Saturday morning to see a *60 Minutes* producer standing there with Morley Safer personally asking for an interview that Dad declined.

No wonder the piranhas were in a frenzy. One of the juiciest aspects of the case was the alleged affair angle. It was rumored in the press that Hailey Sutton had been sleeping with a contractor named Mark Disenzo, who had been working on the beach house the year before. A *mob-connected* contractor, the papers were not so reluctant to point out.

Disenzo, a thuggish though handsome guy, would probably have been a media star by now if it weren't for the fact that he, too, was dead.

A month almost to the day of Noah's murder, he wiped out on his motorcycle on the Verrazzano Bridge doing a hundred and thirty. My father had looked into it, and I overheard him tell one of his investigators that there had been more coke in Disenzo's system than blood when he spun out and hit the rail.

No doubt about it, the case had pretty much redefined the term *sensational*. When my dad announced Hailey's arrest at a press conference at the end of July, the networks had actually interrupted their broadcasts. They'd even cut away from a Mets day game. A *Time* magazine cover with Hailey's face on it appeared the next week.

Though my dad's lips were airtight about the case, there had been leaks, and they were doozies.

Apparently, there were no witnesses and no murder weapon but there was DNA evidence. A hoodie allegedly belonging to Hailey had been found in the garbage of a neighboring property. It was speculated that on it was blood splatter belonging to Noah.

There was also apparently some extremely damaging testimony to come out from Hailey's maid, Jailene Mercado, who was holed up at an undisclosed location. Jailene was a forty-year-old woman from the Dominican Republic, and the Spanish network Telemundo had gotten in on the media frenzy by promising her her own TV talk show.

I looked at the hordes of journalists standing outside in the cold.

"Now, this," I mumbled to myself as I blew into my hands, "is how to do a bring-your-kid-to-work day."

22

I bought a bottle of water and a doughnut from a food truck and stood with the crushing crowd of reporters out in the cold near the courthouse's front entrance. I'd already had my sister, Erin, call in sick for me at school. My dad had told all of us to stay the hell away from the trial, but there was no way I was missing this. No way that I wasn't going to be there to see what happened and to support my dad.

I'd finished my doughnut and was licking at the last of the chocolate stuck to the waxed paper when I saw the reporters getting all riled up. Something was definitely about to happen. They'd been standing around, stamping their feet, shooting the breeze with one another, and then all of a sudden, they were all moving en masse, grabbing their cameras, running toward the street at the end of the plaza.

As I watched, a Chevy Suburban with tinted windows pulled up to the curb across from the courthouse, and all of its doors popped open at once. Then Hailey Sutton emerged from the vehicle in the midst of three bodyguards.

The clicking paparazzi camera flash packs strobed off Hailey and her entourage like white heat lightning as they crossed the gloomy plaza. There was something strangely graceful in the way the massive body of backward-walking, hollering reporters and techs moved in sync with Hailey and her forward-moving entourage. With the soundtrack of the cha-cha-ing castanet-like clicks of all the cameras, there was a sort of festive ritual quality to the whole scene.

Yeah, I thought, watching in awe.

The running of the bullshitters.

And even though we were on opposite sides in this, I couldn't deny how striking Hailey looked between her bodyguards and the paparazzi. Wearing Chanel shades and an immaculate white wool coat, she looked like she had stepped out of *Vogue.*

As the plaza media tango passed by me for the door, I quickly deep-sixed the water bottle into an overflowing garbage can when I saw who was coming up behind the crowd.

The short, feisty fiftysomething woman crossing the street, schlepping several case-file-filled bags, gave me an eye roll as I stepped up to her.

"Hey, Mrs. Fisker, let me help you," I said as I took one of the overflowing bags from my dad's secretary.

"Terence Rourke, you awful brat! What are you doing here? Don't you have school?" she said as she hurried for the farthest door to the left away from the reporters.

"My mock trial coach gave me permission. Can you help me get in?" I said as I opened the courthouse door for her.

"As if I don't have enough to do. Take this bag here. I'll try, I guess. C'mon."

"He's with me, Jimmy," Mrs. Fisker said to a bald mean-looking court officer, holding a clipboard beyond the metal detectors.

Jimmy looked at me and rolled his eyes as he reluctantly let us by.

"Okay, you're in," she said. "If you tell anyone, I'll deny it. Trial's upstairs in 3A. Run! Tuck yourself in at the back and look like you belong there."

23

Courtroom 3A was a high-ceilinged room paneled in pale yellow wood. It looked like a chamber-music hall or even a modern church with the packed gallery benches standing in for pews.

After I scored a space along the wall five feet from the door and craned my neck out to see over the heads, I got another good look at Hailey.

Her lawyers had probably advised her to dress as approachably as possible, but the navy blue designer sheath dress she was wearing accentuated her silhouette such that she looked nothing short of stunning. All really good-looking women have a kind of haughty air about them, and Hailey had that in spades.

Speaking of standouts, I thought as I looked at her lawyers.

She had three of them, Justin Mortain, Bruno Tully, and Byron Seager, and they were all from one of the country's top law firms.

Mortain was a famous criminal lawyer who had defended a popular director from doing time for a drunk driving fatality, and Tully had been an adviser to two presidents.

But Byron Seager was the most concerning.

I'd already seen him in two TV interviews, and he radiated decency and balance and charm. He was witty, sincere and had a kind of boyish, small-town look to him. Except he wasn't what he appeared. At only thirty-one, the Jimmy Stewart look-alike was the finest, most ruthless mercenary trial lawyer in the country. He had already somehow saved a car company and a Wall Street bank from existential-level lawsuits that they completely deserved to lose.

What was even more discouraging for my dad and his case was that all of Noah Sutton's billionaire family—his son, Julian (from his first marriage), his two brothers, Nelson and Henry, and his sister, Brooke—were sitting directly behind Hailey and her dream team.

Dark-haired Nelson Sutton, the eldest in the family, was tall and barrel-chested and had a kind of brawny, almost thuggish look to him, more like a cement truck driver than a billionaire.

The remaining siblings, on the other hand, thoroughly looked the part. Brooke was dressed to the nines, her salon-perfect hair and makeup and dark stylish pantsuit and jewelry all effortlessly on point.

Henry was even more photogenic and wealthy seeming. Almost as handsome as Noah with highlights of blond in his thick brown hair, Henry could have easily played himself when they made the movie.

No doubt about it. My dad had not counted on that. He, like anyone, had assumed the rich and famous Sutton family would be eager to see justice served in the case of their brother's violent murder.

Especially considering the fact that the accused was none other than his brand-spanking-new sketchy younger wife.

He'd thought wrong.

From almost the outset, the Sutton family had made it well known to the press that they felt the whole incident was nothing other than a tragic murder by an unknown assailant and urged that Hailey not be prosecuted.

Why this was the case wasn't easy to figure out. They didn't like Noah so much? Or maybe that after the three-ring media circus of the funeral, they simply wanted to save their extremely famous and powerful family from yet another trial? Yet another trip through the tabloid media mud?

No one knew. But there they sat behind Hailey, supporting her 100 percent.

After fifteen minutes, Judge Edward Mathiassen entered the chamber. A short dignified-looking man with neatly parted white hair and a neatly trimmed white mustache, Mathiassen had already garnered some gripes from the media as well as the defense attorneys for not allowing a camera in the courtroom.

For that reason alone, he seemed somewhat sane to me.

Mathiassen wasn't through clearing his throat to get the proceeding underway when Hailey's lawyer Byron Seager leapt to his feet.

"Your Honor," he said, "may we please approach the bench?"

What? I thought.

"Already?" Mathiassen said.

Seager gave him his best Honest Abe apple pie–eating smile.

"Yes, Your Honor, if you would humor us."

There was a low murmuring through the room as all of Hailey's lawyers and my dad huddled by the side of the judge's bench. They spoke for a while, and things seemed to get heated at one point. But then they dispersed back to their tables.

"Bailiff, please let in the potential jurors for the voir dire," Mathiassen said.

The door behind me opened, and everyone turned as thirty potential jurors marched in and headed for the jury box.

24

I was in my dad's study reading one of his law books when he finally came back home that night around seven.

"Terry, what are you doing in here?"

"What happened today at the beginning, Dad?"

He paused for a moment and then finally smiled and shook his head at me.

"Why do all my kids have to be nuts?" he said.

My dad and I had been tight ever since I was little. I was, after all, probably the quietest of my loud family, and I would often follow him around like a puppy. I was also usually the only willing participant in whatever chore or activity he needed some help with.

Plus we were both big fans of mystery shows. On Saturday

afternoons when everybody else went out to play, I'd sit by his feet and watch whatever reruns were on with him. Episodes of *The Twilight Zone* and *Alfred Hitchcock Presents*, and lots of detective shows like *Perry Mason*.

As we watched, my dad would lecture as to what he would have done to prosecute the cases and how the detectives would have fared in real life if they had to bring the cases to trial.

Everybody else groaned when my dad did this, but not me. He had been so proud of me in freshman year when I joined the mock trial team that he would even come to our practices and coach us.

"So, what happened?" I said.

He poured himself a drink. His drink. Pabst Blue Ribbon served in a wineglass. It was a nod to his own father, our grandpop, who had been born in Ireland and had been a cop in the Bronx and would drink it at cookouts when he came to visit. "We're in the Hamptons," he would say, and the wineglass was "to class the place up, dontcha know."

"Terry, I don't know why I should tell you any of this, but I will as long as you promise to keep it to yourself."

"Of course, Dad. What happened?"

"Well, son, frankly, we were sandbagged. Our evidence was stolen. Hailey's hoodie as well as the two bullets recovered from Noah's skull mysteriously grew legs. The cops lost them. Put the word *lost* there in quotes."

"What! No! When?"

"Three days ago. There was some kind of break-in at the evidence room and everything we had on Hailey walked out the front door of the Village of Southampton Police Department. The hoodie, the bullets, all of it."

"No! Unbelievable! Somebody stole it? Who?"

"Who knows? Though it is unbelievable. And yet true. One of your patented unsolved mysteries."

"This is a disaster!"

"Not completely."

"How?"

"At the sidebar, the defense complained that we hadn't sent them our discovery. When I told them the evidence had been stolen, they immediately asked for a dismissal, but the judge denied it. He actually did us a solid. He's allowing the autopsy to be put into evidence even though we don't have the actual bullets anymore."

"But aren't you toast now? The DNA evidence on the hoodie? That was your ace in the hole!"

My dad smiled.

"Don't worry, kid. We still have a few tricks up our sleeve."

25

"Would you please state your name for the jury?" said my dad.

It was Monday of the following week. The jury had been selected, the opening statements made, and the full courtroom was on the edge of its collective seat as the real trial officially began.

It was so quiet and tense that when someone opened the door to the hall behind me just about every head shot back anxiously toward it.

"Would you please state your name for the jury?" my dad said again as my intimidating court officer buddy, Bald Jimmy, silently closed the door behind him.

"Jailene Mercado," Hailey Sutton's maid said.

The papers had been right about Ms. Mercado. She was a

nice-looking lady, though more than a little overweight. In a black turtleneck and houndstooth skirt with her burgundy-highlighted brown hair tight in a bun, she looked very polished and professional.

"Ms. Mercado, what do you do for a living?"

"I'm a maid. I worked for Noah Sutton for seven years. Since 1992."

Her Dominican accent was pretty thick, but I thought she spoke English quite well.

"How did you get the job?" my dad asked.

"Through my uncle Freddie. He was a doorman at Mr. Noah's building in Manhattan. Mr. Noah had fired his old maid and asked my uncle if he knew anyone."

"Could you please walk us through the early morning of July 5, 1999?"

"I had taken my vacation the week before back to my parents in Santo Domingo and was coming back from the airport, from JFK."

"You were coming back to Noah's house on Meadow Lane?"

"Yes."

"In a taxi?"

"No, a car service. Mr. Noah's service he told us to use. It was a Lincoln town car."

"What time did it pick you up?"

"Around 6:00 a.m., and we arrived at the house at about 7:00. Maybe 7:15."

"How did you get in?"

"I used my security code at the gate. I didn't buzz because my coworker Hortencia had told me there had been a big party, so I didn't want to wake anyone up."

"The driver dropped you off at the front door?"

"Yes, with my bags. Then I let myself in."

"How? With a key?"

"Yes, with my key."

"The front door was locked?"

"Yes."

"Was that uncommon?"

"No, Mr. Noah was very security, um…"

"Conscious?" my dad said.

"Objection," the defense lawyer Byron Seager said with a charming little smile.

"Sustained," the judge said.

"Noah Sutton liked to keep the doors locked at night?" my dad asked.

"Yes," Ms. Mercado said.

"Okay, so you went inside the house. What then?"

"I went to the buzzer and opened and closed the security gate for the radio car."

"Did you see anyone inside the house? Anyone awake?"

"No. I came in with my bags, and it was quiet and dark with the shades down. I was about to go downstairs to my room when I noticed that the light was on in Mr. Noah's office."

"Was the door to his office open?"

"No, but it has a glass…"

"A glass front? Like a French door?"

"Objection."

"Enough with the leading, Counselor."

"Please continue, Ms. Mercado," my dad said.

"I saw the light and thought maybe Mr. Noah was up, and I could tell him I was back, but—"

That's when she lost it. I watched as my father tried to console Ms. Mercado by handing her a box of tissues.

"Can you tell us what you saw?"

She took a deep breath and nodded, wiping at her eyes.

"As I got to the door, I saw Mr. Noah's legs on the rug through the glass. He was on the floor half under his desk. He was in his underwear, and when I got closer, I saw the blood."

26

A sudden loud murmur went through the courtroom, and the judge called for order.

I watched as my father went to the prosecutor's table to check his notes before he resumed his questioning.

"Did you enter the office at that point, Ms. Mercado?"

"No."

"What did you do?"

"I screamed and ran. Ran out of the house. But then I thought maybe Mr. Noah needed help, so I went back inside and ran upstairs to get Miss Hailey."

"Was Hailey Sutton in her bedroom?"

"No."

"Where was she?"

Ms. Mercado shook her head.

"I don't know," she said.

"Did the bed look like it had been slept in?"

"Yes, it did. It hadn't been made up."

"What did you do then?"

"I ran downstairs and called 9-1-1 from the kitchen."

"Okay, Ms. Mercado. Now, I'd like to fast-forward a little and go over the testimony you made to the police later that morning when you were interviewed at the station house."

As my dad said this, I held my breath, my heart thumping.

Because this was where it was going to get interesting.

I actually knew what was up next. My dad's best friend, Detective Marvin Heller, had arrived at my house three nights before for a strategy session, and I had listened in by the door of my dad's office and heard every word.

Marvin Heller was the first arriving detective, and as soon as he came on the scene, he quickly whisked Ms. Mercado away to the station.

And received a bombshell.

During questioning, Jailene Mercado had told him that she had seen a gun in a drawer in Hailey's closet two weeks before when she had gone to the room to change the sheets.

Not only that, Marvin had shown Ms. Mercado a book of guns, and she'd ID'd the pistol she had seen in Hailey's closet as a blue-steel Smith & Wesson Model 52 semiautomatic with walnut grips.

The reason why this was such a bombshell was because a Model 52 was a special target pistol that shot .38-caliber wadcutter bullets.

Which was the same exact type of round found in Noah's head.

What was also completely incriminating was the fact that under the brief amount of questioning Hailey had been subjected to before her army of attorneys had arrived, she had been asked if she possessed a gun, to which she had said no.

Knowing all this, I held my breath some more as my leg started bouncing up and down. I sat waiting for Ms. Mercado to now nail Hailey Sutton to the courtroom floorboards.

"When you arrived at the station house, Ms. Mercado, you were interviewed by Detective Heller. Is that right?" my dad said.

That's when it happened.

"Wait!" Ms. Mercado suddenly blurted out. "I need to tell you about that now. I need to tell you all about that."

"Tell us all about what?" my dad said, baffled.

"What I said at the police station."

"We're getting to that, Ms. Mercado."

Jailene Mercado looked at my dad and then over at the jury, then down at the floor. She looked like she was about to cry.

"I need to tell you that I lied. I lied to the police. About the gun. I'm so sorry. There was no gun. I make the whole thing up."

"Your Honor, pardon my French, but what in the green hell is this?" Byron Seager said as the courtroom exploded in an uproar.

"Quiet! Order! Order!" the judge yelled. "Ms. Mercado, your job is to answer questions. Nothing else."

"But I talk to a priest. A priest," Jailene Mercado said, bursting into tears. "I need to tell the truth, the whole truth, the real truth. Now."

27

"Dad," I said that night as he came into his office, "she's a lying sack of—"

"That's enough, son. Quite enough," he said as he plopped down in his chair and closed his eyes.

"And how do you know?" he said, taking a sip of his PBR. "If I didn't know better, I might think you were listening in by the door three nights ago when Marv was here."

"Dad, how can she do this? How can she suddenly say that she didn't see a very unusual gun in the house? A gun that she identified out of a book at the police station with Marvin. A gun whose very unusual bullets were found in Noah's head. It's completely frigging impossible!"

"She's been paid to lie, son. That's how. She saw the gun. Sure as I see this ice-cold beer I just poured to soothe my aching soul."

"Dad, you have to prosecute her now. You need to throw her lying butt in jail. You just have to."

"I'll get right on that with the judge, Terry. I'll say, 'Judge, my seventeen-year-old son says I have to throw Ms. Mercado's ample butt in the hoosegow.'"

"I'm eighteen now, Dad."

"That's right. My bad. Duly noted," he said.

"Talking to a priest," I said. "She should be excommunicated. It's unbelievable!"

"*Unbelievable* is the word," my dad said.

"How can you be so calm, Dad? They've got you cooked, don't they?"

He took a sip of his drink and licked the suds off his upper lip.

"Nah, I'm not done yet, son. They don't have me beat just yet."

"But you're out of options. First, they steal your evidence, and now this! This is the most screwed-up trial in the history of trials. It's over, isn't it?"

He shook his head with a funny private smile on his lips.

"You leave it to me, Terry, my boy," he said. "Two outs, bottom of the ninth, two strikes, but I still got the bat, kid. No worries. It ain't over till the old man sums up."

28

At ten o'clock the next morning, the courtroom hushed as my
father stood and approached the jury.

He stopped before them and closed his blue eyes and put his
weather-beaten fisherman's hands together as if he were about to
lead the courtroom in prayer. He stayed like that for a moment.

From my place along the left-hand wall in the back, I nervously passed a hand through my hair as I watched him.

What was he waiting for? What was taking him so long?

The bright, hot courtroom was completely silent. The air
stilled. When a woman in the last bench ahead of me coughed, a
bunch of people shushed her. My dad in his dark blue suit looked
very small against the judge's blond wood bench behind him.

Then he opened his eyes and began his closing statement.

"I've been thinking about everything that's been happening to all of us during this trial. The pressure we are all under. You, me, the judge, the defendant, of course.

"All of us have been under such a strain. Because everyone is watching us. Everyone in New York. Everyone in the country. Heck, I saw a BBC news van when I was coming in this morning. Maybe everyone in the world is now tuned in to see what we will do."

I smiled. My dad really was a charming son of a gun when he wanted to be. A special person. You just liked him. Everybody did. His blue eyes and workingman's face and easy smile. Plus he was so damn smart.

That's what his little smile was about. His secret weapon. He would win this case with nothing but his simple and true Irish blarney charm.

Please, God, I prayed, crossing my fingers. *Please.*

"I was thinking about all that," my dad continued, looking wistfully out at the packed court, "and about what happens after. To all of us. Whichever way this goes. And then it occurred to me. I was wrong.

"Because this case isn't about you, and it isn't about me. It isn't about the judge or even the defendant. It's not about the media, and it's not even about the watching eyes of the entire world.

"This is all about a man. A man who had once been a baby and then a toddler and then a schoolboy and then a teenager. A man who was a son and a brother and a husband and a father. A man who people loved and who had loved other people. And it is that—"

My dad tapped the jury rail with his finger softly.

"That man, Noah Sutton. That poor man—whose full life was violently and viciously and painfully taken away from him on the morning of July 5 in his own home—it is that man that we are all here for.

"We have come here for him. To speak for him and to stand up for him no differently than we would speak for and stand up for our own sons and brothers and husbands and fathers if they were brutally and horrifically taken from us."

My father paused again as he looked straight up at the coffered ceiling sadly as if he could see Noah Sutton up there in heaven.

"Who could do such a thing?" he asked quietly as he looked back down at his feet. "Who could raise a heavy pistol and point it at the head of a man—a sleeping man—and pull the trigger. Feel the jerk of the kickback, hear the clink of the spent casing. See the round strike flesh and bone. Then do it again. Not once but twice?

"We have heard in this courtroom the deposition of Hailey's maid, Jailene Mercado, taken on the morning of July 5 hours after the murder. In that testimony she admitted she had seen a gun in the closet of Hailey Sutton. On the morning of July 5 hours after the murder, Ms. Mercado identified this very type of gun from a book of guns."

My dad went to the evidence table and lifted a binder with the photograph of the Smith & Wesson Model 52 semiautomatic on the front page.

"Out of all the hundreds of guns in the book, she identified this quite distinctive type of gun, a Smith & Wesson Model 52. The very same type of very specific target gun that is known for shooting the very same target round wadcutter bullets that were found embedded in Noah Sutton's brain.

"Now, the other day we all sat here and heard Ms. Mercado attempt to change her statement on the stand. Which Ms. Mercado are we to believe? The one rushed down to the police station after seeing her employer brutally murdered? Or the composed, some might say professionally coached and polished, Ms. Mercado who sat here and told us she'd somehow made the whole thing up?

"We are actually supposed to believe this? Really?"

The binder landed with a dramatic clattering bang as he tossed it back onto the prosecutor's desk.

"Or perhaps not. Perhaps, we need to believe her original statement that actually makes common sense."

29

My dad slowly approached the jury box again and leaned against the rail as he tented his fingers.

"Because, as science dictates, there is no effect without a cause and no action without a motive. In any murder without witnesses, before we can find out who the perpetrator is, the question arises as to why. Why was Noah Sutton murdered? Who would want him dead?

"We've heard testimony in this courtroom concerning his wife Hailey's behavior prior to the murder. We have heard from witnesses that she was having an affair with her contractor, Mark Disenzo, a man with a criminal history of violence and, most alarmingly for our case, illegal gun possession.

"And we have heard testimony that Noah himself was also having an affair and, on the very night of the party, was seen dancing with and kissing other women in front of several witnesses. Some say he had even been swimming with a few of them."

I smiled despite the tension, as my father was referring to me.

"At this party, we have also had witness testimony given that Hailey Sutton was intoxicated.

"With all this evidence in hand, we can surmise the following most plausible explanation for Noah Sutton's murder.

"Hailey was intoxicated when she saw her husband disrespecting her with other women at the party, and it galled her. Maybe it was the drinking that fueled her rage, but whatever the case, at some point in the early morning hours, Hailey took the gun—the gun Jailene Mercado had seen in the marital bedroom two weeks before—and Hailey went down into Noah's office, where he was sleeping, and she shot him twice in the head.

"We have heard testimony that when the first police arrived they did not find Hailey in the house. Not in her bed. Not on the scene. Then after ten minutes, when the police arrived back from their safety check on the guesthouse, they suddenly did see Hailey, looking very awake and wearing workout clothes, including running shoes.

"Where had she been? After she had committed her crime, Hailey sobered up a little and simply, like all remorseful killers, decided to try to cover up her crime, so she left with the gun and got rid of it. She was still in the process of this cover-up and had not yet returned when the first police arrived.

"These are the facts of the case. This is why I, and any other reasonable person with knowledge of the facts, can only conclude beyond the shadow of a doubt that that woman—"

My dad pointed at Hailey Sutton.

"—killed Noah Sutton.

"I know it is hard to believe on the face of things that this beautiful young woman would be capable of such an act.

"But beauty often has a side effect called pride. Noah hurt that enormous pride, and this beautiful reckless hustling young woman decided he wasn't going to get away with it anymore."

Hailey had stayed completely silent and graceful throughout this accusation, but at the word *hustling*, she bristled in her seat and a murmur quickly spread throughout the courtroom.

"In a minute, you members of the jury will have to go into that room and deliberate and come up with a verdict. What I do not want you to do is to think about what *I* think about your decision or what the defense thinks about it or the judge or the reporters or the world.

"What I want you to do is to think about what the man we are all here to stand for thinks about it. Because the reporters will soon leave and your lives will return to normal. Your vital connection to and responsibility for Noah Sutton—who can no longer speak for himself—will be with you for the rest of your life."

30

The steak house on Main Street in Riverhead was one of those old-fashioned dark wood cave-like ones. I mean, it was really dark. Whenever anyone came in or out of the place, the suddenly sunlit doorway looked like the light at the far end of a mountain train tunnel.

Yeah, I thought as I nervously sat there with my father. Or was it the light from an oncoming freight train?

We were about to find out.

It was around one thirty in the afternoon, the third day after my dad's summation, and the fate of Hailey Sutton was now in the jury's hands.

The jury had gone to deliberate two days earlier, but there was still nothing by one o'clock when the judge had called for lunch.

In some cases, the jury asked to see the evidence or to have testimony provided for them again, but in this case, there was none of that.

Was that good? Bad? There was no way to know.

"C'mon, Terry. Eat up," my dad said, gesturing at my cheeseburger.

My school was closed for a teachers' conference, so my dad had actually let me come to court with him officially for the first time.

"Fine," my dad said, cutting my burger in half with his steak knife and commandeering it.

Some upbeat jazz music suddenly emitted from the speakers over our booth. But I definitely wasn't feeling it.

"How can you eat, Pop?" I said, watching him. "The only thing I feel like chewing is my nails."

"Sean!" someone called over.

In the dimness, we looked over. It was the bartender, holding the phone toward my father.

"Hold those nails," my dad said as he got up.

"Afternoon. Are you Mr. Rourke's son?" a voice suddenly said from the steak-house shadows beside the booth as my dad got on the horn.

It was some voice, Southern and honey smooth and deep with an almost musical quality to it.

Holy shit, I thought as I turned and watched, starstruck, as Xavier Kelsey stepped into the table's candlelight.

I'd seen him at the trial sitting behind the Suttons. He was quite the standout with his signature tortoiseshell glasses and bow tie. I'd read an article in the paper that said he had been hired by *Vanity Fair* to cover the trial.

Up close, his sharpened-to-a-point goatee gave his baby face a crafty fox-like quality, I thought. As did the intelligence in the eyes behind the glasses.

As I managed a nod, the Pulitzer Prize–winning author

smiled as he stepped in close enough for me to smell his mar-
tini lunch breath.

"I have been through many a summation," he said, "and I
must say, your father's was as compelling as I have ever wit-
nessed. You should be proud of him."

"I am," I said.

When I looked over at the bar again, my dad was on his way
back. I tried to read his face, but there was nothing. He looked
about as emotional as a man rolling a trash can up his driveway.

"One more thing," Kelsey said in his honey drawl. "I saw
you at the trial and you seem quite familiar to me. I never forget
a face. Ever. It's driving me crazy. Have I not seen you somewhere before?"

I suddenly noticed that the overhead boppity-bip music was
really working up a frenzy as I looked up at him.

He had seen my face. From the opposite side of a bar. Near
the end of the night at Noah's party, I remembered refilling his
champagne glass.

But as I had no desire to be a *Vanity Fair* exclusive beneath
the headline *Sutton Slay DA's Underage Son Attended the Party!*,
that was for me to know and Kelsey never to find out.

So, I just shook my head.

He moved on for the door just as my dad arrived back.

"What did he want?" my dad said, watching Kelsey walk
away. "Don't tell me you told him anything."

"Dad, come on," I said. "How stupid do you think I am?"

"As you're one of my crazy sons, I'll have to take the Fifth
on that one. You want that wrapped up?" he said, taking out
his wallet.

"No, thanks. What now?" I said.

"Put your coat on," he said. "The jury's back."

31

We came in through the rear entrance of the courthouse to avoid all the press.

Jimmy, the not-so-jolly giant court officer, was there in the back corridor sipping a coffee and I gave him a wink as we went past.

We were some of the first ones back, so I was able to score a front-row seat near the left-hand wall.

Hailey Sutton returned with her lawyers in tow a moment later. I guess I must have been gaping at her there in the empty courtroom or maybe she just caught the family resemblance to my dad because as she went past, she gave me one holy hell of a dirty look.

The room quickly filled back up, and then the judge appeared.

I felt like I was going to explode five minutes later as the jury door opened but no one appeared even after a minute.

But my dad just sat there. Every time I glanced from the open jury door to him, he was still placid and poker-faced, still stoic and completely unruffled. When he spotted me looking at him, it was his turn to give me a wink and a warm, dimpled smile.

I looked over at Hailey, beautiful and dark and snooty. She was wearing a deep green sharply tailored wool dress the exact color of her eyes.

But when the jury finally piled in, I saw the snootiness disappear.

As the jurors found their seats, I watched as Jimmy took up position to the right of the jury box with another large younger court officer. It was a place neither of them had stood before.

They were there to immediately take Hailey into custody if she were found guilty, I realized.

I watched as Hailey suddenly noticed the officers as well. She didn't actually swallow as she looked at them, but I saw her cut a longing glance back up the aisle at the courtroom door.

As the foreman finally stood, it was so quiet you could hear the nervous rattle of the paper he was holding.

Hailey bowed her head and went white like she was about to toss her cookies.

She wasn't the only one, I thought, as I puffed out a huge breath, my hand gripping hard on the arm of the wood bench I was sitting on.

"Foreman?" the judge said.

The foreman of the jury was a very heavy pale white fifty-something man with dyed black hair and big glasses. I'd forgotten his Polish name, but I did remember he was a civil engineer who worked for the town of Hempstead in Nassau County.

Engineers relied on logic, right? Reason? I thought. *We had this, right?*

"Foreman, has the jury reached a verdict?" the judge asked.

I, as well as everyone else in that room, held my breath as the foreman brought the paper up before his eyes. I was gripping the bench even harder now. So hard one of my knuckles suddenly cracked.

"No, Your Honor," the heavy engineer finally said. "We have not."

I slammed back into my seat as if I'd been shoved.

What?

I watched Judge Mathiassen cast a quick panicked look at the packed, now loudly murmuring courtroom.

"Foreman, as I instructed you yesterday, this case is of grave importance to the community. Can't you deliberate some more?" he said.

"No, we cannot, Your Honor," the foreman said, just as nervous. "Two of the members of the jury are not in agreement with the rest, and we just spoke about it, and the holdouts are adamant. They will not be moved."

The white-haired judge looked very, very weary. He took off his reading glasses and rubbed at his eyes. He opened his mouth to say something. But then closed it again and lifted his gavel instead.

"Then I have no other option but to declare this proceeding a mistrial," he said as the courtroom erupted.

No! I thought. Mistrial?

Wrong! Wrong! It was all wrong.

I looked for my dad, but there were too many people around him to see his face. I couldn't imagine how bad he felt, how devastated.

I looked over at Hailey. She was ecstatic and beaming. Over the back of her lawyer Byron Seager's bespoke suit, I could see her smiling with her eyes closed.

Truly, it was like she'd just won the World Series. Or an Academy Award, I thought, seething at the bull crap of it all. I couldn't stop shaking my head in anger as her friends and family and even Noah's family all hugged her as her lawyers patted her on the back.

I knew that a mistrial meant she could be tried again, but this was a blow. A hard one. After all that, my dad had lost. The damn thing had been open-and-shut. But they had stolen his evidence and lied and cheated about everything.

And they had beaten him. They had beaten my dad.

What bastards, I thought as my eyes suddenly filled with hot tears.

It stung all right. The worst thing possible had happened.

Or so I had thought.

But I was wrong.

It wasn't the worst thing possible. Not by a country mile.

I didn't know it then, but the worst thing possible was already on its way, coming at me and my family like a runaway train.

PART TWO

UNBURIED TREASURE

32

"Mommy! Why are we still here?" Angelina said, rubbing at her eyes as she woke from her nap. "My legs are hot, Mommy. And this isn't the beach! Why are we still in the car?"

I sighed as I finally put the car in Drive and whipped a quick U-ey on Meadow away from the Sutton Glass House.

"Exactly, Mommy," I said, shaking my head at my wife. "Why do you do these mean things?"

We went back to the house and parked and saw that some of the family were at the pool as we came across the park of grass along the side of the house. But as we had promised Angelina that we'd take her straight to the "lotion," as she referred to it, we just waved to everyone as we found the teak stairs for the beach.

Angelina splashed in the swash for a bit, then begged for me to take her out into the waves. At least in the beginning. After the first one plastered into us and she got a pretty good taste of the seawater, she changed her mind.

"Yuck, Daddy! Take us back, take us back!"

Soothed from her ill-fated "lotion" adventure with a juice pack and a dry towel, Angelina was completely absorbed in full *Bob the Builder* mode with her pail and shovel beside our towel ten minutes later when my wife turned to me.

"And?" she said.

"What do you mean, and?" I said, looking out at the water.

She didn't say anything. But I knew what she meant. I still wasn't done with the story. I still hadn't told the hardest part.

The Aftermath.

I sighed.

"After my dad lost the trial, pretty much the entire Village of Southampton turned on my family. We had always worked in the village. My mom part-time at the library, me at the country club, Tom at the biggest restaurant in town as a waiter. Erin had babysat half the kids in town, and Mickey and Finn had always worked at Grogan's, the ice cream shop next to the movie theater. We knew everybody, and everybody knew us. Or at least we had thought so. But we had thought wrong because every single one of us was almost immediately fired."

"No. All of you? What! You've got to be kidding me. They actually shunned you? Like a collective shunning?" Viv said.

"Yep. Small towns are small towns even if everybody is loaded. And the Suttons' pockets were the deepest of all. My mom's hours were cut down to hardly anything. My summer application at the country club, which had always been a formality, was returned by mail with a form rejection letter. As was Tom's and Mickey's and Finn's applications at their jobs. Oh, they had excuses. Too many staff this year, business was slow, yada yada. But it was a punishment."

"That's unbelievably cruel."

"And it wasn't just our jobs either. I got along with pretty much everybody. The kids at the country club, the surfers, the summer New York City kids. But all of a sudden around town, people I used to say hello to walked past without acknowledging my existence. And Mickey got really screwed. He wanted to go to West Point. It was his lifelong dream, and he had the grades and was on the baseball and basketball teams. He was just waiting on our local congressman's letter of recommendation. It never came."

"They needed to rub your noses in it," Viv said.

"That's exactly what they were doing. Worst of all, my dad got fired. After the trial, my dad's boss lost the election for district attorney, and the new jerk who came in gave him the boot. He'd worked there for fifteen years—was the best lawyer there—and they turned on him. He got a new job that he hated as a real-estate lawyer, but we all started to worry about him.

"He'd never been a teetotaler, but after work, he was coming home later and later. Sometimes his MG would be parked on the lawn. And bottles of Jameson were starting to appear beside his PBR empties in the garage. He thought he had just been doing his job, seeking justice. That at the very worst, the blowback would end with him. He never realized that they would come after us as well. He felt he had done it to us. Failed to protect us."

I felt Viv's hand on the back of my neck as I looked out at the water. A large wave was breaking. When it crashed and fell, it landed so hard I could feel the rumble of it through the sand.

"I was coming in the front door when I saw Erin on the phone," I said.

"I saw her red face, the pain and the tears on it, and immediately, a chill went down my spine. I finally got it out from her that Dad had gone fishing and there had been an accident at Flying Point Beach, and I flew out the door.

"I borrowed my neighbor's car, and when I got to the beach,

I saw all the Village of Southampton police four-by-fours and the ambulances. I saw the pontoon police boat in the water and several cops in the surf struggling with something."

My wife leaned in, hugging me now.

"As I tried to get around a cop who was stiff-arming me to keep me back, like in a dream or something, Tom was suddenly there beside me. He punched the cop with a quick loud pop to his jaw, and then we were in the surf with the cops. That's when I saw my dad."

"Oh, Terry," Viv said as she cried into my shoulder.

"He was in his clothes, soaked, and his skin was all wrong. He looked bloated. There was a huge bruise at his left temple. His blue eyes were open, but they were lifeless. He wasn't moving. I remember the pontoon's outboard whirring like crazy to keep the boat steady in the choppy surf, and Tom rushing in to grab Dad's legs to bring him ashore."

I took a breath and swallowed hard, just wanting to get to the end.

"Tom went under the surf then, and when he popped up, I could see the despair in his face. I wrapped my arms around him. Can you imagine? Your big brother? His heart was ripping in two. Both of our hearts. 'Somebody, please help us,' he kept sobbing in my ear."

I held my wife tighter.

"But nobody helped us, Viv. Nobody. The waves just kept hitting us and the blazing sun just kept burning down."

33

An hour later, we were back in our room. Lunch was already over, but the incredibly awesome staff, seeing that we had missed it, had made us up a picnic basket, brimming with sandwiches and treats and juice packs and sparkling water.

We were just finishing up when Viv and I noticed an itinerary sheet being slipped under the door to our suite.

Instead of black tie and tails for dinner, tonight was going to be jean jackets and shorts. There was a huge Fourth of July fireworks display in Montauk scheduled for 9:00 p.m., and Tom, ever the outrageous host, had arranged for a party bus to escort the lot of us to dinner at a famous outdoor lobster joint in East

Hampton and then on to the festivities like we were all going to the prom.

I had showered first, and after I got dressed, I decided to clear my head while the girls got ready. I was downstairs in the formal living room on one of its half-dozen couches reading a coffee table book about an hour later when Viv came down the *Gone with the Wind*–sized staircase hand in hand with Angelina.

"Where is everybody?" she said.

"A bunch of them are down in the playroom. We're waiting on Tom. He's going to be down in a minute was the latest text."

"How long ago was that?" Viv said.

"Oh, about an hour ago," I said as I held up the book in my lap to show Viv. "You have to see what I found here. Listen to this, honey."

Viv and Angelina sat down on the couch across from me.

"Ready for a story, Angelina?" I said.

She nodded.

"'In reports afterward, the doorman would recount how he had actually seen the man in the tattered green Norfolk jacket that very morning as he came in for his morning shift. Originally, the sad, almost forlorn-seeming figure lingering around on the Eighty-Eighth Street side of the building hadn't struck him as being that out of place. At times, the down-and-out would loiter there on the building's sidewalk exhaust grates for the heat, and if none of the tenants were around, he would tend to look the other way.'"

"Mommy, I'm so bored," Angelina said.

"Who wants to play *Laser Rabbit*?" Viv whispered, taking out her phone.

"Really?" I said as Angelina seized the phone that she was only allowed to play with on very special occasions. "You call that parenting, Viv?" I teased.

"Mommies need vacations, too, thank you very much," Viv said, tossing a throw pillow at me. "Keep reading," Viv said.

"'But at nine thirty that morning,'" I continued, "'as the door-man was holding open the door of the Mackenzies' new Mercer limousine, he spotted the man in the tattered green coat again coming around the corner with rage in his eyes and a large black revolver in his hands.

"'Mrs. Mackenzie had just stepped out from beneath the aw-ning when the first shot rang out. The doorman, dashing past her to seize the attacker, knocked Mrs. Mackenzie into the gut-ter as the second shot went wide, gouging a chunk out of the Mercer's sideboard three inches to the left of Mrs. Mackenzie's startled face.

"'Mrs. Mackenzie miraculously had only been wounded in her left hip and would recover quickly. The identity of the at-tacker and motive for the attack were quickly discovered by arriving detectives as the shooter, an Italian immigrant and an-archist named Giuseppe Rogasta, began to scream, "Death to Capitalists," as he was cuffed.

"'It was after this family trauma that Mr. Mackenzie made the decision. To take his sensitive wife out of Manhattan and place her year-round at their favorite summer town in the quiet quaint Village of Southampton on Long Island's south shore.

"'But no normal house would do for his beloved Margreth if she were to live on the shore year-round. Fifty acres of prime beachfront was promptly purchased and Sandhill Point was born.'"

"Sandhill Point?" Viv said.

"That's the name of the estate here," I said, excitedly show-ing her the cover of the book.

On it was a black-and-white photograph of the house's black-and-white-tiled foyer. *SANDHILL POINT* was embossed over the top of the picture, and on the bottom it said, *House of Dreams.*

"It's a book about the house itself," I said. "Apparently, this place is not just beautiful, it's really famous. It was built by this guy, Arthur Mackenzie, a robber baron–era steel magnate who was a partner of Carnegie."

"Tom didn't mention that the house actually has a name," Viv said, looking up at the elaborate chandelier. "And how romantic. The man had it built for his beloved wife as a sanctuary. What was her name again?"

"Margreth Mackenzie," I said, flipping through the book. "She was the one who painted all these seascapes displayed throughout the house."

"Even the one in our room?"

"Yep. It was one of her passions, the book says. Not only that, but the house was designed by McKim Mead White, the same architects who designed so many of the famous Newport mansions and the New York Public Library building. The landscape architect who did the gardens, or as the book calls them, the Formal Entrance Court, also did the grounds for the Lincoln Memorial."

"That is so cool," Viv said, smiling. "Look at us. We're living like robber barons. No wonder it's so expensive."

"Not only that, but so many rich and famous people have stayed here, it's not even funny. FDR summered here for a couple of seasons in the thirties. Eisenhower. Jackie O was here for parties and sleepovers when she was a kid. Your butt could actually be parked right where hers was. Much of the antique furniture is the same."

Viv wriggled in her seat and laughed.

"How exclusive!"

"Mick Jagger stayed here in the seventies. Clint Eastwood. Dennis Hopper. Andy Warhol. And get this! Xavier Kelsey used to summer here for decades."

"No way! Your favorite writer!"

"Mommy, *Laser Rabbit* is too hard. I'm hungry," Angelina said, pouting.

"So much for the high life," Viv said, standing. "Text your

crazy brother again, Terry, and tell him we all have hungry kids to feed and if he doesn't get his twenty-first-century *Great Gatsby* butt down here pronto, we're all about to forget about the reservations and head to a Mickey Dee's."

34

"I hate to bother you, Oscar," I said the next morning to the old man bent at the locked door beside us.

"Oh, no, Mr. Rourke. Please, it's no bother," Sandhill Point's longtime head groundskeeper, Oscar Womack, said, continuing to go through his huge key ring.

As we returned from the Montauk fireworks the night before, the house manager, Robin, greeted us with some nightcaps. When I asked her about the coffee table book, she had explained that Sandhill Point's original groundskeeper, Oscar's grandfather, had actually written it.

So I woke up early and tracked down Oscar to get the deluxe Sandhill Point historical tour.

We started out in the garden. After we went through the maze, he showed me where Eisenhower had beaten MacArthur at a game of horseshoes and the hidden gazebo where all the summering debutantes used to neck with their beaux. After that, we went into the kitchen, where he pointed out the antique silver safe, along with the old call bell box that Margreth and Arthur Mackenzie had used to summon the servants.

Now at the end of the tour, we were at the pool house, where Oscar said he was going to show me something I was really going to like.

I expected there to be a guest suite or something. That's why my jaw immediately dropped as I saw there was a pool *inside* of the pool house instead. It was some imperial ancient Roman bath-looking thing the size of a basketball court beside several hot tubs and a glassed-in sauna.

Even the men's changing room we were now standing in was a jaw-dropper, like it could accommodate a state university instead of a private residence.

"Honestly, Oscar," I said. "If you can't find it, we can try again tomorrow. You've already been so nice."

"No, please," he said, smiling. "If you'll humor me, I'll find it, Mr. Rourke. I like playing tour guide whenever I get the chance. Would you be surprised to hear most people who come here couldn't give one whit about this wonderful old place?"

He tried another key.

"No. Most guests just want to take pictures of themselves in front of their fancy cars in the drive. And the amount of times we've heard threats of it being sold to contractors to raze it and rebuild! Rebuild? I say. It would be like painting over the *Mona Lisa* to use the canvas."

He pointed up at the vaulted blue-and-gold mosaic-tiled ceiling as the lock finally clacked.

"How could anyone improve on *this*?" Oscar said as he opened the door.

There was a blast of dry heat and the faint sweet smell of water rot and chlorine as Oscar led me down a narrow staircase. At its bottom along the yellowish paint-cracked wall of a corridor he led me down, I suddenly noticed the gallery of pictures.

They were old black-and-white photographs of Gilded Age rich people. Women in wedding dresses. A debonair-looking fellow playing a piano in front of an enormous Christmas tree. My favorite was an elegant silver-haired gent in a topcoat and tails with a silk hat, cigar in his mouth, holding a puppy.

"Those are the old Mackenzie family photos," Oscar told me as we walked along. "Grandpa really loved them. And they loved Grandpa back, especially old Mrs. Mackenzie. She gave him a precious silver picture frame from Tiffany's as a gift every time Grandma had a new baby. They really treated him like one of the family. Imagine? Who would do that? They were a real class act, I'll tell you. When he retired, they threw him a party at the Rainbow Room in New York City. First time in my life I ever tasted real French champagne."

Oscar led me past a humming, low-ceilinged room filled with gauges and dials and a stainless-steel electronic board.

"All this stuff is new for running the pools," he said. "They had a team from Germany come in to install everything. It'll tell you the pH level in the pool and automatically adjust the chlorine. Top-notch stuff."

After the pump room, we began to walk past several open doors in the right-hand wall.

"What's in there?" I said, peering into one room with dusty tarps everywhere.

"Those are the last of the old Mackenzie family belongings and furniture. The remaining heirs keep claiming they're going to have an antique appraiser come to take a look, but it never happens. Just a lot of hot air. No one seems to care about any of it."

I nodded. I knew from Tom that the estate had been sold five years ago to the hotel company that was now renting it out during the summers as a private resort.

When we reached the last door at the end of the corridor, Oscar opened it and clicked on a light. Inside was a small concrete room ceilinged with dusty overhead pipes. Beneath them were piles of ancient clutter. There were old wood paint-splattered ladders and rolled-up rugs. On top of the deck of an ancient 1980s treadmill against the right-hand wall were a bunch of sea green copper sconces piled into milk crates. The sour antique-store smell of rot and dust was cloying.

"And here she is," Oscar said.

35

"Here what is?" I said, glancing at the junk.

Oscar suddenly pointed to a card table and folding chair on the left-hand wall.

"I present Sandhill Point's pièce de résistance," he said.

"Um. That's real nice, Oscar, real nice," I said, looking around the jail cell–like concrete room, trying to figure out the joke. I was having trouble.

"You said you liked Xavier Kelsey, the writer, right? Well, this was where he did it. At least in the summer. This was his writing studio and that there was his desk."

"You've got to be kidding. Xavier Kelsey used to write here? No! In this horrible hot basement? Not even at a real desk?"

Oscar clapped his hands as he let out a loud laugh.

"Yes, can you imagine?" he said. "Out of all this wonderful estate—all its unparalleled rooms and gardens and views—he chooses this dump and a rickety folding table."

"How?" I said. "Why?"

Oscar shrugged his bony shoulders.

"Beats me. Everybody thought Kelsey wrote in his suite. I think I even read that once in a magazine article. What a load. We all knew better. I saw him myself one morning in '79 right after I got out of the Navy. I came down to fix a leak, and he was sitting right there at that card table, his cigarette sticking out sideways from the corner of his mouth and banging away on one of those old black Royal typewriters."

Oscar shook his head, remembering.

"Rat-a-tat-tat! The volume of it. It sounded like a Thompson machine gun. And did I mention that he was in his underwear?"

"No!"

"Yes," Oscar said, punching at his leg as he shook with laughter. "No shirt and in his skivvies, sitting on that metal folding chair. It was a sight. I guess all writers are supposed to be kind of nuts."

He pointed up at a coat hanger that hung from one of the pipes.

"See. That's the hanger he used. He'd come down here at six every morning, dressed in a nice button-down shirt and Bermuda shorts. And I guess he would then, um, get comfortable and write all morning. Then when he came back up at noon for lunch, he was dressed again pretty as you please. Go figure."

"That's something," I said. "It sounds like Kelsey was quite the oddball."

"Oh, no," Oscar said. "Aside from this quirk, he seemed perfectly sane. Charming. Mannerly. Remembered everybody's name, always had a joke when he came to the garden, a real gentleman. Though he did like his cocktails."

I smiled as I remembered meeting Kelsey at the steak house awaiting the verdict in Hailey Sutton's trial more than twenty years ago.

"The Mackenzies were very fond of him," Oscar said.

"He must have left them out of his infamous tell-all short story," I said.

"Say again?" Oscar said, turning toward me.

"Amazing, Oscar! A famous writer working right here. This house couldn't get more special," I said quickly.

I realized Oscar must have known nothing about the highly publicized scandal Kelsey had been involved in at the end of his writing career. Over a decade ago he had switched gears from true crime and written a very thinly veiled piece of fiction in the *New Yorker* revealing a lot of extremely embarrassing gossip and secrets about his very real and very powerful acquaintances from the Upper East Side and the Hamptons. He'd lost a lot of friends over it.

"So true," Oscar said, smiling.

An electronic ditty suddenly went off loudly in the little room.

"That's my timer for the irrigation system," Oscar said as he took out his phone. "I need to check one of the heads that's gone screwy. Well, that's about it, Mr. Rourke. I hope you enjoyed the tour."

"Oh, it was great, Oscar, really. Thanks so much. Do you mind if I poke around a little down here? I'd love to check out the photos and stuff some more."

"Sure thing," Oscar said. "Like I've said to others, you can even sit in Kelsey's chair if you'd like, but please keep your clothes on."

"Will do," I said.

36

When Viv suddenly opened the door of our suite's huge walk-in closet, I was on the floor in midyawn beneath the empty hangers with my laptop. Her puzzled gaze focused on the three items on the hardwood beside me: my phone, a lamp I had brought in, and a stacked ream of old yellow-edged paper.

"There you are," Viv said, yawning herself.

I groaned as I saw that the sun was just coming up beyond the sliding glass doors behind her.

Uh-oh, I thought.

"What time is it? And what are you doing? When did you wake up?"

"Well, to be perfectly honest, I haven't been to sleep," I said sheepishly.

"What!" Viv said. "You've been up all night? Terry! How could you? I told you we were getting out early to go to that water park with all the kids today. We have to leave in like half an hour. You're going to be a zombie!"

"Don't worry, Viv. I'll do a coffee IV drip," I said, yawning again as I stood. "It doesn't matter. Because you're not going to frigging believe this."

"Believe what?" she said.

I knelt and picked up the fat stack of paper I'd found in the pool-house basement the day before.

"Look!" I said, holding up the manuscript.

"'Untitled by Xavier Kelsey,'" Viv read aloud. "What is that?"

"They're looking for this," I said.

"Who's looking for what?" she said.

About an hour after Oscar had left, I'd found the manuscript in the storage room where Kelsey wrote. Inside a trunk were stacks of enormous leather-bound accounting ledgers belonging to the Mackenzies. I'd gone through two and was taking out a third when I saw a fat envelope sandwiched in the middle of it.

It was four hundred pages, old onionskin-like paper covered in single-spaced imperfect type.

"This is Kelsey's only novel, and everyone—every publisher in New York—has been looking for it ever since he died. They call it the missing Kelsey manuscript. Don't you see? This is it! I found it. I'm telling you."

"Slow down, slow down," Viv said.

"Okay," I said. "You remember that scandalous short story he wrote about all of his famous friends?"

She nodded. "The one Oprah interviewed him about?"

"Exactly. Well, that was just chapter one. They've been looking for this—the rest of it—for the last ten years. It's a tell-all about these socialites. How everyone is sleeping with everyone else and viciously backstabbing and gossiping. Folks are going to go bananas!

"They've been scouring the weeds since Kelsey died. And here it is, right here in your husband's hands!"

"For real?" Viv said, finally looking at it.

"For really real," I insisted. "But that's not it. That doesn't even matter. Get this, Viv. With the manuscript are these notes. Notes for a *new* book."

I took a deep breath as I fished the last three pages out from the bottom of the stack and showed her.

"Look! Kelsey was going to write another true-crime book called the *Sutton Slay* about Noah Sutton's murder!"

"Get out!" she said, peering at the sheets.

"Yes," I said as I pointed. "Here's the outline. See, it's Dad's old case. All the witnesses, all the players involved. There's even supposed to be a chapter about my dad! Kelsey was going to dredge up the whole thing again."

"Wow. That's crazy. How far did he get?" Viv said.

"I'm not sure. He must have still been working on it when he died. All I have is this handwritten outline—he always wrote his outlines longhand. And see, at the bottom here he wrote, 'Must bring files out from New York.' There are files!"

"That's amazing, Terry. That's so crazy. I knew your dad's case was a big deal, but wow."

I stared at the manuscript in my hands.

"What do you think I should do with this, Viv? This novel is sheer publishing gold. Maybe I should…"

Angelina came in like a sleepwalker then, trailing Skippy, her cheese doodle–colored stuffed monkey.

"Mommy, are we going swimming now?" she said.

"Maybe you should get dressed at the speed of light," my wife said, bringing Angelina back toward her bedroom, "and we'll talk about it."

37

They say that the journey of a thousand miles starts with the first step.

And mine was almost a real doozy.

"Watch it, chump," said some mean-looking young jackass on a grungy messenger bike as he almost hit me going the wrong way down Seventh Avenue in NYC's Greenwich Village.

"Thanks," I mumbled at the dope's back as he wove through the Ubers and taxis. "You have yourself a real nice day, too."

It was a little before eleven o'clock in the morning, and I'd just emerged from the steep Number One train subway stairs into the hot muggy gray rain that was drizzling down on lower Manhattan.

I went for the cover of an empty phone kiosk and stood there breathing in the dirty smell of rain off the city sidewalk, trying to catch my bearings.

I needed to catch them.

Because all of a sudden, things seemed to be heading in a brand-new direction.

As part of the Rourke reunion festivities, Tom had arranged to take everyone into NYC for a day trip. The over-the-top extravaganza consisted of a trip to the zoo, then lunch at Serendipity, and then a Central Park buggy ride to the Disney play *Frozen* in Times Square.

But from my all my internet searching about Xavier Kelsey for the past two days, I realized that there was something else in NYC.

Or, more precisely, someone else. Someone farther to the south down here in Greenwich Village.

Which was why I'd just left everybody at the zoo beneath its famous animal clock with promises to catch up with them at the theater. Needless to say, by the look on Tom's face, I'd be lucky if anyone would be talking to me by then.

I stared out at the grittiness of downtown as it began to rain harder. To the south down Seventh Avenue, above the taxis and water towers, stood the gray-blue-spired prism of the Freedom Tower.

Staring up at it, I remembered coming down here with my buddies in high school back in the era when there were still two towers. We'd sneak beers on the LIRR and come down to the bright city lights looking for what teenage boys everywhere have looked for on lazy summer weekends since the dawn of time. To fulfill some vague urgent summer fever dream of girls and bars and concerts and fights and fireworks and adventure.

And here I was now, more than twenty years later, not for pleasure but for business.

Unfinished business, I thought, thinking about my father as I hefted my backpack and came out of the kiosk and started walking east down West Fourth Street through the rain.

Two minutes later, I slowed as I turned onto a leafy section of Waverly Place, a block from Washington Square Park. The address I'd gotten off the internet turned out to be a redbrick town house behind freshly painted black wrought iron. I saw there were bunches of flowers all down its stoop and pressing up against the gate.

Is this really a good idea? I kept wondering as I stood staring at the house.

I wasn't sure. I was leaning toward no. Because I'd been a cop long enough to know how reality worked, how rich people's worms got put into cans for serious reasons. And how opening those cans could be quite hazardous to the health of the person holding the can opener.

So, I knew if I started this, I was going to be swimming against the tide here, probably the heaviest I'd ever face. Probably all by myself. My eyes were wide open about it. I wasn't walking into this blind.

But then I realized it wasn't really about that, was it? It wasn't about the odds of success. Or even about what I wanted.

In the end, it was about what *needed* to happen. And whether I had what it took to make it happen come hell or high water.

I stood across the street, stalling some more. When I read the last of the glued-on flyers and faded graffiti on the lamppost beside me for the second time, I was finally out of options.

"Here goes nothing, Pop," I mumbled as I crossed the street and rang the buzzer at the town-house gate.

I waited, looking through the black iron bars at all the flowers. Up close, their scent was surprisingly strong. It was an odd thick heady smell I'd never encountered before, sweet and spicy almost like licorice.

After three full minutes, I rang the buzzer again. And waited. And waited. Nothing.

I was stepping off the curb to leave when I heard the static crackle behind me.

"Yes?"

"Mr. Brody? Does Mr. Brody live here?" I called into the box.

"Maybe," the box said. "Who's there?"

"You don't know me. My name is Terry Rourke. I found something, Mr. Brody, that I believe may have belonged to Mr. Kelsey. I sent an email to Mr. Kelsey's literary agent about it this morning."

I stared at the silent box.

"What are you talking about? Who is this? What email?"

"I have a manuscript, sir. I have—"

The box let out an electric screech.

"Say again?"

"I have Mr. Kelsey's novel. The one that's missing. The one everyone has been looking for. I found it."

I waited, staring at the box.

Then the gate buzzer sounded like bacon frying as it popped the lock.

38

Xavier Kelsey's former companion, Lucas Brody, was a handsome sharp-featured vaguely Asian-looking guy in his midforties. He was wearing a navy blue Under Armour T-shirt that showed off a massive chiseled chest and remarkably defined and veined muscular arms.

There was a suspicious look on his taut bodybuilder's face when he answered the door at the top of his stoop. He also seemed sort of sleepy.

I looked at his hugely dilated pupils. As a Philly PD street narc, I knew stoned when I saw it.

Wake and bake without a doubt, I thought.

"You don't appear particularly bookish," Brody said to me as he stood there, sizing me up with his glazed eyes.

"Well, don't judge a book by its cover." I smiled.

"Especially a missing one?" Brody said with a catty eye roll.

I'd read a bit about Brody in one of the articles that came out after Kelsey's death. Many old friends of Kelsey apparently hated this younger man and considered him nothing but a cold and vicious gold digger.

When Kelsey died of a heart attack, his blue-blood family back in Kentucky actually demanded an autopsy, I suddenly remembered as Brody beckoned me in and closed the door.

Then I instantly almost turned around and fled.

In the foyer just inside the door was a candle-filled alcove, and inside the alcove was the most amazingly hideous African mask I had ever seen.

"Say hello to Dolly," Brody said casually as we passed it.

No, thanks, I thought, turning my head away from the massive demonic face that looked like it was made of dead grass and dried mud mixed with who knew what.

Past the primitive art installation, his house was a virtual ideal of the concept *richly furnished Manhattan apartment*. It was a soaring *Architectural Digest* centerfold of just-so rugs and modern furniture and massive modern-art paintings.

"Okay, so let's see it," Brody said.

I removed the first page of the manuscript from my bag and handed it to him. He plopped onto a couch and clicked on a lamp as he found some glasses. I found a seat on a perfectly simple and beautiful gray flannel reading chair across from him and waited.

When he was done with the page, he suddenly sat up and looked at me.

"Where did you find this?"

"I'm not really at liberty to say."

"Are you representing someone?" Brody said, squinting. "You're not a lawyer?"

"No, but I am representing someone," I lied on the spot. "All I can say on the matter is that this was found at an antique shop somewhere in the Northeast. It was inside an old accounting ledger."

He thought about that for a bit.

"How…Nancy Drew," Brody finally said, biting his lip as he stared at the floor. He glanced back at me sort of contemptuously.

He didn't seem too impressed by me. I liked that. It was best he think me a lowly messenger.

"This person you represent wants…? Wait. Let me guess. Lots of money?"

I shook my head slowly.

"What, then?" Brody said, sitting up straighter.

"A trade," I said.

"How's that?"

"They want a trade," I said. "The manuscript for Mr. Kelsey's research on his last book. The one that he was working on when he died."

"The *Sutton Slay* book?"

"Exactly," I said.

"Why would someone want all that crap?" Brody said.

I shrugged.

"Who knows? But this could mean a lot of money for you, Mr. Brody," I said. "The missing novel of Xavier Kelsey markets itself. You and I both know that. You'd have publishers at your mercy. You could make headlines. It would be the book of the year."

I saw a smile briefly play on his gold-digging lips.

"If it's real," he said.

I took out the rest of the manuscript, which included Kelsey's handwritten outline, and stood and handed it to him. When I sat back down, I checked my watch and crossed my legs.

"Please, Mr. Brody. Everyone knows Kelsey handwrote all of his outlines. Have a look," I said. "Take all the time you need."

39

I looked up from the pages in my lap and pointed my face at the dusty Montauk-bound LIRR train window beside me. It had stopped raining and the sun was setting. It looked like we'd just come out of the tunnel into Queens.

"Let's try it again there, buddy," said a redheaded conductor hovering above me in the jostling aisle to my left. "Ticket, sir?"

"Oh, I'm sorry," I said, almost knocking the papers to the floor as I fished my ticket out of my shorts' pocket and handed it over.

"That must be something good you're reading there," the conductor said as he clipped and left.

"Unbelievable," I said quietly to myself with a slow shake of my head as I finally slipped the pages back into the open cardboard file box sitting between my feet.

Suffice it to say, Brody had leapt on my offer to trade the novel manuscript and outline for the *Sutton Slay* files, which were worthless to Brody since Kelsey had never begun writing the actual book.

We'd just spent the afternoon sweating our way through the town-house basement, where the remains of Kelsey's things had been stuffed.

The *un-air-conditioned* town-house basement.

But it had actually been worth the grime and sweat, I thought as I patted at the dusty lid of the old file box lovingly.

Because if I wanted to know more about my dad's old case, I'd just found the mother lode.

In magazine interviews I had read, I learned that Kelsey's writing process was to first gather as much information as possible. "Getting the groceries," he had called it. For a full year, he would do nothing but research, absorbing everything humanly possible to know about a subject. Only then would he take another year to write, or what he called "weave together" all the material.

He died before he had begun the weaving process, apparently, because there was only a mound of research and his outline.

But what research!

In the box were neat rows of glossy binders, and in each binder were dossiers of information on everyone who had anything to do with the Sutton case. Some people were familiar but others I had never heard of. Ones that my father had never mentioned. All the suspects and witnesses. The police and all the lawyers. There was even a thick one about my father that I didn't have the guts to crack. At least not yet.

The detail was just incredible. There were addresses, phone numbers, email addresses, places of business. There were even illegally obtained credit card statements and internal phone company records in some of them. All the information had obviously been compiled by some top-notch corporate detective agency Kelsey had hired. It didn't say which one because all the letter-heads had been redacted like in a CIA file.

What was getting me so excited as I sat there was that I knew I really had something here.

Looking at all the info, I realized that it wasn't just research for a book. Instead, it was a detailed cold-case file that could contain the missing link to finally putting Hailey Sutton back on trial and vindicating my father.

One pretty much set up on a tee for an interested cop like myself to come along and solve.

I looked at the box and then out the window.

"I'm going to finish this, Pop," I whispered as the speeding shadow of the evening train flickered over the sunset faces of the old buildings.

"If it's the last thing I do," I said.

40

The train in front of us broke down on the Montauk line north of Bay Shore, so it was actually quite dark when I finally got back to the house. I was walking through the shadows just before Sandhill Point's massive circular driveway, dreading how much Viv was going to cream me, when I heard the sound.

I dropped the file box in the bushes near the front steps as the high whine, a kind of thunderous industrial trilling, suddenly came from the back of the house.

I sprinted across the crushed shells beneath the porte cochere's elaborate arch and had just made it to the side lawn when I saw it.

"Oh, shit," I said.

Out of the night past the edge of the beach at about the height of an elevated subway train suddenly emerged a large helicopter. It was one of those corporate ones, big and fat and white with sleek red and blue pinstripes. I watched it flare up and hover and begin to descend.

"Tom, you incredibly crazy son of a bitch," I said to myself with a smile as I ran toward it.

The chopper had just landed on the grass between the house and the pool by the time I got to where everybody was standing on the sundeck.

It was my turn to gape at them now. The entirety of my siblings and in-laws and nieces and nephews were all in their Sunday best atop the marble side steps of the house. Everyone was holding champagne flutes. Robin ran over and handed me one as I arrived beside Angelina and Viv.

My mom, half amazed, half terrified, in a silvery dress, came over and laughed as she squeezed my hand and gave me a kiss.

Viv tried to say something, but it was impossible to hear her over the quivering roar of the helicopter.

Like everyone else, I just stood there rooted to the stone steps, gaping at the rumbling aircraft. With the whole back of the house as well as the grounds floodlit, it looked like something out of a magazine shoot or a scene in a James Bond movie maybe.

Just as I thought this, as if on cue, Tom came running out of the side of the house in a three-piece suit. As dapper as Fred Astaire, he descended the marble steps and dashed to the chopper and popped the door. He really hammed it up on the way down, of course, as everyone laughed.

Who is it? I was about to scream at Viv, but then I realized who it was as the chopper's door slid wide and a small cute strawberry blonde woman stood cowering in it.

It was Tom's wife-to-be, Emmaline Fullerton, I suddenly realized as I remembered her photo from the save-the-date card that had been stuck to our fridge for the last several months.

She made quite the entrance, didn't she? I thought as I stared wide-eyed at the aircraft.

Or at least my brother was making sure she did.

With her were two similarly stunned-looking impeccably dressed young men. They were her two younger brothers, Toby and Gordon, I remembered Viv telling me. Tom helped them all down out of the helicopter and then suddenly scooped Emmaline up in his arms and carried her across the lawn.

As he carried her up the stairs, the chopper pilot gave us a thumbs-up from behind the canopy. We all cheered, especially all the Rourke boy cousins, as it lifted back up into the dark sky.

"You're absolutely nuts, just incorrigible," Emmaline said, punching at Tom's chest as he finally let her down in front of us.

"Emmaline, this is the fam," Tom said casually. "Everyone, this is Emmaline."

She gave us all a little wave, still looking quite flustered.

"When you said you had a ride waiting for us at the airport, I thought you were talking about a car, you incredible idiot," she said.

"A car?" Tom said, frowning. "I thought I told you, honey. They changed the town ordinance. Cars aren't allowed anymore. At least not in Southampton. You'll just have to get used to flying, I'm afraid."

But even Tom couldn't hold it in. He burst out laughing when he saw how ridiculously startled Emmaline looked.

"He's a madman, isn't he?" she said, staring at us as he buried his face into the nape of her neck. "No, really. This is how he introduces us? Some kind of practical joke? He knows I hate flying. Who would do this? I think he may truly be an actual lunatic."

"You're right. He is, Emmaline. But now he's your lunatic, so good luck," I said, and everyone laughed.

I decided I liked Emmaline. She was a character like Tom.

You could tell. Nothing like the stuffy London banking executive I had expected. She would give Tom a run for his money.

I looked around at the lit-up estate, the Parthenon of the pool house, the massive lawn, the flashing red lights of the departing helicopter.

And clearly, Tom had a bit of that, I thought, shaking my head.

As we all started meandering back toward the house, I stopped for a moment and turned and looked north up the beach. About a dozen houses up, I saw the lights there on its dark curve.

Staring at the lights of Hailey Sutton's glass house, I thought about how Tom was probably accomplishing his mission. He had no doubt pissed her off with his little low-flying chopper gag.

But was that such a good thing? I suddenly wondered.

I was lifting the flute to take a sip of the champagne when I paused. Instead, I left the glass on a stone railing as I kissed my daughter on top of her head. Then I took my wife's hand and headed back into the house.

41

Past the Coast Guard station in Montauk at the end of a little drive called Star Island Road is a secluded bayside parking lot. On weekend nights when I was in high school, kids often used to park in it with their significant other to *watch the submarine races*, to quote the term of the time.

On a beautiful unseasonably cool morning two days later, I pulled my Honda into this same lot and shut off the engine and got out of my car. I didn't see any racing submarines, but at the end of a dock at the far end of the lot, I saw the tall mast of an old fishing trawler swaying back and forth against the cloudless sky like a branchless tree in a soft breeze.

Then as I came around some hedges that rimmed the lot, I

looked out at the water and smiled as I saw a guy in a sea kayak paddling in.

"My goodness, little Terry Rourke. Look at you," my dad's old friend and partner Marvin Heller said as I helped him onto the dock.

"You look great as always, Mr. Heller," I said to the short and handsome sixtysomething Black man as we pulled in his kayak.

"Don't I, though?" he said with a grin as he patted at his close-cropped gray hair. "I keep telling my wife how lucky she is to have her own personal Denzel with a gun and a badge around."

I laughed as I helped Marvin toss his kayak into the back of an old faded red Nissan pickup.

"You're a cop, too, I hear," Marvin said as we sat on the tailgate. "Your dad sure would be proud of you, son. Be proud of all of you guys. Tom most especially. Not because he hit it big. But because he's finally getting married. He was always worrying about him. That boy drove him crazy. Just crazy."

I laughed.

"You can say that again," I said.

"So, Terry. What's up?" he said. "I didn't think I'd see you until the wedding. What can I do you for? Looking for some sea kayaking tips?"

"Well, Marvin, I was wondering about something," I said. "About your and my dad's old case, the Sutton case."

He blinked at me, looked truly surprised.

"The Sutton Slay?"

I nodded.

"Now that I'm back home, I was thinking about giving it a fresh look," I said.

"Is that right?" Marvin said to me after another long moment. "You're a cop where now again? Boston? No, Baltimore?"

"Philly," I said.

"Philly," he said. "They don't have enough work for you to

do down there in the City of Brotherly Love, huh? All those crimes solved? And aren't you on vacation?"

"The case is pretty ripe for a new looking over, wouldn't you say, Marvin?" I said. "I was wondering if you could walk me through it from your perspective as the homicide lead. See if I can get a better picture."

"You sure you want to do that, Terry? Get into all that old stuff?"

I smiled.

"You don't have to talk to me if you don't want to, Marvin. But I've made up my mind. In fact—"

I handed him a photograph I'd taken from one of Xavier Kelsey's dossiers.

"I've already started my cold-case investigation."

"What's this?"

"That's Jailene Mercado's house," I said.

"Hailey Sutton's maid? Our star witness?"

I nodded.

He whistled loudly at the five-bedroom, five-thousand-square-foot house.

"It's down on Jupiter Island in Florida," I said. "She paid one million seven hundred and fifty thousand dollars for it. Records show she owns it outright. She lives there with her daughter. It's got a view of the water, too."

I handed him another photograph of her garage.

He whistled again.

"A Range Rover and a Merc. Doing well for herself. So, you're thinking this proves what? Somebody paid her off?"

"Well," I said, "she didn't hit Lotto, and she doesn't have a job."

He handed me back the photos.

"What do you see coming out of dredging all this stuff up? Putting Hailey Sutton back on trial?"

"It had crossed my mind," I said. "It was a hung jury, after all."

"Sure was hung. By design. Power put its fist down. You don't think it can do it again?"

"What's wrong, Marvin?" I said, looking at him. "I thought you'd be excited about this."

Marvin looked at me, then at the water, then back at me. He opened his mouth. Then he closed it.

"What's up?" I said.

42

"Terry, if you're going to even think about doing this, you need to know a couple of very important things. First and foremost is this. There's a lot—and I mean a lot—of wacky stuff going on around here right now. Especially with the local DA's office and the Suffolk County cops."

"What do you mean?"

"Bad stuff is happening, Terry," Marvin said as he stood from the tailgate and took a look around the parking lot to make sure we were alone.

"Folks looking the other way. People getting their palms greased. There's always been a bit of graft, but never like this."

"I don't understand. How does this affect me reopening the case?"

"Because the DA, the not-so-honorable Nathan M. Wheaton, is the son of a bitch who personally decides who gets tried, or in Hailey Sutton's case, retried, around here. That piece of garbage goes to all the society parties and is known for working far harder weaseling his way out of prosecuting a case against the powers that be in the Hamptons than he does in court. Wheaton actually worked with your father. We both hated that rat son of a bitch. Your dad especially."

"So that means what?" I said.

"It means that photo is a good start, but it won't be enough to chicken wing that slimy piece of work into calling for a new trial. Not even close."

"You gotta be kidding me."

"And not only that," Marvin said, holding up a finger. "You start poking around about Hailey Sutton and her rich friends, you're going to have to look out for Wheaton's troops."

"Troops?"

"The county cops. They're just running wild, I hear. The department has never been in such bad shape."

I thought about that. The Suffolk County PD was no joke. It had over two thousand officers.

"Especially the chief, Dennis Tapley. Son of a bitch is bad news. And he and Wheaton are like Bert and Ernie, buddies from way back."

"Screw 'em, Marvin," I said, shrugging. "I don't care. I'm reopening the case."

Marvin looked at me with concern.

"All right. I'm telling you this because we're like family. But this doesn't get spoken of to anyone, wife, brother, mother, nobody. Agreed? *My* wife doesn't even know what I'm about to drop on you."

I stared at him.

"My lips are sealed, Marvin. What's up?" I said.

"The Feds are working a case against the Suffolk County

DA's office and the department right now," Marvin said. "They brought me in on it about three months ago. About two years ago, there was a bunch of murders along the Nassau County border, prostitutes strangled and dumped on the beach."

"Yeah, I remember hearing about that."

"Well, the FBI hears about it and wants to bring in the profilers to help. Sounds okay, right? Get some help. Let the Feds drain some of their budget for a change. Wrong. Chief Tapley puts the kibosh on it. 'We're good. We got this,' he tells them."

"That's nuts," I said.

"The Feds thought so, too. They look into it. Turns out Tapley himself knew three of the victims socially. Seems that this married man, father of three girls, likes to get his freak on with the Nassau County ladies of the evening. Off the job and even on. That's off the record, by the way."

"Wow," I said.

"Not just that. They start watching him, watching the shifts. It looks like he's got some of his boys on the night shift weekends safeguarding certain cars coming in and out of these big summer shindigs. Driving them in and out like a damn police escort up and down the Montauk Highway."

"That's insane. Drugs?" I said.

"Sure seems like it. Drugs. Prostitutes. VIPs who don't want to get pulled over for whatever they got in their possession. Use your imagination. Whatever somebody with no scruples and a disposable endless wad of hundreds wants or needs come a sultry Hamptons summer's night.

"And they've been to Hailey Sutton's place, kid. One of the main stops on the party circuit."

I couldn't believe what I was hearing. Since my father died, it seemed like all hell had broken loose.

"Who's running the case against them? Why haven't they arrested people yet?"

"Still climbing up the food chain. They want Tapley himself. And the DA, Wheaton, too, if they can bag him."

As if this wasn't going to be hard enough? I thought.

The DA's bad? And the county cops?

"This is unbelievable," I said.

"It is what it is, Terry. By the way, you actually might know one of the FBI agents on the corruption case. She's a townie. About your age. Went to Our Lady."

"Yeah? What's her name?"

"Frazier."

"Courtney Frazier?" I said, surprised.

"That's the one." Marvin smiled. "Not surprised you know her. She's a looker."

I nodded. I remembered her all right.

"She was a couple of years ahead of me, in Mickey's class," I said. "I worked with her over at Beach Point Country Club. We were lifeguards together. She still lives around here?"

"Oh, yeah. Never left. Her husband just opened up a popular restaurant in Amagansett last year," Marvin said. "But she works out of the FBI office in Nassau, so if you really need to do this, then get reacquainted pronto. You should definitely talk to her.

"She's got people in the DA's office feeding her info. Good people. Maybe they can help you with reopening Hailey Sutton's case from back channels. Or who knows how. You're going to need some kind of alternative way of getting this done. Because you go into the DA's office right now, he's going to shoot you down."

I followed Marvin as he walked around to the cab, took out his phone, and gave me Courtney's number.

"Remember now, Terry. If you start poking into the business of the powers that be, the Meadow Laners, you make sure your six is being watched. These people play for keeps. And stay the hell off the phone. You know those dirt box things you can use to snatch up a cell on the job? They got 'em, too."

"Wow," I said.

"*Wow*'s the word. They've all got illegal wiretaps going. Everybody in the DA's office and the department. Even on each other it's getting hot. To see if people are ratting each other out. I know one detective who's under his car with the grease monkey every time he gets his oil changed, checking for bugs."

"I appreciate the heads-up, Marvin," I said as I took out my notebook. "Now, about the case. If you could start from the beginning."

Marvin laughed.

"Stubborn one, huh?" he said, sighing. "Just like your old man."

43

"Alert, alert! This just in!" I said upstairs in our room in the beach house that night an hour after Angelina had fallen asleep. "I think I finally got this nailed down now. Or at least most of it."

I stood up from the desk in our luxurious master suite that was now covered with my dad's case. There were folders and binders and copy paper everywhere. On the bureau and desk, the bed and the mini fridge. There were several piles of print-outs on the floor.

"Okay, Viv. Are you with me? Do I have your undivided attention?" I said as I lifted up the whiteboard that I'd bought at Staples in Riverhead that afternoon.

"Wait. Not just mine," Viv said, smiling from the bed. "The baby's kicking."

I went over and put my hand on her belly and laughed as I felt it.

"You gotta be kidding me. Even the next generation of Clan Rourke is excited about going after this cold case, huh? I love it," I said.

After dipping out on the gang in the city and almost missing meeting the bride-to-be for the first time, I was grateful to be back in Viv's good graces. She had even somehow managed to smooth things over with Tom and the others.

"Okay, without further ado, here's what happened with the *State of New York v. Hailey Sutton*."

"No, wait," Viv said, grabbing her carton of Chubby Hubby off the nightstand. "Okay, ready. Go."

"On July 5, 1999, a call went into the village PD at 8:31 a.m.," I said, pacing around the room as I read from my notes. "Responding Village of Southampton police officers, Timothy Page and Raymond Gabrielson, arrive at 8:43.

"They both get there at the same time in separate patrol cars and get buzzed into the estate. The maid is waiting for them outside in the driveway, and they go in and find the deceased, Noah Sutton, in the left wing of the house on the floor of his office."

"Not in bed?"

"No. Either he woke up and came downstairs or he actually crashed there on the couch the night before. He slept in the office sometimes, the maid said, especially when he and Hailey were fighting. He'd been spending a lot of time in the office in the weeks leading up to the murder, she said."

"Continue," Viv said.

"Noah's in his boxer shorts, no shirt, facedown between the couch and the desk, blood pooled on the Persian rug. There were two shots to the right side of his head. One in the temple and one farther back, right above his ear. There was plenty of blood but no brain matter. Often with head wounds, the thick skull bone slows the acceleration of the bullet considerably. The bullets, two .38-caliber rounds called wadcutters, were still lodged in his brain."

Viv shuddered. "What's a wadcutter?"

"It's a kind of practice or target bullet. They're not really common in shootings. They made a big deal about that fact at the trial."

"Was there evidence of a struggle?"

"Not definitively. There seemed to have been a bit of a struggle that was over quickly."

"Like, 'Hailey? Honey, what the hell is that in your hand?'"

"Exactly."

"Where was Hailey when the cops showed?"

"This is where it gets interesting," I said. "When Officer Gabrielson asked where the lady of the house was, the maid said she didn't know. She'd run straight to Hailey's bedroom directly after she saw Noah, she said, but Hailey wasn't there.

"The maid speculated to the arriving cops that Hailey could have been in the guesthouse. But she was afraid to check without the police. When the responding officers went to the house with a key, they found the sleeping party guests inside alive and well."

"But no Hailey?"

"No. Only when the officers return to the house at around 9:12 a.m. do they find Hailey sobbing beside her beloved Noah in the office."

"Where had she been?"

"No one knows, but the officer noted that she was wearing sneakers and workout clothes, not pajamas."

"That would also come up at the trial?"

"Yes," I said. "That was prosecution point number one. Where was Hailey Sutton when the cops showed up?"

"This is fun," my wife said, spooning some more ice cream into her mouth. "Keep going."

"Prosecution point number two," I said, "was what detectives found in the garbage next door."

"I know this one. Hailey's hoodie with blood on it," Viv said.

"Noah's blood, to be precise," I said. "And what really should have cooked Hailey's goose was when the detective, Marvin Heller, who arrived at 9:20, asked her if she or her husband owned a gun. She said no."

"Which was a lie because the maid had already told the cops she had seen a gun," Viv said.

"Precisely," I said, pointing to where I had written **Hailey Lies** on the whiteboard.

"Then there's Hailey's background," I said. "Hailey was from backwoods Wisconsin originally and had worked her way into a very shady real-estate management firm in Manhattan. She worked there for three years, going from assistant to full broker. Her boss went to federal prison for bribery three months after she left."

"She get charged?"

"No. She was the one who ratted him out."

"That's how she originally met Noah, right?" Viv said. "She was his broker?"

"That's right," I said. "She sold him a huge penthouse on Central Park West."

"Wonder how she closed that deal," my wife said.

"There were certainly nasty rumors about that, but nothing compared to the rumors concerning her affair with the contractor that was doing work on Noah and Hailey's house, a contractor with Mob ties from Brooklyn named Mark Disenzo."

"That just makes no sense," my wife said. "Hailey bags one of the most eligible bachelors in the world and then cheats on him with a Mob contractor? Was it really even true? About the affair, I mean. Could your dad prove it at the time?"

"Yes," I said. "Dad didn't do speculation. The house gardener testified on the stand that he had seen them through the guest-house window one morning in flagrante delicto."

"Gotta watch those glass houses, Hailey," Viv said, shaking her head.

44

"But it sounds like an open-and-shut case," Viv said. "How the heck did Hailey get off?"

"The evidence went missing," I said.

"Oh, right. I forgot," Viv said. "Go on."

"The case then hinged on the maid," I continued. "Detective Marvin Heller was nobody's dummy. He quickly whisked the maid away to the station for questioning the day the body was found. He tried to get Hailey to come as well, but then a carload of Sutton family lawyers showed up moments later, and Hailey was sequestered and never spoke to the police again."

"They can do that? Just block access?" Viv said.

"They sure can. You have the right to remain silent, right?"

Viv shook her head. "So what did the maid say at first?"

"During questioning, she said she had seen a gun in Hailey's closet in the bottom drawer two weeks before and that it had scared the hell out of her. She identified it as a blue-steel Smith & Wesson Model 52 semiautomatic pistol with walnut grips."

"Wow, that was specific."

"She picked its picture out of a gun book Marvin Heller showed her. What made it so significant and plausible was that Model 52s are mainly target-shooting pistols that shoot—"

"Wadcutter bullets?"

"Bull's-eye," I said.

"But then she went back on what she had said."

I nodded. "Yes, it was the final straw in Dad's case. On the stand, she said she had made the whole thing up. After talking to a priest, she said she was told she had to tell the truth now."

"That's ridiculous. She picks the perfect gun out of the book and then says she made it up?"

"Exactly. And here's what lying bought her," I said, showing Viv the photos of Jailene Mercado's Florida villa I'd shown Marvin earlier.

"Isn't that enough to reopen the case?"

"No, not yet," I said.

45

"So what kind of case did the defense present?" Viv asked.

"Somebody else shot Noah," I said. "Somebody at the party. A lot of weird people in and out of the house that night. Maybe Noah interrupted a burglar. There was nothing missing, but why stop a good BS story? And their ace in the hole was the defendant herself, Hailey Sutton."

"How so?" Viv said.

"She was twenty-five, beautiful. Just a sweet defenseless grieving widow. How could she be a stone-cold killer?"

"That's not right," Viv said. "And the jurors fell for it?"

"Just two of them, which was all it took. When my dad got a chance to question them, they both said the same thing. They thought that Hailey had more to lose than to gain by killing her husband and coupled with the fact that Noah's family supported Hailey made them think that she was innocent, as well."

"Why did the Sutton family support Hailey?" my wife asked.

"I don't know. That's a great question. They really did support her, too. They paid for her ridiculously expensive lawyers and sat behind her at the defense table every day. No one really knows why."

"So what now?" Viv said.

I waved at the dossiers strewn about the bedroom.

"I'm going to interview all the people in Kelsey's files. I'm going to start with the staff and work my way in toward Sutton family members just like the way Kelsey outlined it for his book."

"What will you say to them? That you're a cop?"

I shook my head.

"Viv, I know it was a million years ago, but I did major in journalism. I'm going to fib and tell them I'm a journalist and that Kelsey's publisher hired me to finish his book. Twenty years can loosen a lot of people's tongues. Give people perspective. Grudges can live a long time, especially for employees. Who knows, maybe I can shake something loose."

"But, Terry, I don't know. This sounds like it could be dangerous."

"You think going undercover in the blue-blood Hamptons is dangerous?" I said. "You should try it in North Philly."

"You don't need to remind me," she said, steamed. "You should try waiting up nights for you to come home. Or wondering if you're not."

"Viv, I can handle it," I said. "You know I can. I know it's a pain, but can you hold down the fort with Angelina and the wedding stuff while I take a stab at this? It really means a lot to me."

My wife laid her spoon down on the nightstand with a click.

"I will," Viv said finally. "On one condition, Terry."

"Name it."

"You promise that after this vacation, you'll take me on vacation."

46

I was a little bit beyond a mile past the main drag of Amagansett on the Montauk Highway when I hit my clicker and pulled into a drive beside what looked like an abandoned farm stand. The noon heat rolled in as I zipped down my window and took a look around. It took me a minute to see that there was a dirt road leading to a field behind it, and I followed it past some fruit trees and a small cornfield, and then I saw the main building.

It looked like an old rambling clapboard country house you'd find somewhere in the middle of Iowa, but then when I got a little closer, I could see the sparkling bay and the shoreline right behind it.

I parked in the almost completely empty lot to the left of the restaurant and walked toward the bayside entrance. Along the path outside, I could see the tables on a terrace that overlooked a little fountain-filled English flower garden set up along the shore.

I stopped for a moment and looked out at the sweeping water view. The scenic property had to be worth a not-so-small fortune.

Inside, the dining room took up almost the entirety of the house's bottom floor. Everything was crisp and clean and white, white wainscoting and white tables with white and pale purple flowers on them.

A busboy I met led me into the kitchen. And at the other side of it, through the doorway of a cluttered closet-like office, I spotted my old friend and coworker Courtney Frazier with her back to me, talking on the phone.

Marvin Heller had been right. She certainly was a looker. Tall and blonde and blue-eyed. Even after all this time, she was still as pretty as I remembered.

To say that I had been at one point in my adolescent life infatuated with Courtney Frazier would not have been far off the mark. Every young male at the country club, from the caddies to the lifeguards to the country club kids, and even some of their creepier fathers, was smitten with Courtney Frazier sitting there up on her lifeguard chair, swinging her whistle.

It was pure fantasy all right. She saw me as a kind of little brother. She'd call me "Little Rourke" all the time at work even though I was a full lifeguard just like her.

I'd actually entered a club tennis tournament in her honor. The staff wasn't even really allowed to participate, but I'd seen that some jerk named Graham Ericson, whom Courtney was rumored to be dating, was on the sign-up board, so I put my name right under his.

It was only when we were put head-to-head in the first round that people told me to get ready to be destroyed because Graham Ericson, some Rob Lowe look-alike, was actually on the Junior tour.

He destroyed me all right. In almost straight sets. *Almost.*

I'll never forget the two games I took off him. He didn't expect that. No one did. I remember people mumbling when it happened in the first set. And then more people came over to watch, including Courtney.

I couldn't serve for my life, but I had played with my brothers and could hit back pretty hard, especially with my forehand. The first game I took from Graham, he smashed at the net with his racket. The second game I took, he actually tomahawked it into the fence and screamed.

When he did that, I looked over and made lingering eye contact with Courtney. I remembered she had looked back at me sort of shocked and touched. Or at least maybe. It never led to anything, of course, but she knew what I was doing. At least I fantasized that she did for the rest of that summer.

When Courtney suddenly put down the phone and turned in her chair, a look of surprised joy shot across her pretty face as our eyes met. A calendar came loose off the door as she leapt up.

"Terry!" she said as she gave me an unexpectedly huge hug. "Terry Rourke, you're back!"

47

The water view off the restaurant's back terrace was even more amazing than the one in the front. Under our outside table's umbrella, a sea breeze softly rang my water and wine glasses together with a musical chime as I took another bite of my lemon chicken.

"This place you guys have is incredible," I said to Courtney, sitting across from me. "I remember your dad's steak house was awesome, but this is, wow, another level."

Courtney smiled.

"Yeah, we lucked out. My husband, JJ, is a chef and he was burning out commuting into the city. My dad knew the old lady, Mrs. Korkowski, who was selling. There were all these huge bids, but she sold to us because we assured her we were going to keep the farm going."

I nodded, knowing my local history. The Hamptons was mainly an Irish and Polish farming community before the 1970s, when Wall Street people found it and started buying up everything. My father had actually moved out here from the Bronx, having loved the wonderful weekends and summers he spent on his uncle's farm in Bridge Hampton.

"Special Agent Farmer Courtney," I said. "Life's pretty funny, isn't it?"

"You're telling me, Terry Rourke. Here he sits, the Roger Federer of the Hampton Bays, all grown up."

"You bet," I said, sipping the white wine, which was even better than the chicken. "And when I'm not scoring from the baseline and kissing the Wimbledon trophy, I'm in Philly central booking with a collar. And you're a Fed because…? Let me guess. They have a really good lap pool down in Quantico?"

She laughed.

"Actually, I went to NYU law school and found myself in the Nassau County prosecutor's office. About nine years ago, I started to get bored. An agent I knew said they were hiring, so here I am."

"So did Marvin tell you what I'm trying to do?"

"Yes. You want to reopen the Noah Sutton case," she said, peering at me closely. "Talk about a bombshell. Why, Terry? I mean, why now?"

"I found something," I said. "Some new evidence. A cache of it, actually. I want to see if I can shake something loose."

"Wow, a cache? Really? Marvin mentioned some photographs of the former maid."

I nodded.

She looked at me very closely.

"Where'd you find this, eh, cache?" she said.

I smiled at her. "A little birdie dropped it off."

"Of course. I've heard of those. A seagull, I presume? Out there on Meadow Lane?"

"You heard, huh? The Rourke family reunion."

"Crazy, fun townie family done good suddenly scoops up the biggest white elephant on Meadow Lane for the summer?" Courtney said. "Yeah, people are talking, Terry. I don't know who more. The beautiful people who come in who find it incredibly droll. Or the townie staff faithful who think it's the coolest thing that's ever happened in the history of Long Island."

"There you go," I said, smiling. "I'll have to tell my crazy brother his plan is working. Anyway, Courtney, Marvin thought we might be able to help each other out due to the, um, sensitive situation currently going on at the DA's office. He thought a less direct route in getting the Sutton case reopened was probably my best bet. That maybe you could help me there."

"Marvin's a smart man," Courtney said. "I know one of the good ADAs at County. I'll contact them and see what they think. I can also coordinate between you and them if you or your little birdie finds anything else. Would that help you out?"

"That would be amazing, Courtney. That's exactly what I'm looking for."

"As I'm sure Marvin told you, you have quite a rough row to hoe in front of you here," she said. "District Attorney Wheaton's up to his neck in shenanigans with a lot of heavy hitters in the village, including Hailey Sutton, by some of the rumors. So, you're going to have to come up with some pretty undeniable evidence in order to pressure him to reprosecute."

"I've heard. It doesn't matter. I'm still going to give it a crack," I said.

Courtney took a small sip of her wine and nodded.

"I understand, Terry. I remember your dad and your brothers and Erin and your sweet mom at the library. What happened to you guys after the trial was just disgraceful. You're an old friend and a damn good cop. I hope you find what you're looking for. I really do. I'll be pulling for you."

I squinted at her.

"Who told you I'm a good cop?"

She smiled. "I've heard about your antics down there in Philly. Your buy-and-bust records. How you like to be the UC in the stings. Quite the actor, I hear. I also heard about your combat medal."

I glanced at her. Back in 2014, I shot and killed a meth dealer, a biker who had drawn down on my partner. The idiot thought we were these two guys who had robbed his spot the day before. My old partner was a captain now. I still had nightmares about it where my gun jams or I'm out of ammo and it just goes click.

"I have my little birdie friends, too, Terry," Courtney said with a wink.

48

When I got back to the beach house, at first I was puzzled at the dozens of cars parked along Meadow Lane in front of it. Then I heard the cheering, and I zipped down the drive and parked and ran upstairs to get changed.

I'd just come down to join everybody already out on the immense side lawn beyond the pool as a big dude in an umpire's uniform yelled, "Okay, batter, batter, batter!" in a booming voice.

I'd made it, thank goodness. The first official Rourke-Fullerton family reunion softball game was finally underway.

Like everything else Tom had in store for us, all stops had been pulled. He'd had a mesh backstop brought in and chalk lines laid and even a DJ. As the music started along its baselines, a crowd of about seventy-five people sitting on beach chairs and beach towels let out whistles and hollers of approval.

The two teams were quite a combination of cousins from both Mom's and Dad's sides, as well as some of Emmaline's relatives who had begun to arrive from England for the upcoming wedding.

I glanced over at the formal old-money behemoth of a house and smiled as I wondered what Margreth Mackenzie of Sandhill Point would have thought about the mix of Brits and firemen and finance gurus getting buzzed on suds here out on its hallowed grounds. Not much, probably.

Or who knew. Maybe she would have loved it. Maybe after a few gin and tonics, Margreth was a beach blanket party animal, hoop skirt and all.

As people still milled around slowly, I decided to grab an adult beverage myself. A few minutes later, I was sitting in a folding camp chair beside Viv, balancing it on my knee. Between sips of my ice-cold Sam Adams, I watched to my right beyond the curve of the beach where a couple of sloops were cruising south out there in the hot hazy blue distance of the Atlantic.

Then my attention was pulled left as I watched Angelina, squealing and running around like mad with the rest of the kids as they played Frisbee with a couple of Labradors.

"Happy?" Viv said beside me as she took an ice cube out of her cup and flicked it onto my neck.

Sweet blue billowing smoke from a whole mess of sausage and peppers getting happy on the grill behind me washed over me as I took a healthy hit of my icy Sam Adams.

"Definitely getting there, babe," I said as the heavy rockabilly bass line of Springsteen's vintage "Pink Cadillac" started pounding from the speakers.

"Now first up, fresh to our shores, the pride of England, Toby Fullerton," the DJ announced.

Watching Emmaline's younger brother Toby do some very low swings with the bat in the on-deck circle, my brother Mick called out from third.

"My good man, quick tip. This is softball, not golf!"

"Jolly good!" Toby called back as he stepped into the batter's box. "Ready!"

I'll say. When my brother Tom threw the first pitch in low, Toby surprised us all. He must have played cricket at school or something because he freaking clobbered it. If the stadium of grass had a wall, it would have gone over the right field one.

As I watched the right fielder turn around as it sailed over his head, it was looking like an inside-the-parker for sure.

Then I turned back and saw what Toby was doing.

"No, stop!" I yelled as I saw him running for third base.

"Toby, no! It's the other way!" I cried. "Come back! Come back!"

He was around third heading for second when he realized his error and started back. He'd passed home plate and was half a step to first when they finally got the ball back in.

"You're out!" the ump cried as everyone burst into laughter.

"Hey, Tobster," my brother Tom said over the merriment. "We drive on the right-hand side of the road here as well, okay? Just FYI."

"I'm afraid I don't know what to say," Toby said to me as he returned to our dugout.

"It's okay, Toby," I said, patting him on the shoulder. "You really creamed that one. You'll know next time where to run. Also remember, don't run with the bat. You're supposed to drop it."

"You are too kind, Terence. Next time, I will do my uppermost," Toby said, bowing his head.

"Next up," the DJ said over the speakers, "the Rourke family's youngest son, Terry."

"That's you. C'mon, dummy," my brother Mickey called to me with a grin from third base.

"Yay, Daddy!" Angelina said as I set my feet into the batter's box.

I wiped my sweaty hands on my blue T-shirt as Tom, on the mound, tossed the ball up and caught it behind his back.

"This guy ain't got nothing, folks," he called out.

I gave a practice swing to the aluminum bat and set.

"Bring it, you crony capitalist," I said.

In came the glowing yellow-green softball, high and fat. I swung and whiffed at it. Nothing but air. Everyone groaned.

"Philly fan fans and misses," Tom called out. "What did I tell you, folks?"

I let a few balls go. Then I tipped one off the end of the bat, a wimpy pop-up between first and the plate that Tom dived for but thankfully missed by a hair.

Strike two. Not good, I thought, watching Tom get back to the pitcher's mound.

Everyone laughed a second later as I pointed dramatically with the bat out to the sailboats at sea à la Babe Ruth.

Why I did that, I didn't know. A little overconfident advice from Sam Adams maybe.

But as the next pitch arced in toward the plate, time seemed to slow down as I kept my eye on it.

Then I swung from the hip the way Dad had taught me, and there was the sweet feel of incredibly solid contact as I connected with a loud whump. Even I couldn't believe how high I had launched one to left. The left fielder ran out and then ran in and then out again as it went over his head.

I put on the jets and went for three and whooped with elation as I got in right under Mickey's diving tag.

"Safe!" roared the umpire.

"No way! He was out!" Mickey complained as he threw his hands up.

"Mom, you were right there," Tom said to our mother, who was sitting just off the bag. "He was out, right?"

"Ah, get over yourself, Tom. The throw beat him, but Mickey flubbed the tag. He was safe."

I gave my mom a big hug and kiss on her cheek as everybody cheered and started cracking up. Even the umpire.

"I always suspected you loved him more, Mom," Tom said, shaking his head. "But now it's confirmed."

49

I was standing by the keg after the game had ended when the commotion started.

Up by the front of the beach mansion, there was some loud beeping, like trucks backing up. We watched as a couple of our cousins came jogging across the grass from under the porte co-chere.

"What's up?" my brother Tom said, putting down the keg pump spout.

"Hey, everyone! Listen up," one of them called out. "Some asshole cops are towing cars up on the road."

"What?" Tom cried. "You have to be kidding me. I bent over backward to get the permits. I had my lawyer call twice. It's been completely cleared with the town. This is complete bullshit."

"Yeah, well, looks like no one bothered to tell the cops," our cousin said with a shrug. "And they're taking cars."

I immediately followed Tom across the lawn. As we reached the end of the driveway by Meadow Lane, we saw it was true. Two tow trucks were hooking up cars parked along the shoulder as a third one arrived.

There was a uniformed cop there as well, wearing aviator shades and sitting on the hood of a police cruiser across the road. I knew he was some kind of brass by his crisp white shirt and black tie.

I followed Tom across the street toward the cop.

About six-one with broad enough shoulders, the man had some size on him, I noticed. But he wasn't really in shape. He was soft in the middle and sort of pear-shaped.

"What's the problem, Officer?" Tom said as we stepped up. "We cleared the event with the town. I have the permit right here on my phone. There must be a mistake."

"It's 'Chief,' not 'Officer,'" he said, casually straightening his tie. "Chief Tapley. And I'm not from the town. I'm from the county."

I couldn't believe it. Marvin wasn't kidding. Tapley was definitely not on the up-and-up.

"But it's right here, Chief," Tom said, offering the phone to him. "Please, if you would just take a look."

"Get that shit out of my face unless you want to watch it land in the bay," Tapley said nastily.

"What?" Tom said, confused.

The smirk that slowly crossed Tapley's face had some real mirth in it, I saw. Like other psychos I had unfortunately worked with from time to time on the job, this loo-loo seemed to have a real high opinion of himself.

And he was truly enjoying this.

"I'm from the county," he repeated. "You need a hearing aid? This is my county."

"Oh, the county," Tom said, peering at him. "I get it now. Let me see. Do I genuflect now or bow? Salute maybe?"

Tapley removed his shades as his smile disappeared. His eyes were cold and gray as sheet metal.

"You tone down that smart mouth," he said. "This is a county park police matter. Permit or no permit, you're blocking access to Shinnecock east county park, and I will do what I need to do to render the situation safe."

"Shinnecock east! That's three miles away down Meadow Lane!" Tom said, pointing.

"Doesn't matter," Tapley said. "The blockage is here and we've gotten complaints."

Just as he said this, a vehicle approached from the direction of the beach.

It was a fancy blue Mercedes SUV, I saw as it slowed. One of those really expensive safari-style things.

The woman in the Mercedes looked pretty fancy and expensive herself. She was dark-haired and regal and perfectly tan in a black bandeau bikini top and matching wrap and floppy beach hat. A Hermès Birkin bag with a little dog in it sat on the passenger seat beside her.

It must have been the Sam Adams I'd just drunk, because even after she lifted her Chanel shades, it took me a second to realize we were all standing there staring at Hailey Sutton.

"Thank you, Chief," she said before she tore off in the six-figure Merc down Meadow Lane in a demure grumble and puff of sand.

"Oh, I see," my brother said, watching after her.

"Yeah? You see what?" Tapley said as Tom stepped another foot closer to him.

"Tell me, Chief. She paying you in cash?" Tom said. "Or maybe you boys at the county got one of those electronic Square things now for your iPhone to take American Express payments."

Tapley's mirthful smile was back.

"You got a problem with me, why don't you take it up right here, Rourke?" Tapley said, pointing at his chin. "I'll even give you the first shot. Or maybe you're not your poor old dearly departed drunk of a daddy's son after all. Wall Street made you soft, did it?"

I grabbed my brother just in time as he lunged forward.

Tapley smiled some more as he slowly slid his sunglasses back on.

"Guess your little brother got the brains in the family, Rourke. Because that would have been the worst mistake you ever made."

"It's all right, Tom. Calm down, dude," I said as I pulled Tom with all my might back onto the other side of Meadow Lane into the driveway.

"How do you like that, Terry? Hailey Sutton herself!" Tom said as he broke free and began pacing back and forth on the seashells.

"Tom, come on now. You saw that cop. He's baiting you and he's fricking evil. He's working with Hailey. It's all a setup! He's also loving every minute of messing with us. He's begging for you to do something so he can nail you."

"Oh, he won't have long to wait, then!" Tom screamed as he kicked half a foot of expensive gravel into the hedges.

PART THREE

THE COLD HARD TRUTH

50

Beyond the dark shore of Connecticut, the lights of New London winked in the warm summer night like a diamond necklace.

Then the Orient Point ferry's horn sounded from the top deck beside me as it lurched to a stop.

From the ferry's top rail, I stood looking across the boatyard as a deckhand clattered a ramp down onto the concrete dock.

I smiled as I watched the first cars disembark into the shadowed old whaling town.

Because I was really finally doing this, I thought as I came down the steps and off the ramp.

I was finally reopening my dad's old case.

It took ten minutes of winding through New London's funky

narrow streets past old brick buildings and art galleries to find
the neon lights of the bar I was looking for on Green Street
called Joe's Tavern.

The joint really made pains to put the *old* back in *old-school*,
I soon realized. Not only did a blast of classic Cheap Trick hit
me as I pulled open its door, but the empty barstool I found a
moment later was on the back wall between the restrooms and
an old *Wizard of Oz* pinball machine someone had managed
to get through a 1983 wormhole. Even the waitress who came
over and asked if I wanted to see the pub grub menu had high
eighties hair.

As she went off to get me one of the three-buck Schaefer
cans that were being advertised, I perused the photographs on
the dark wainscoting beside me. They featured a lot of sailors as
well as some submarines from the base that was just across the
I-95 bridge in Groton, CT. There was also a bunch of photos
of some old-timey dude with a mustache who turned out to
be Eugene O'Neill, the great Irish American playwright. According to one of the photo captions, he had a house outside of
New London and had done a lot of drinking right here at Joe's.

After I was done with the decor, I checked out the people.
There were maybe two dozen in the tiny place, which made
it pretty packed. There were college-aged kids in the rows of
booths beside me, but most of the guys at the bar seemed older.

The J. Geils Band replaced Cheap Trick on the radio as the
waitress brought my beer. I gave her a five and popped the top
and sipped, watching the patrons glued to the BoSox-Rays game
up on the TV to the left of the door.

I was three-quarters through my beer, imagining that the sea-
soned folks at the bar were all tortured struggling playwrights
contemplating our long day's journey into night, when I suddenly spotted a guy I hadn't noticed before, sitting at the bar
up near the door.

My can of beer made a clicking sound as I placed it on the windowsill beside me and smiled.

Because it was Darren Ross, Noah Sutton's old limo driver, the man I had come here to see.

51

Target acquired, I thought as I watched Darren watch the game.

I'd done my homework on him from Xavier Kelsey's folders. Ross had been sleeping in the staff apartment in the basement of the Sutton house on the night of the murder. He had been on my dad's interview list, but like most of the staff, he had had massive amounts of legal representation from the get-go, so it was never pinned down what he may or may not have seen that night.

Xavier Kelsey's detective agency notes about Ross said that the New London resident was a regular at the tavern and talkative. I was hoping they were right.

Each dossier contained an extensive background preliminary on each of the interview targets. It seemed like they had all been surveilled extensively, but none of them had actually been contacted. Kelsey himself, like any other good investigator, insisted on making that initial contact personally so that he could get their first crucial reactions. But he had died before he'd ever had the chance.

With that in mind, I sat and observed Darren. He was a short yet kind of tough-looking character, stocky, in a long-sleeve black T-shirt and camo shorts. He had a sharp kind of GQ sidewall-style haircut that was definitely younger than his forty-four years of age.

Darren was originally from Boston, his file said, and he had gotten the job working for the Suttons through an uncle who had worked on one of their estates in Wellesley.

Darren had left Hailey Sutton's employ six months after the trial and seemed to have done a bunch of bouncing around after. Suspiciously expensive bouncing around. Photos posted on his Facebook wall showed him backpacking through Europe, Asia and even New Zealand. He'd lived for over a year in Bali, it said.

In 2008, he'd come back to the States and owned a small bar in Hoboken, New Jersey, for a while before it went belly-up. The lifelong bachelor had one bust, a possession with intent to sell some weed back in 2012 down in North Carolina, where his sister lived.

I thought that the best angle of attack on Darren was the implication of him making some money by talking to me. The riskier side of the appeal-to-greed approach was that the file said some of Darren's family members still worked for the Suttons up in Beantown. Another sister of his was a lawyer attached to a Sutton law firm also in snooty Wellesley.

But what was in my favor, at least maybe, was the fact that in every workplace there are factions. Some people like the boss, some people hate him. If Darren had liked Noah and disliked Hailey, then maybe he would talk to me for that reason alone.

I stood and headed toward the bar.

I had to find out.

52

When I was finally able to sidle my way in between Darren and one of the playwrights at the bar, I saw that the Sox's five-run deficit was in danger of ballooning now that the Rays had two on and no outs.

"Are you kidding me?" I said loudly up at the screen. "Take the guy out already! What's the holdup?"

"Exactly," Darren said. "Exactly."

In addition to the beer in his hand, I saw there were a few empty shot glasses in front of him. So far, so lubricated, I thought.

"Hey? Darren?" I said as I offered him my hand. "Darren Ross?"

Darren's eyes squinted as he gave me a weak smile.

"I know you?" he said.

"No. Name's Terry Rourke. I'm a journalist. I'm writing a book about the Noah Sutton case, and I was wondering if I could ask you a few questions."

He looked at me. I looked back at him.

I'd interviewed enough people on the job to know a few things. One of them was how to detect fear in a person's body language.

Do they swallow or clear their throat? Do they start blinking more than normal? What's their breathing like? Is it louder? Or even slower like they are trying to control it? Do they suddenly start sweating? Where are the hands? Do they try to hide them to prevent you from seeing them shake?

Darren's standing expression didn't change much, but I did notice two pretty common tells. He started blinking pretty rapidly as he placed his beer down and he also put his hands under the bar.

My question had made Darren anxious.

Good, I thought.

"You serious?" he said.

I nodded.

"Here we go again," he said, shaking his head.

"There's money in this, man," I said. "I've got a book deal lined up and an agent hooked in to all the true-crime shows to market it, Darren. We've got people in Hollywood chomping at the bit."

He squinted at me hard.

"I've already spoken to Jailene Mercado," I said, leaning in as I lowered my voice. "But every new detail is money. I could cut you in on a point or maybe even two or three if you have something good."

He swallowed as he looked down at the bar and very deliberately took a sip of his beer. In the gap between classic rock songs, you could hear the pinball machine in the back ring out the electronic bars of "Over the Rainbow."

I could tell Darren's brain was going a million miles a second. He definitely knew something and was considering it, weighing his options.

"They fired you a few months after the trial, Darren. What was up with that?" I asked.

That's when it happened. Something in his eyes suddenly shut like a window.

Dammit, I thought as I saw it. I could have kicked myself. I'd pushed him. Too much too soon.

"No comment with all that stuff, friend," he said with a laugh.

"But you were there at the house the night Noah was murdered. Don't you care?"

"Get lost," he said without even so much as another glance in my direction. "I'm watching the game."

53

I'm not sure exactly when it was that me and all my brothers had first heard "Tubthumping," Chumbawamba's timeless ode to getting back up again.

But I do know from that second on, it had become our family anthem.

That's why the next day at around noon after my Connecticut strikeout, bright-eyed and bushy-tailed and wired on my third cup of coffee, I was on the other side of the Sound again in North Salem, New York, an upscale rural town in Westchester about thirty miles north of Manhattan.

Even following my GPS, I got lost twice before I found the right curving back road I was looking for. The address I slowed in front of two minutes later was a small and sort of 1970s-era spacey and flat modern house on a rise above the twisting un-paved road. It was probably expensive because of the moneyed location, I thought as I sat staring at it, but it definitely needed some work. The grass needed mowing and the faded yellow paint on the house was peeling in places.

The residence belonged to the second target on my interview list, a man named Jeff MacBay.

Jeff's file said he had been the live-in tutor for Julian Sutton, Noah's son from his first marriage. I actually remembered seeing the teenage Julian at the trial. It was hard not to. He had definitely inherited his father's good looks and fit right in with Noah's photo-genic siblings sitting behind Hailey in the courtroom.

What was also positive was that I was able to call Jeff and con him into believing I was a journalist working on Kelsey's true-crime book about Noah's murder. Turned out Jeff was a big fan of Xavier Kelsey and was very receptive to speaking with me. Unlike Darren, the grump, Jeff actually sounded pumped and a little giddy about it.

Originally, we were going to meet at the Starbucks over the Connecticut state line in Ridgefield. But when I was on my way, he told me he was working from home today, and if it wouldn't be a bother for me, I could come to his house.

"No problem at all," I said to myself as I parked.

I sat for a moment in the car game planning. I didn't want to blow it like I'd blown my chance with Darren Ross. I decided I needed to be as relaxed as I could so I didn't spook him like I'd spooked Darren.

I really needed to pump Jeff for what he knew because he was one of my majorly important targets. Like Darren Ross, Jeff had actually been at the house on the night of Noah's murder.

It was really muggy as I got out of the car. My new writerly sport coat was sticking to my back by the time I came around the rear of the house and rang the bell to Jeff's basement office as instructed.

When the door beside the bell opened, I was surprised to see how big Jeff was. The soft voice on the phone didn't seem to fit with the six-five kind-of-overweight headbanger whose long hair was now going to gray. The metal hair went with a turquoise medallion on a black choker-like necklace that he wore. But for all that, in his khakis and button-down blue business shirt, he seemed gentle enough. He had a composed quality about himself.

"Mr. Rourke?" he said.

"Pleasure to meet you, Jeff," I said as we shook and he let me in.

It was neat inside but smelled dank with an old basement smell that reminded me of kids' games and sleepovers. Ping-Pong and Twister and Connect Four. He sat me down in his office. There were books everywhere.

Jeff's file said that he had hooked up with the Suttons through his mother, who had been a beloved teacher of Noah's at his New Hampshire boarding school. Jeff was just a year out of college at the time of the murder, and after Noah's death, he'd been fired.

Since then, he had gotten out of the education business altogether. His LinkedIn showed he was a design director at a cutting-edge architecture firm that specialized in high-tech office spaces now.

"You mind if I take some notes?" I said as I took out a Moleskine.

54

"No, please go for it," Jeff said as he sat behind his chrome-and-glass desk. "Xavier Kelsey. Wow. I've loved his books ever since I was in high school. I'm really glad you're doing this. Writing a book, I mean. There's so much stuff about all that happened that is just plain wrong. It's high time we get the record straight. I felt so bad for Julian when his father was killed. The media circus and everything. I still do."

"Tell me more," I said as coolly and calmly as I could. I slowly took out a pen and clicked it.

"These rich kids. People don't realize how isolated they are. Noah was nice enough, but let's face it. Like most of the Suttons, he was pretty self-centered. And the new wife, Hailey. She just ignored Julian completely. Treated him like the furniture. Actually, she probably treated the expensive furniture better."

"No one liked Hailey?" I said.

"No," he said. "None of the staff. After the shooting, Julian went to live with his mother's relatives, who he hardly knew."

"Shifting a little from Julian, what was Noah like?" I said.

Jeff passed a large hand through his thinning hair.

"As a boss? Noah was cool enough, I guess. Wasn't mean or anything. But he was distracted, you know. You get up at that level, you have a pretty packed social calendar. Lunch and drinks with these people and weekends here and there.

"New York people, Boston people, Washington people, Hollywood people. He even knew a bunch of people from London and was always going there. It's pretty insane how busy their lives are when they don't even have a job."

Jeff folded his arms.

"He wasn't just aloof with the staff either. His son, Julian, was a pleasant kid, earnest and friendly and completely cooperative. But Noah just looked right through him. Julian really liked Dungeons and Dragons. I was the one who told him about it. He'd never heard of it before. That's how sheltered he was."

Jeff looked down at the floor, remembering.

"I'll never forget what a kick he got out of it."

I was starting to like Jeff. He was open and almost childlike. I especially liked that he looked like a guy incapable of not answering a question fully, truthfully, and thoughtfully.

I clicked my pen again. A little quicker this time. Time to squeeze him like a ripe lemon.

"So, did you wake up that night, Jeff? Your room was on the east wing, right? Did you hear the shots? Did you see anyone? Did you know if Hailey was there? Please give me everything you can remember about that night."

As he opened his mouth to respond, there was a sudden chime from somewhere in the house above us. Then a door slammed.

"Jeff! Hey, where the hell are you?" came a voice from up-stairs a few seconds later. "Help me with all this crap."

"My wife," Jeff said with a comical grimace. "I'll be right back."

As I waited, I could hear a somewhat heated conversation.

No, please, I thought as I stared up at the dingy drop ceiling. *I'm so close.*

The heated convo ended after a minute, and then a moment later, I looked over and was crushed to see not Jeff, but a short, wiry woman with blond hair appear in the office doorway instead.

"Yeah, hi. Jeff had to run an errand. So I'll see you out."

No! I knew it was too good to be true!

"Sure," I said as I pocketed my notebook.

When I stepped out the back door that she flung open for me, I turned.

"Please tell Jeff thanks a lot and that maybe we'll talk some other time," I said.

"Yeah, how about I don't?" she said. "And how about you stop bothering people about some tabloid thing that happened a million years ago? I know how you jackals like to feed off unsuspecting people. It's not right. Leave Jeff alone or I'll call the cops. He's a nice guy. Too nice sometimes."

The little battle-ax definitely had a point in there somewhere, but I still couldn't resist a final needling.

"But in the end, ma'am, don't the people have a right to know?"

"You have two minutes to get off my property," she said as she slammed the door in my face.

Well, I thought as I came back around the path to my car. At least she didn't beat around the bush.

"So?" Viv said when she picked up the phone. "How'd it go?"

"Strike two, babe," I said from my cell as I put the car in Reverse down the unpaved drive.

"Strike two."

55

Running late for my next interview, I was already out of the car and halfway across the drive toward a little house on a wooded lot in Farmingville when I noticed the large dog on the porch. It was a dalmatian, I saw, and stopped in my tracks as I heard it start to growl.

"Dempsey, who do you think you're kidding?" the former Sutton family chef, Peter Morales, said to his dog as he pushed open his screen door.

After insisting that I call him Pete, the pudgy affable middle-aged Hispanic dude brought me through a huge vegetable garden around to his backyard, where some lawn chairs were arranged around a firepit. As I sat, I noticed that beyond the backyard was a vast cemetery. We both turned as Dempsey arrived in a jingle and lay at Pete's feet.

"Been here about two years," Pete said. "My wife is superstitious about the graveyard and still not right with it, but look."

He gestured out at the fading gold light on the cemetery lawn and the headstones and the treetops.

"Look at how they keep the grass. And it's so peaceful. I don't drink anymore, so I like to come out here and chillax."

From his Kelsey file, I'd read how Pete had been a very young man the night Noah had been shot. Only nineteen years old. He'd originally been from some hellhole neighborhood in the South Bronx but had started out in NYC restaurants as a dishwasher and prep cook when he was fifteen. By eighteen, he had been the line cook at a new place down in SoHo when Noah came in one night and visited the kitchen to compliment him on the meal. Six months later, Pete was working for him for the summer out at the Glass House and living there. His file said that he ran the grill at the Spring Lake golf club now.

Pete grinned as he looked over at me.

"So, you're writing a book about Noah Sutton, huh? About time someone did. They told us if we talked to anyone at the time, we'd be sued. They were extremely serious about it."

"Who's they?"

"Hailey Sutton's lawyers. They were such pricks. Especially this one obnoxious skinny white guy with a thousand-dollar suit and a Boston accent. He said he'd go after our families. I felt like going after him with a piece of pipe. Man, those snotty Red Sox fan types boil my blood."

"Me, too. Go Yankees," I said and laughed.

"Exactly. I'm so pumped you're doing this. I watch all these true-crime shows and wonder, where the heck is the Sutton Slay? Let me ask you, have you spoken to anyone in the family yet?"

"No, just some staff. I thought I'd start on the outside and work my way in."

"That's a good strategy. I wouldn't think they'd want to talk to you. Especially Hailey."

"What was she like?"

"We hated her. When Noah first brought her home, she was cool with everyone just like he was. But after the marriage, she became lady-in-waiting Sutton, and we were given new itineraries and rules. No member of the staff shall speak to Mr. and Mrs. Sutton without being spoken to first. Imagine? I wanted to pack up my knives about a week after she moved in. Who else have you contacted?"

"Darren Ross."

"Ah, that little creep. I hated that guy. What a little boot-licker. Hailey and him got along swell. Who else?"

"Jeff MacBay."

"Jeffie, yes. I liked him. Weird but nice. Like a little kid trapped in a big guy's body. We were roomies when we went to Noah's apartment in the city and down in Palm. How is he?"

"He's married up in Westchester. He's an architect now."

"Really? Wow. What did he tell you? Anything?"

"Truthfully, not much."

"Okay, so what do you want to know from me?"

"What everybody wants to know," I said, staring at the head-stones. "What happened that night?"

56

"I wish I knew, man," Pete said. "I wasn't even there that night. The guests weren't the only ones having a good time. I'd gotten lucky and had gone back to one of the catering waitresses' houses in the Bays. This little Italian girl. No, wait. She was Portuguese. I remember now. Amanda was her name. Hot!"

I actually knew that already from my files.

"What do you think the deal was, Pete?" I said. "The staff knows everything. What do you think happened?"

"Okay, here's what I think. For my money, I think it was the contractor, Mark Di-something."

"Mark Disenzo?" I said.

"That's the guy. Something to do with him. He did it himself or had a buddy do it. Always hanging around after hours, waiting on Hailey. Had a real thing for her. Rumor had it that they were together before Hailey married Noah. Which was why he got the job. Why else hire a firm all the way from Brooklyn?"

I stared at Pete. That was new.

"So you think Disenzo shot Noah? You don't think it was Hailey?"

"I mean, it could have been her, sure. But out of everybody who was around at the time, if you took a vote and said who here is actually capable of putting two bullets in another human being's head? Disenzo would win in a landslide."

Pete patted his dog.

"He was mobbed up or at least sounded like he was. He fronted like a Gambino or something. He had this mean, really deep gravelly voice. His fuggedaboudits and the vicious way he treated his guys who were working on the addition seemed pretty freaking authentic to me."

"Walks like a duck…"

"Precisely. I can't believe this. Think *Dateline* would do a piece based on your book?" Pete said.

"Who knows? Maybe even a movie," I lied.

Actually, that might not be a total lie, I thought.

The press probably would want to do something. Especially if I actually managed to slip Hailey's elegant wrists back into a lovely set of cold steel cuffs.

"A movie? Imagine? My wife would go nuts."

He patted at his gut.

"Me and Dempsey here need to start running around the block. Gotta get ready for my close-up, huh? Oh, did you talk to Robert yet?"

I peered at him. I'd practically memorized Kelsey's files, and there weren't any Roberts in it.

"Robert? Robert who?" I said.

"Robert Holm. He was Noah's good buddy from the city.

They played poker together and went fishing. One night, they knocked back a bottle of something and ended up putting an ATV in the ocean.

"Robert was so freaking mad when Noah died. They said he got into a little scuffle with one of Noah's brothers in the parking lot at the wake. He hated Hailey's guts, as well. I remember him at the funeral. He seemed really ripped up. More than Hailey and the rest of Noah's family combined."

"Who was he to Noah? A family friend?"

"Yeah, he was his roommate in college or something. He was a good guy. He was a lawyer, people said, but he was just a normal Joe six-pack kind of guy like you and me. He was funny. He would bust Noah's balls mercilessly. He knew Noah and his family really well. He'll be jazzed to spill the beans. He was Noah's pal. I can't believe you haven't spoken to him."

Spoken to him, I thought. I haven't even heard of him.

Pete smiled.

"See how I'm helping you now? You tell the producers, I'm the man. This crazy Rican wants major screen time."

57

The heavy road construction on the Grand Central Parkway was somewhere between East Elmhurst and Astoria Heights, and in the blinding glare of its construction light cart, a battle was underway.

It was between an old dump truck and a black Maxima, and they were playing chicken to see which vehicle was going to be the next one through the bottlenecked shoulder ahead of me. I had my money on the Maxima at first, as I'd heard the guy scrape the guardrail twice. But then the dusty dump truck just kept coming, kept upshifting and downshifting and shrieking his old brakes in his valiant quest to edge forward while somehow keeping his door-sized fender from touching the Nissan.

As I watched them go neck and neck and centimeter for centimeter to see who was going to shave a millisecond off their commute, you'd think I'd be frustrated.

On the contrary. As a native Long Islander, even after all these years, there was no amount of road rage and no volume of city traffic that could faze me in the slightest.

Which was why I had woken up so early that morning for my drive into the city to interview Robert Holm.

It was about 8:30 when I arrived at his Midtown office on the sixth floor at the New York Catholic Archdiocese building on First Avenue and Fifty-Sixth Street.

It was only when he opened the door to his small office and I saw the collar that I realized that the small bald fireplug of a man was actually *Father* Robert Holm.

"Yeah, surprise," he said as he sat me down and closed his door. "I'm a priest. It's been three years now. I started out here as a lawyer doing social work, but then one thing led to another. This God guy is pretty relentless. If you stay around Him long enough, He starts to get His hooks in."

Holm's office was tiny, but it had good furniture, especially the desk, a dark shining mahogany number with a tooled red leather top and ball-and-claw feet. His view looked north up First Avenue at the on-ramp for the traffic-filled Fifty-Ninth Street Bridge. The priest silenced the honking horns by shutting a window and insisted on making us some French press coffee.

As he was pouring me a cup, a hard smack of thunder exploded from somewhere in the muggy steel-and-glass Midtown blocks to the west like a car bomb. Rain began pelting at the window as he sat.

"So you and Noah were roommates?" I said.

"Yes, Mr. Rourke. We were roommates at Dartmouth."

"Actually," I said, sitting up a little straighter. "Before we get going, Father, I have a little confession to make."

"Ha ha, confession, priest, that's pretty funny. What is it?"

"I'm not a writer. I'm a cop."

He peered at me. "Why are you telling people you're some-one who you aren't?"

"My father was the ADA who prosecuted Hailey Sutton and lost all those years ago. I've reopened the cold case and intend to get her retried. But I don't want her to know just yet. I need to gather evidence. If she figures it out, she'll pull up the draw-bridge. She'll start paying people off to keep their mouths shut."

"Like last time."

"Exactly. Also, I'm actually a Philly cop and really have zero jurisdictional authority up here in New York."

"I see. You've been telling people you're a writer to try to sneak up on Hailey Sutton?"

"Yes."

He laughed.

"Good," he said. "You keep doing that. Just might work."

Father Holm leaned back and looked up at the office ceil-ing. "You hear that, Noah? You have a new detective on your case, brother."

58

I smiled.

"So, you and Noah were good friends, Father?"

"Best friends in college. We were roommates and both on the rugby team, which was something, since Dartmouth was nationally ranked. I was the hooker, the tip of the spear when the teams scrum. You know who gets to be the hooker?"

"No."

"The slowest and smallest guy on the team. And also the dumbest. I got my collarbone broken for me during the national championship."

"Ouch. But did you win?"

"No," he said and laughed. "Cal completely crushed us that year. Me literally."

"Was Noah any good?"

"Okay, I guess. He rode the bench mostly."

"He was better at the parties after?"

"Yes. So, you met Noah," he said, smiling. "We loved beer and AC/DC and trying to pick up girls. We both had learned a little karate, and after the bars closed, we would have heated but hilarious karate fights in the room. Shirts off with a tie around the head. There would be bowing. Man, you had to see the bruises. I went out drinking with him when his girlfriend dumped him. It was on the night before one of my finals, and I failed the class and had to take a summer one."

"That's what bros are for."

"Yeah, we were definitely bros. I think he really appreciated that. I wasn't from money, didn't give a care about his prominent family. My dad was a beer truck driver outside of Minneapolis. We just goofed together, watched football."

"And you remained friends after college?"

"Yep. Once or twice a month, we did poker games and Yankee games. There was actually a large group of Dartmouth rugby alums in NYC who we hung with. I still go to a dinner we have every year."

"A lot of priests?"

He laughed. "No, just me. The rest all work on Wall Street. Shocker."

"So, what do you think happened that night to your friend, Father?"

He stared at his coffee cup. "I've thought on this a lot over the years. And I think deep down it had to do with...his family's company."

What!

I had been convinced that the name Mark Disenzo was about to come out of his mouth. Or definitely Hailey.

His family's company?

I looked at him and mentally raced through my notes.

"Cold Springs Chemical?" I said, remembering the boring-looking file in the Kelsey box I hadn't read yet.

"I mean, don't get me wrong. Hailey is obviously in this. Up to her salon-plucked eyebrows. But it had to do with the family company. Had to be. Especially when you look at what happened after."

"What happened after?" I said.

Father Holm stared at me for a beat. "Oh, you don't know about all that, do you?"

He stood and went to the coffee maker and dumped out the grinds into his wastebasket.

"Let me put on another pot, Mr. Rourke. You're going to like this, but it's going to take a little while."

59

I saw my gas tank light go off as I was coming across the Fifty-Ninth Street Bridge with the departing commuter traffic, so I put SIRI to work.

I was guided to a station in nearby Long Island City, Queens, and after I gassed up, I parked and decided to call Viv.

As I waited for her to pick up, I stared out from under the giant metal jungle gym beneath the bridge at Midtown Manhattan.

The incredible view looked like it was from a postcard. It had stopped raining, and the city's steel-and-glass towers were shining there across the East River like a new car in a showroom. You could see the Chrysler Building and the UN and the Empire State dead ahead.

The Empire State Building looked especially cool. Like a movie poster. Like King Kong would appear in a second and start climbing.

After the score I'd just made, I actually felt a little like King Kong. Which was why I was calling Viv before I got back on the highway. The intergalactic level download of info I'd just bagged couldn't wait another second.

An Amtrak train rolled out from a train tunnel to my left as Viv finally answered.

"Honey, tell me you're pulling into the driveway," she said.

"No, not even close, Viv. I'm sorry, but I need your help. I need to download what I just heard from this guy, Robert Holm. It's huge. A completely new angle on the case."

"Wait. Slow down," my wife said. "Let me get some paper so I can take notes."

"First, how's my little angel?" I said.

"Little devil, you mean. She's bad. Very bad."

"What? Why?"

"I just put her in time-out. When I came into her room after the pool a minute ago, do you know what she was doing? She was in the buff, throwing her wet bathing suit up at the ceiling fan!"

"Hahaha! No!"

"Yes, can you imagine the boldness? She'd turned the fan on somehow and was trying to get her wet suit stuck on the blades. No way is that my side of the family."

"Oh, that's hilarious. Yeah, that's Rourke DNA without a doubt right there."

"Okay, I'm ready now. What's the new angle?" she said.

"Now, remember how the Sutton family originally made its money?"

"The grandfather was a bootlegger or something."

"That was in the olden times. The modern Suttons made all

their dough from a Long Island chemical company the father bought in the sixties called Cold Springs Chemical.

"Over the years, Cold Springs Chemical made acquisitions and became bigger and bigger to the point where it is now one of the country's biggest privately owned corporations. It's not up there with Dow or DuPont just yet, but close. It's massive."

"I've never even heard of it."

"Neither did I. That's because it's private. You can't buy stock. Plus it's very discreet. Also, a lot of its operations are offshore. They have facilities all over Canada and South America and are apparently moving into the Middle East. Anyway, when the father died, each of the four Sutton kids got an equal piece of the company.

"Well, almost equal. The three eldest children, Nelson and Henry and Brooke Sutton, got 24 percent apiece, while Noah, who was the father's favorite, got 28 percent. Nelson and Henry, who were very close, ran the company, and the other two, Brooke and Noah, just lived off the billion-dollar-plus-a-year proceeds, jet-setting about."

"Sounds like fun."

"You'd think so, right? But as these things happen, after the mother died, Brooke started getting in a huff about how much the company was really making and if the oldest two, Nelson and Henry, were paying themselves too handsomely."

"Oh, boy."

"Noah, who was the baby of the family, really didn't care about it, but his sister, Brooke, did. So, she eventually got a bunch of lawyers together and started a coup to oust the two oldest brothers from the helm."

"How sisterly," my wife said.

"Now, because Nelson and Henry together had a 48 percent hold of the company to Brooke's twenty-four, she really had only one move for a successful coup."

"To get Noah's deciding shares?"

"Exactly. And both factions were wooing him to determine who would ultimately control the company."

"So, what happened?" my wife said. "Whose side did Noah choose?"

"He never got the chance."

60

"Did your dad know about this rivalry within the company?" Viv asked.

"Not that I can tell," I said. "The family wouldn't talk to anyone. They just surrounded themselves with lawyers. Also, like I said, this was a private family company, so the dispute among the siblings was being handled internally by an independent mediator."

"So, what does this new info mean? Noah could have been killed by his own family?"

"Well…maybe. I guess. But the really important point here is Noah's will."

"Go on."

"Well, it seems to explain much of what happened after Noah died. When Noah was killed, he left everything to Hailey, the house, his family company shares, everything."

"All the more reason for Hailey to kill Noah."

"True. But if the primary beneficiary, in this case, Hailey, was deceased or convicted of Noah's murder, then the secondary beneficiary would get the shares."

"Makes sense. Who was the secondary beneficiary?"

"Father Holm doesn't know. Noah never said. Could have been his ex-wife, his son, one of his siblings. Who knows?"

"Wow. So that explains why the Sutton siblings were so supportive of Hailey."

"Exactly. They needed Hailey to be exonerated so that each faction could continue to persuade her to sell her shares to them. Henry was Hailey's biggest cheerleader, putting together the dream team of lawyers and sitting in on all the meetings."

"So did Hailey sell her shares after the trial?"

"No. In the end, she just kept the shares and the massive income stream exactly the way it was, and the brothers retained control."

"That's cold, Terry. How could they do that? They didn't care at all about their murdered brother? They didn't care that his wife had blown him away? Just the company? Just the money?"

"It is ice-cold, Viv."

"So it didn't matter to them that the jury was hung?"

"Not then, but it does now. This news is huge for our case."

"How?"

"Once we bring up this bombshell at the new trial, then a jury will see that the family support had nothing to do with them believing in Hailey's innocence."

"And had everything to do with greed."

"Right. The Suttons had an extremely strong motive of material benefit and gain from Hailey beating the case. Which could also be used to explain the highly suspect theft of the forensic evidence. No one knew that hundreds of millions or even billions of dollars were riding on the case."

"Do you think the DA will take the case now? I mean, what else could they want?"

"I don't know. Maybe. But we're definitely getting closer."

"Don't say *maybe*. I want you back now, Terry. I love your family and all and even weddings, but it stinks around here without you. I almost feel like throwing my wet bathing suit onto the ceiling fan with all your running around."

"Not without me there, you won't!" I laughed. "Don't move a muscle. I'm on my way."

61

When Viv's foot poked my left knee pit for the second time, I reluctantly opened one eye and saw it was still dark.

Then the soft soothing cool pillow I was sleeping under was lifted, and I heard my phone vibrating.

"Just leave it," I groaned as her foot worked on my right knee pit.

I waited until Viv rolled over before I reached out slowly and saw it was a text from Special Agent Courtney Frazier for us to meet up.

"I'm about to just smash it with a hammer, Terry," Viv said as I sat up.

It was dark when I left and just daybreak when I pulled in beside an old barn on the edge of Courtney's family farm restaurant in Amagansett. I saw that there were two other vehicles already parked at the side of the beat-up barn. One of them I actually recognized. It was Detective Marvin Heller's red Nissan Frontier pickup truck.

Seeing it, I wondered if I was going to hear some good news that the case was going to be reopened. I had already told Courtney all about my new findings from Father Holm. How the money and power-grabbing machinations of Noah's family had cast the case in an entirely new light.

I spotted Marvin just inside the door of the abandoned structure along with Courtney. There were two other new people there, as well. A tall fortysomething white guy with curly brown hair who was wearing a suit, and an attractive fair-skinned woman in her midfifties who was wearing a workout hoodie and patterned leggings.

"Are you sure no one was following you?" Courtney said to me.

"I'm positive. What's up?"

"You're being surveilled," said the pale fiftyish woman.

"Terry, this is the assistant DA of Suffolk County, Katrina Volland, who's working with us on our Suffolk DA corruption case."

"Nice to meet you," I said. "I'm being followed? Are you serious?"

"You went into the city yesterday, right?" Volland said.

"Yes."

"So did one of the county undercover cars of Suffolk County police chief Dennis Tapley, who we have a tracking device on," said the tall man in business clothes.

"Terry, this is Assistant Special Agent in Charge Walter Marino," Courtney said. "He's my boss who's in charge of the RICO case against the Suffolk County DA."

"Pleasure," I said, nodding at him as I tried to absorb what I was hearing.

"I told you this place has gone crazy," Marvin said. "And Chief Tapley is the craziest one of the lot."

I remembered the sociopathic look on Tapley's face as he screwed with me and Tom back at the house. The coldness in his eyes.

Then I thought about Viv and Angelina and the rest of my family.

This wasn't good, I thought. I didn't like this at all.

62

"Terry, we've been having some trouble moving forward with our corruption case," said ASAC Marino. "So, we've decided to shift our focus and resources."

"We'd like to get behind you and your cold case, Terry," Courtney said. "We think that if we can get Hailey Sutton back on trial, we can negotiate with her to give up Chief Tapley."

I remembered how Hailey had shown up right as Tapley was towing all the cars.

"So, it's really true? You think Hailey Sutton is siccing this Tapley guy on me?" I said in shock.

"Remember I told you about all these crazy parties?" Marvin said. "Well, I've been asking around and Tapley moonlights security at her parties."

"It's obvious Hailey and Chief Tapley are thick as thieves," Courtney said. "We get Hailey, we feel we can get Tapley."

"And then with Tapley, he'll give us Wheaton," ADA Katrina Volland explained.

"But it's cards-on-the-table time, Terry," FBI ASAC Marino said. "If we're going to help each other, we need to know more about what you're doing."

"Off the record, right?" I said.

Courtney pointed up at the blue sky coming through the missing rafters.

"This look like a courthouse deposition to you, Terry?"

"Okay, good point," I said. "Here's how it happened."

It took me about ten minutes to spill all the beans about how I had found the Kelsey novel manuscript at the beach house and how I'd exchanged it with Lucas Brody for the extensive private investigation files concerning Noah's case.

"Why didn't you tell me all this before?" Courtney said.

"Because there's illegally obtained records in the case files. Credit card statements. Phone logs with local usage details. I don't know who did Kelsey's investigating, but the son of a bitch broke about every privacy law there is. Do you want to look at the files?"

"No, no. You keep them for now at least," ASAC Marino said. "We touch those files, the case is over. Fruit of the poisoned tree. We couldn't admit anything in court."

The FBI agent looked at me and nodded to himself.

"The way you're playing this is actually perfect. You keep feeding Katrina anonymous information. That's the best way."

"But if you're going to continue your investigation, and they're watching you, you're going to need some backup," Marvin said as he patted me on the shoulder.

"What are you saying?"

"Me and you are partnering up now," Marvin said. "I can run cover for you. With Tapley watching you, you're going to need someone watching your six."

"Okay," I finally said, looking at everyone. "I have no problem working together. You got it. But what about all the stuff I just got off Father Holm concerning the family company and Noah's will? Isn't that good enough to move forward with a retrial?"

"Under normal circumstances, I'd bring it to Wheaton," Volland said. "But this thing has to thud when it hits Wheaton's desk. He has to have no way out of it. He needs to believe that if he doesn't prosecute, it will be leaked to the press, and he'll look bad."

"He's slimy but political, Terry," Courtney said. "He can be moved, but we're still going to need to come up with a little more, I think."

"If you still want to do this, that is," Marvin said. "With the county now watching you, it could be some trouble for you, Terry."

"They're not even cops anymore. Just crooks with badges," ASAC Marino said, the concern in eyes sincere.

"Tapley, especially, is a nasty character," said Marvin. "He's paranoid now, as well. He knows or at least suspects we have an investigation open on him."

"So, what do you think, Terry? You want to keep going?" Courtney said.

I looked around the barn. The back of it was collapsed and the weeds were coming in, nature taking back over. Beyond it in the green field, there was a rusted flatbed from the fifties surrounded by black-eyed Susans.

The whole barn smelled like flowers, I suddenly noticed.

Like a floral shop, I thought as I tried to decide. Or was it maybe more like a funeral parlor?

I smiled at Courtney.

"You better believe I want to keep going," I finally said. "All the way back to the Arthur M. Cromarty Criminal Courts Building or bust."

63

Even during the day, the perfect stretch of beach between the summer mansion and the Atlantic was as serene as a meditation video.

At six o'clock in the morning with the sun cracking the sky above the waves, it made you feel like taking up yoga. Or like maybe you were the last person on earth.

Good, I thought as I came down Sandhill Point's private stairs and closed the security gate firmly behind me.

I knew the village police department patrolled the beach at night to bust people who tried to camp out on the million-dollar sand, but thankfully, I didn't see anybody.

Or, more importantly, I didn't see anyone seeing me.

I'd been extremely vigilant ever since I'd been told about the county car trailing me. I'd actually stood watch with binoculars for over an hour the night before from one of the spare bedrooms facing Meadow Lane, looking for any sign of surveillance.

I'd seen nothing, but that was actually more disturbing, I thought. I knew from experience all the ways one could be watched by the police with electronic cellular surveillance. Heck, some departments used drones now.

A minute later, I came up off the beach and waved at the pair of headlights that flashed off to my left in Road D Beach's small parking lot.

"Morning, Terry," Marvin Heller said, handing me a huge cup of 7-Eleven high-test before I hopped into the back of his Nissan pickup and scrunched down.

"Milk and sugar okay?" he said as he backed out onto Meadow Lane.

"Perfect, Marvin. Thanks." I smiled from the rear compartment. "How we looking? See any lights?" I said as we made the left onto Halsey back for the village.

"Nah, we're good," he said. "Seems like the world's still sleeping. Even the corrupt bozos at County. Where you headed today, Mr. Investigator? Or should I even ask?"

"Need-to-know basis only, Marvin. Got to keep this as covert as possible," I said.

"Aye, aye, Agent X," he said.

Ten minutes later, Marvin dropped me off at the Enterprise car rental place at the small airport in West Hampton, where I picked up the Maxima I had reserved online the night before.

It took me about half an hour to drive over to Port Jefferson through the light traffic, and I was able to catch the eight o'clock ferry to Bridgeport, Connecticut. I stopped once for another coffee and an Egg McMuffin outside of Fairfield and spent the rest of the morning driving across Connecticut into New York State.

I arrived at my destination around ten fifteen, slowing as I came up on the large sign just off the wooded two-lane road in Otisville, New York.

**US Department of Justice
Federal Bureau of Prisons
Federal Correctional Institution**

64

With the grass and strolling paths running between its un-assuming glass-and-concrete buildings, the federal prison camp at Otisville looked more like a corporate park or a college than a jail. If it weren't located next to a real jail with fences and razor wire, you probably couldn't even guess its purpose.

As I pulled into visitors' parking, I spotted a half dozen deer grazing in the grass alongside the razor wire for the real prison.

"Prisoner name," said a hard-faced female clerk behind a desk as I walked in through a door that said Processing.

"Gittenger. Louis Gittenger," I said.

This cold-case target from my Xavier Kelsey files was a bit of an outlier since he had no firsthand knowledge of Noah or of the night of the murder. But Gittenger had dated and even lived with Hailey Sutton in the first few years after Noah's murder. His perspective into the whole thing as a confidant of Hailey's could be very interesting, I knew.

Gittenger arrived ten minutes later escorted by a prison guard.

I introduced myself and we sat at a concrete picnic table in the center of the sunny yard. Gittenger was a slim nice-looking guy of about fifty. He had freshly cut hair and bright brown eyes, and even in his prison jumpsuit he looked the part of the high-end Manhattan real-estate broker he used to be. He had a very calm and confident way about him.

Which made some sense, I thought, as he was in jail for being a con man.

Gittenger's simple yet effective scam was to take out a mortgage on a property, usually a million-dollar listing on the Upper East Side, and forge documents to say that he actually owned it free and clear. Then with those false documents, he would take out a home equity loan with a different bank. He had stolen over eleven million bucks before all the cards started to fall.

"And you want to know something really funny? I didn't have any of the money when I got popped," he said, smoothing a hand over the warm concrete tabletop. "Not a dime. I gambled away the whole eleven million. I hope they never let me out of here. It wouldn't just be better for society, it would be better for me. I'm my own worst enemy."

"So, what was dating Hailey Sutton like?"

"In a word? *Fun.* We made each other laugh. We'd actually been coworkers in the early nineties before she bagged Sutton. And the sex. Yow. Electric."

"Did she have any contact with the Sutton family when you knew her?"

"Not that I recall. She's a major shareholder in Cold Springs Chemical, so I remember her going to some meetings. But Hailey never considered me the type of boyfriend to bring home to meet the family."

"How about the contractor, Mark Disenzo?" I said as I remembered Chef Pete's theory. "Did she ever talk about him?"

I watched as Gittenger's eyes lit up like Fourth of July sparklers.

"So, Kelsey got my letter after all."

I quickly tried to remember a letter in Gittenger's file. Nothing came to mind, but I went with it anyway.

"Why do you think I'm here?" I said.

He nodded.

"One night when she was talking to her mother, I rifled through her stuff in a file cabinet in her office. I found a DVD. You know what was on it?"

I shook my head.

"The security video from the gas station. She and Disenzo were in her Porsche at the Mobil on Hampton Road in Southampton Village. I looked at the time signature. Date 7/5/99. Time 8:11 a.m. I thought about taking it, then thought again as I heard her coming up the stairs."

"So, you're saying Hailey was with Disenzo the morning after the murder?"

"Yes. During the famous missing time, she was with Disenzo. I saw it with my own eyes."

"You sure?" I said.

"I get it. I'm a convicted con man. But I'm good with numbers, as you may have guessed," he said, smiling. "And that's what I saw."

"You think this means Hailey got Disenzo to do it?" I said.

"I do," Gittenger said. "I really do."

"Did you stop dating her then?" I said.

"No way. Are you kidding? We were having a blast playing house. Plus she had a whole lot of that Sutton money, and frankly, I wanted to get at it with both hands."

"Did you?"

"No," he laughed. "Not even close. She was tight with her money all right. Every time I tried to get her to invest in some real estate, she'd ask me about my strategies and bring up six points as to why she wouldn't do it. Good points, too. She could read a spreadsheet faster than a CPA. Shrewd."

"How'd it end?"

"Sadly and abruptly. One day she said I had to move out, and then she just stopped answering my phone calls. That was right around when the Feds started their case against me, so I'm thinking she might have been told by them that I was about to be indicted."

"That's where the fairy tale ended," I said.

"Yeah," Gittenger said, laughing. "I romanced the Evil Queen and then I ended up in the dungeon."

65

Viv and Angelina met me at the West Hampton Airport Enterprise, where I returned the car. I didn't see any corrupt crazy cops trailing us to the beach house, which was good.

When we got back to the house, we went across the backyard and straight down the stairs to the beach again.

Viv had already gone over the latest wedding-related affair we were to attend that evening, dinner for the bride Emmaline's whole family, including her father and mother, William and Bea Fullerton, who were arriving from London.

Tom was arranging a beach clambake for us all, and as we got closer to the water, we spotted an army of caterers already out there atop the bluff. They were putting out Irish linen–covered tables and setting up striped cabanas and string lights. The serving tables were resting on hay bales, and rumor had it that there would be fireworks.

Viv sat on a towel as I took Angelina out past the waves with me into the "lotion" again. We did better this time, and I actually taught her how to do a little bodysurfing. After she tired of swimming, I just lay there in the swash with her as she played with her Barbies in the muddy sand.

It was that golden moment they talk about. The sky light and the water going from blue to black. In the twilight, the beach mansion over the grassy bluff looked like something out of a storybook.

I turned my gaze to Viv, who looked just as amazing, tan and beautiful and positively glowing. I couldn't believe what a lucky man I was.

Then I thought about what Courtney had said in the barn about the empire starting to strike back, and I wondered if I was pushing it. I'd dived into the case with both feet and made some progress, but it was going to get harder, I knew. The higher up the food chain you went with an investigation, the heavier the pushback. The people I would be talking to now were closer to Hailey, and it would be more difficult to get anything from them.

Plus I'd been lying to people, misrepresenting myself. That could get me into trouble with the Philly PD brass, some of whom weren't exactly my best buddies.

It had been a head rush finding out about Kelsey's investigation and his files.

I looked over at my beautiful little daughter talking to herself as she played in the sand.

Maybe I needed to roll it back some, I thought. But I was getting so close to the truth.

We stayed out a little longer than we should have, so we had to hustle our butts back to the room for showers and sprucing up before we were ordered to head out to the front steps.

It was downright ridiculous, of course, for all of us to be standing there in sport coats and dresses in the front formal court while waiters served champagne like we were starring in a modern version of *Downton Abbey*.

However, as Tom explained, it wasn't for us but for Emmaline's very formal, well-to-do British aristocratic parents, whom Tom had never met. All the stops had to be pulled, Tom had said, as William Fullerton, Emmaline's dad, was actually *Sir* William Fullerton.

Sir or no sir, I really thought they were going to be a couple of stiffs. Three bags full, sir. William especially.

And as he emerged from the limo, it looked like my prediction was true. He was decked out in three-piece Savile Row despite the heat, and Sir William's nose was literally raised into the air like he was staring up at the sky as he came across the seashells. We all watched breathlessly as he halted at the bottom of the steps and sniffed up at the thirty-thousand-square-foot mansion behind us.

"This will do, I suppose," he said in his clipped British accent. "And all of you are staying where now?"

Tom stood there wide-eyed with his mouth open, unable to speak. I'd never seen him so nervous. Or so stunned.

Then William finally broke character and gave Tom a wide grin as he seized his hand.

"Gotcha, son!" he cried as we all laughed with relief.

66

After a truly great dinner and a laughter-filled evening with the Fullertons, who were all as funny and sweet and charming as Emmaline, Sir William maybe even more so, I woke up at seven, just in time to see a message appear on my phone.

An hour later, I was in a conference room on the top floor of the new modern federal courthouse building in Central Islip.

On my left was Special Agent Courtney Frazier, and across from us was her boss, ASAC Walter Marino, along with Marvin Heller.

Funny and sweet and charming was yesterday, I thought as I looked at their grim cold faces.

"Ready?" Courtney said as she stood.

"Ready for what?" I said.

"You'll see," Marvin said as Courtney led us out of the room and into the hallway.

Ten feet from the end of it, Courtney opened a door, and we all entered a room the size of a walk-in closet with a mirror in it. The mirror was one-way and on the other side of it was a person I couldn't help but immediately recognize.

It was Noah Sutton's old chauffeur, Darren Ross.

He sat on the other side of a beat-up table, desperate-looking and sweating, a far cry from his demeanor during my interview with him at the bar. His hands were pulled inside his T-shirt and he needed a shave.

"What the...? What's he doing here?" I said.

"He got busted on a drug deal three days ago up in Boston," Marino said. "Mexican heroin. Pretty major weight."

"You don't say."

"When we heard about it, we reached out," Courtney said. "He wants to cut a deal, Terry. Turns out it's just like you told us from the Kelsey file. Ross was there that night. Not only that. He saw something. Something you're not going to believe."

"You have to be kidding me. He knows what happened to Noah Sutton?" I said, wide-eyed.

"Yes, Terry," Courtney said, nodding. "Not only did he see what happened that night, he's willing to testify in exchange for leniency."

"That's amazing," I said. "So, c'mon already. Tell me what happened. Was he involved or something?"

"I'll let him tell you," Courtney said as she left.

A moment later, Ross seemed to jump through the glass as the door behind him clacked open and Courtney entered the interview room and sat.

"Hey, Darren. I know we've been through this already, but just one more time. So, you were there that night in the house. How did it happen again?"

Darren Ross took his arms out from underneath his T-shirt and took a deep breath.

"Staff usually stayed in the guesthouse, but there were guests over that weekend, so they had us down in the basement. We were all day-drinking at the concert along with everyone else, so Jeff MacBay and I headed back around seven or so and crashed. I'm not sure what time it was when I woke up hungover and thirsty like you wouldn't believe. We weren't supposed to go into the kitchen after hours when the Suttons were there, but I'd done it before, so I snuck upstairs."

He sighed.

"I was in the kitchen about to pull open the fridge when I heard the sound. I really didn't think anything of it because it didn't sound like a gunshot. It was just two clicks no louder than a stapler maybe or someone snapping their fingers. Maybe even less than that. Even so, I walked to the door. The kitchen had a swinging door with kind of a porthole in it like you see in a restaurant, so I took a peek.

"That's when I saw him holding the gun in the dining room doorway. He had his head down, and he was unscrewing something long off the front of it, which had to be the silencer, right?"

"Who did you see?"

"It was Disenzo," he said. "It was Mark Disenzo."

"No way," I said.

"You're sure? It wasn't too dark that early?" Courtney said.

"It's a glass house," Darren said. "The sun wasn't up yet but the sky was lit. I saw him plain as day."

"Then what happened?"

"Then I saw Hailey arrive next to him and they said something to each other I couldn't hear, and then they both left," Ross said.

67

The next two days were some of the best I had spent at the house since we'd gotten there. We swam in the ocean and boogie boarded. There was a Disney night for the kids in the immense basement theater. My brother Finn's wife, Stephanie, and my sister Erin's son Billy shared the same birthday and we celebrated on the beach with ice cream cake and the construction of an epic sandcastle. It reminded me of the old days and our treehouse fort.

I really got a chance to speak to everyone, to get to know my family as adults. How much they loved their kids, how hard they all worked. I got to watch my mother as a grandmother, how thoughtful she was and patient.

Obviously, my incredibly good mood hadn't fallen from the sky. It was because we had it wrapped up. All my research and sniffing around had paid off in spades.

Disenzo really had done it. With Hailey's approval and assistance. And we could prove it. Ross was going to testify to the whole thing.

Hailey really was going down once and for all and there was no way, no how, for even a corrupt district attorney to stop it.

Because of my thorough satisfaction and happy anticipation at these facts, when, two days later on Monday after breakfast, I received a phone call on my cell phone, I was very reluctant to pick it up.

When I saw it was a New York City 212 area code, I figured, why bother? We had plenty to go forward now. Enough with the case. It was time to participate in the family again and pitch in.

But in the end, I relented.

"Hello?" I said as I finally thumbed the Accept button.

"May I speak to Terence Rourke?"

"Can I ask who's calling?"

"It's Father Holm. Robert Holm."

"Father," I said, smiling, remembering the fireplug priest. "What can I do for you?"

"I've done nothing except think about Noah's case since you left. So much so that I reached out to somebody. Somebody much more intimately involved in Noah's death than me."

"Is that right?" I said, wondering who he could be talking about.

"The good news is they said that they would love to talk to you. If you're still interested."

"Who is this somebody?" I finally said.

"Julian Sutton," Father Holm said.

"Noah's son?" I said, almost dropping the phone.

"Yes," Father Holm said. "Noah's son."

68

Julian Sutton's apartment was at One West Sixty-Seventh Street, a stone's throw from Central Park.

It was an amazing prewar Tudor structure with a doorman and a sunken cream marble lobby and hand-painted murals. As the doorman announced my presence to Julian the next morning while I stood in its lobby, I saw that above the Gothic wrought-iron elevator doors, it even had those little half-moon indicators from black-and-white movies that moved like a hand on a clock to show the elevator's progress.

Julian's apartment wasn't just on the eleventh floor, I saw as I stepped out. It *was* the eleventh floor. A smiling friendly Filipino maid was waiting by the alcove's only door.

Once inside, I was immediately blown away by the apartment's incredible double-height ceilings and windows. A spiral staircase in a corner led up to a catwalk paneled with brimming bookcases.

"Thanks for coming, Mr. Rourke," Julian Sutton said suddenly from behind me.

Julian was shorter and stockier than his father, Noah, but had the same great California blond hair and looks. In his rumpled chambray shirt rolled up to the elbows and old faded jeans, there was an artistic air about him.

"Let's sit by the window," he said, leading me past a photography studio set up in a corner with light stands and a black velvet background.

I soon realized why. Outside the huge window the newly refurbished copper dome of a church was backgrounded by a green sea of Central Park trees. The white towers of Fifth Avenue in the distance beyond them looked like something out of a movie.

"This is a beautiful apartment. These ceilings. Is it a duplex?" I said as we sat across from each other on two facing couches.

"All of the apartments are duplexes," Julian said with a nod. "The place was built at the beginning of the previous century as an artists' residence with high windows to catch the light. My mother bought it after the divorce. It was her favorite place in the world. When she died, she left it to me. Now it's my favorite place in the world."

Julian looked at me closely.

"So Father Holm tells me you found Uncle Xavier's notes," he said.

"*Uncle* Xavier? Xavier Kelsey? You knew him?" I said.

"Oh, of course," Julian said with a smile. "Xavier was very good friends with my father. That's why he started the book. He actually asked my permission before he started. But you must know all this already, don't you?"

I shook my head.

Julian looked confused.

"But you're picking up where Xavier left off, right? That's what Father Rob said. Xavier interviewed me for his book for two days. He sat right where you're sitting."

I stared at him. I thought Xavier had still been in the gathering information stage. This was the first I had heard that he had actually interviewed anyone.

"He interviewed you?"

"Yes, for hours. He had a tape recorder. He had to actually change the tape. Don't you have his files? I thought Father Rob mentioned that."

"I thought I had all of them," I said. "But there aren't any tapes. Did he discuss the book with you?"

"Yes. He said that he was sick, but he knew that he had to do it when he heard about the other deaths."

69

I stared at Julian for a long moment. Now I was becoming completely confused.

"Deaths?" I said. "What other deaths?"

"You don't know about Philip's death? My friend Philip Oster?"

I blinked at him silently. I had thoroughly sifted through Kelsey's files, and there was no mention of a Mr. Oster.

"That name is not familiar to me," I said.

"Philip was my friend from school. He had come up from the city that night for the party and stayed over. You don't know about Philip?"

"No."

"Oh, my, you don't know, then. I'm not sure what to say. I thought you knew. I thought that's why you were doing this."

I stared at him. I felt weird all of a sudden.

I had thought I had a handle on all of this, but there was something, something big, that I didn't know, and as I sat there, for some strange reason it suddenly scared me.

"Please, if you could explain, Julian. I don't know what you're talking about."

He looked out the window then back at me with an expression of unease mixed with something like pity. I felt my heart begin to beat more rapidly in my chest.

What the hell was going on?

"My friend Philip was at the house that night on July Fourth for the party. No one knew I'd invited him because the both of us had gotten into trouble with some drug thing, and I wasn't supposed to be hanging around him. We partied and he crashed back in my room that night, but he left early, somewhere between four and five. He was gone before the cops arrived."

I took a deep breath. I thought I had known about everyone who had been at the house that night. But now I knew I'd thought wrong.

"After my dad was murdered, I tried to get into contact with Philip, but he kept avoiding me. Then that September, he went away to school in England, where his father lived."

"Do you think Philip had something to do with your father's death?"

"No, no. Nothing like that," Julian said. "Philip wouldn't hurt a fly. He was a total hippie kid, peacenik. But I think he saw something when he left. Something or maybe someone. I think he saw the person who killed my father. In fact, I'm pretty much convinced."

I took a breath. This was huge.

"Why?" I said.

"The following summer, in 2000, Philip returned to the States.

In August, he attended a Paul Simon concert in Massachusetts. When it was over, he said goodbye to his friends and went to get his car. That's when he jumped to his death off the roof of the parking garage."

"What?" I said.

"They said he was distraught over a recent breakup. But he had fallen wrong, Mr. Rourke. If somebody leaps to their death, they would land facedown, right? Well, he was turned the other way, faceup. The way you would land if you were pushed. It looked extremely suspicious."

I took a deep breath, trying to process what I was hearing. *There was another murder?*

"But wait. You said there was more than one death?"

He gave me the strange wide-eyed look of pity again.

"In 2013, Philip's mom was moving and going through some old keepsakes and found a notebook that had belonged to Philip at the time of his death. In the back of it, he had written a phone number."

Julian Sutton bit his lip and looked away, out the window.

"The number belonged to your father, Mr. Rourke. Philip was in contact with Sean Rourke when he died."

I sat there with my mouth open.

"What? My father? This Philip was talking to my father?"

Julian nodded. "They were going to meet. Then Philip died. And then your...father died from drowning. Don't you see?"

I shook my head, my eyes wide. I didn't see anything. I didn't want to see anything.

"Philip must have seen something the night of the murder and finally reached out to your dad once he returned from England."

I sat there stunned.

"Then both of them died in suspicious accidents three days apart."

I felt hot, suddenly dazed.

"That's why Kelsey wanted to do the book. Philip and your

father were about to meet, and someone didn't want that to happen. That was the bombshell Xavier was going to reveal."

My father, I thought.

Murdered? My father murdered?

"No," I said, suddenly finding myself on my feet. "No, you're wrong."

I needed to get out of there. I felt dizzy as I stumbled to my feet.

I almost knocked down the maid bringing the coffee into the storybook living room as I headed for the door.

70

Numb and stupefied, I burst out of the building into the street. Instead of heading to get my car up on Columbus, I crossed Central Park West and started walking south in the shade of the overhanging branches.

It had gotten hotter in the time I'd been inside Julian Sutton's apartment, muggier, the heat off the sidewalk and street palpable and oppressive. After a half dozen blocks or so, I found an empty bench near Columbus Circle and sat in the swelter.

Still out of it, I stared up at the black glass of a building across the street from me for a while. People walked by. A short muscular woman jogging, a Black guy in a beautiful blue suit, a bald guy in a white Adidas jacket and aviators speaking French into an iPhone. I gaped at everything around me like an escaped mental patient. It felt like I'd just taken a blow from a blunt object to the head.

My father, I thought.

Murdered?

I tried to process it.

What did I know about my father's death?

There had been an autopsy. Alcohol in his system, but the cause of death was determined to be accidental drowning.

But what if it wasn't?

My phone clattered to the cobblestones as I fumbled it out of my pocket. I picked it back up and dialed Viv.

"Viv, I need you to do me a huge favor. Are you in the bedroom?"

"Yes. What is it, honey? You okay? You sound funny."

"I'm fine. Bad connection. Viv, in the box with the Sutton case file, there are some of my father's things. I'm looking for his planner, his old planner. Do you see it?"

"No. Wait, yes. I have it."

"Good. Turn to the week of August 6, 2000. Does it say anything?"

"No. It's blank. But there's something on the eighth."

I waited. Please, I thought.

"'Dentist 10:15 a.m.'"

"Nothing else?"

"No."

I thought about that. My father was very organized when it came to work. OCD level. I let out a breath.

"Wait. There's also something on the tenth," Viv said. "'Meet with PO at 9 a.m.'"

PO.

Philip Oster.

I felt like I was about to vomit. Then it wasn't just a feeling.

I jumped up as I puked all over the Central Park stone wall beside the bench.

Murdered. They'd murdered him.

They'd murdered my dad, I thought as I wiped at my mouth with the back of my hand.

"Terry?" my wife said as I ran across the street to get a cab.

71

I was down on Waverly Place, sipping a ginger ale to get the taste of puke out of my mouth as I watched the evening invade the Greenwich Village street in front of Lucas Brody's town house.

I'd rung his buzzer when I first arrived about an hour and a half before, but there was no answer, so now I was watching and waiting.

I figured if Brody weren't out of town, he'd be coming back soon. Or if he were inside and didn't want to speak to me, he'd eventually be going out.

As I waited, I went over everything again and again in my head. But no matter how much I turned it over, things weren't adding up. If Disenzo killed Noah Sutton and then died in a motorcycle accident, who in the hell killed Philip Oster? And most importantly, who in the hell had killed my dad?

I didn't know but it didn't matter.

I ricocheted the empty can of Canada Dry off a garbage pail on the corner and watched it roll clattering into the golden sun-lit street.

Because I was going to find out. I was getting to the bottom of this now, no matter if I needed a pickax, a shovel, and maybe even some dynamite to get there.

"I knew it," I said when I saw a light go on in Brody's ground-floor front window around 8:15.

He was in there. There was a camera beside the buzzer, so he had seen me knocking. But apparently, I couldn't come in.

"Good luck with that," I said, seething, as I continued to wait.

It was twenty minutes later when I saw the delivery guy on the bike stop in front of Brody's place and padlock his ride to the lamppost. I was across the street, waiting, right behind the delivery guy as he rang Brody's buzzer.

"Oh, it's you," Brody said over the departing pizza guy's shoulder as I leapt up the flower-filled stairs.

"I need to speak to you, Mr. Brody."

He reluctantly let me in.

"What do you want?" he said as he left the takeout on the shelf with the devil mask on it.

He had on a pair of beautiful camel-colored shorts and a black silk shirt that was open to the waist, showing off his insanely defined Wolverine-like physique. There was a spot of shaving cream on his chin. He was tanner than when I'd seen him almost two weeks ago.

He was getting ready to go out.

"You left something out," I said angrily. "Our agreement was for all of Kelsey's research. I didn't get all of it."

"What are you talking about?"

"The audiotapes. Kelsey recorded his interviews. I need them."

"My, aren't we pushy now," he said, giving me an arrogant look.

"The deal was for all of Kelsey's materials. I want all of them. Now," I said, staring at him.

"And if I tell you to get lost?"

I got almost nose to nose with Brody and stared at him hard.

I was beyond emotionally wrecked at the news about my dad's potential murder and really ready to hurt someone at that point. He was a muscular son of a bitch, but I'd about had it. I wondered if it would actually come to blows here in his front hall.

"Fine," he said, glaring at me. "It's probably downstairs with the other crap. You're the one who didn't get all of it. Not me. So, don't get all pissy now," Brody said.

"I need the key to the locker," I said, staring a hole through the back of his skull.

He opened a drawer in a front hall mail table and handed it to me.

"Get whatever the hell it is and get out of here. I never want to see you again. Leave me the hell alone, you got me?"

"With pleasure," I said, turning as I headed downstairs into the hot, dark basement.

72

The tape recorder was an old Sony.

Probably state of the art in its day, I thought as I lifted the brick-sized device from Xavier Kelsey's old card table desk back at the beach house in Southampton. It seemed heavy enough to bash in somebody's skull.

It had taken me over an hour to find it in Xavier Kelsey's basement in a shoebox along with dozens of interview tapes.

But the important thing was that I had found it, and I was back now.

Back down under the creepy old steps past the creepy old black-and-white photos where it had all begun.

The sixty-minute microcassettes in the shoebox were Sony,

as well. On the table before me was a stack of them with names written in black Sharpie.

The one I'd just inserted into the recorder said **Sonya Serrano** on it in Kelsey's beautiful handwriting.

I'd already looked her up and discovered on LinkedIn that she was currently a lieutenant in the Nassau County PD.

How that was significant, I didn't know.

I hit Play.

But I was about to find out.

"So," the voice of Xavier Kelsey said in the silence. "Let's talk."

"This can't get back to me. This is just off the record," a woman said.

"Come on now, Sonya," I heard Xavier Kelsey say. "You called me. Tell me, why are we here?"

The hair on the back of my neck stood up as I heard Kelsey's famous charming Southern lilt for the first time here in his creepy basement studio.

I stared at the slowly turning tape reel through the recorder's plastic window.

A voice from the grave, I thought.

"Like you don't know why?" Sonya said. "I already told you on the phone. Now you want me to repeat myself? If I didn't know you better, Xavier, I'd say you were wearing a wire."

You could hear restaurant sounds in the background, the clack of plates and the murmur of people talking, as Kelsey cracked up at that one.

"A wire? Of course I am, darling. If you could speak a little more loudly right here next to my cane? You don't want to talk, that's fine by me. Only we'll have to split the check then," Kelsey said.

"Fine. Okay," Sonya said. "When I worked at the Southampton Village police department, like a lot of small departments, it had a pass-back locker system."

I clicked the tape recorder off and sat up. I rewound the tape and played it again.

"The Southampton Village police department," Sonya Serrano said again.

I was thinking of maybe slapping myself to make sure I hadn't perhaps fallen asleep and was now dreaming.

Because they were talking about the evidence, I realized.

The damning evidence that had been stolen at the beginning of Hailey Sutton's trial.

73

I fumbled and almost dropped the recorder as I let it run.

"A pass-back what? What does that mean?" Kelsey said.

"It means they had an evidence room that was open to the entire department but had wall lockers that could be accessed by only two people, the assignment officer and the assignment evidence tech," Sonya said.

"On the second night of the trial, there was a power outage at the station that forced the civilian desk clerk to exit the premises for several hours. In the morning, the lock on the back door of the department was missing, and they found that several of the lockers had been broken into. Some drugs were taken and a few guns and other items, including the forensic evidence from

Hailey Sutton's trial. Both the plastic bag containing the hoodie and a small envelope containing the bullets were taken."

I actually grabbed my head as she said the words *Hailey Sutton's trial.*

"So, who took them?" Kelsey said.

"Nobody knew," Sonya said. "That is, until I went out on a date with an old partner of mine."

"Who?"

"Dennis Tapley."

"What?" I yelled in the dark.

"Tapley, the current Suffolk County police chief?" Kelsey asked.

"Yes."

"What does Tapley have to do with it?" Kelsey said.

"Tapley showed it to me."

"Tapley showed what to you?"

"The missing evidence bag and envelope."

I closed my eyes.

"Bullshit. The Southampton police evidence bag and envelope from Hailey's trial?"

"Yes," Sonya said. "He showed it to me."

My heart felt like it had stopped, like I'd been hit in the chest with a baseball bat.

"How did he show it to you? Where were you?" Kelsey said.

"His wife was out of town, and we were at his family's place out on Fire Island. We were stoned off our ass, and I started ribbing him, saying, 'You're not such a big deal, head of the Suffolk County cops. Big whoop.'

"He takes me into the bedroom, and we go into a closet with a gun locker in it, and he presses the code and out comes a big plastic evidence bag. It said *Southampton PD* on it, and inside of it was a hoodie. In with the hoodie there was another smaller bag you use for shell casings. In it were the two bullets that killed Noah Sutton.

"Then he just put a finger to my lips and put it back. It was funny because the next morning he didn't even mention it. He was pie-eyed. But he really had them. Hell, he probably still has them. You want a bombshell, there's your bombshell, Xavier. But you didn't hear it from me."

"Why would Tapley take the evidence?" Kelsey said. "Was Tapley hired to take it by Hailey?"

"Who knows?"

"But Tapley has it?" Xavier Kelsey said on the tape.

"Yes. As far as I know, it's still out there at his vacation place."

"When did you see it?"

"The exact date? I don't know. Around the first week of January."

"Why are you telling me all of this?" Kelsey asked.

"Now, now, Xavier. I'm an officer of the law. Do I need a reason to blow the whistle on corruption to expose a crime?" Sonya said.

"Yes, you do. People generally do, in my experience," Kelsey said.

"Fine," she said, letting out a long breath. "When Tapley got the commissionership, he was supposed to put me in as a precinct commander. He didn't do it, so screw him. Turnaround is fair play. I hope he goes down."

"A woman scorned," Kelsey said.

"You said it, pal."

There was the sound of a waiter asking them if they wanted more drinks and some more restaurant sounds, and that was it.

I clicked off the recorder and sat there staring at the concrete wall. There was a hum behind me and then the gurgle of the pool's pump.

I thought about everything.

What I knew. Where this was headed.

But mostly I thought of what I was going to do now.

What I had to do.

PART FOUR

THE BEST MAN

PART FOUR

THE BEST MAN

74

On a clear and warm beautiful evening four days before my brother Tom's wedding, I left the beach house and met up with Marvin Heller at Road F Beach again, and we headed west.

Around 6:00 p.m., we pulled into a full-service fifty-slip marina in East Moriches called Windemere. We came to a stop in the deserted parking lot, and I got out and grabbed the cooler that was in the back.

"You sure you don't need some company on this?" Marvin said as I went up to the driver's-side window.

"No, I'm good, Marvin," I said. "I got this."

"If you say so," he said as he handed me an envelope that I folded and tucked into my shorts pocket.

After I watched him back out and head for the Montauk Highway, I walked with the cooler down the marina's old gray wooden dock and stepped aboard the forty-foot fishing boat at the end of it.

The boat I'd rented was called the *Blues King II*, and it was a 2009 Luhrs tricked out into a fisherman's dream with an in-deck fish box and a bait prep center and three 300-horsepower Verados off the stern.

I untied the lines and got up on the bridge and put out into Moriches Bay, and in ten minutes, I was passing through the heavy currents of the Moriches Inlet into the Atlantic.

About a mile out as I hooked a right to cruise west parallel to the Smith Point County Park beach, I began thinking about my father.

I remembered the time we'd gone deep-sea fishing, and Tom caught a remora, and Dad had taken it off the hook and stuck it fast with its suction cups to the deck. I smiled as I remembered how my blue-eyed old man would start singing out there on the water after a few beers. "Sweet Caroline" was a Sean Rourke standard. But my favorite was when he sang "The Streets of New York" by the Wolfe Tones, about an Irishman from Dublin who comes to New York to become a cop, just like our grandfather had done.

I thought about how my father taught me to throw a punch and to hit a baseball and to tie a tie and to shave and to drive. His big warm hand on my shoulder as we fished side by side.

I thought about the closing statement he had given. How stirring it was. How brave he was. How honest. As I looked back at it now, I realized they must have tried to bribe him.

Then I thought about him out there on the water by himself the day he died. Had another boat come over to him acting in distress? Or maybe a scuba diver had gotten the jump on him before he knew what was happening. Grabbed him from behind and dragged him under.

As I cruised along, I suddenly realized the real reason why I had come home.

Because originally, I wasn't going to. Despite it being Tom's big day, I had planned to blow it off. After I got my life going in Philly, I had never looked back. Why start all that up again? I had thought. All that pain.

But at the last second as I lifted the phone to tell Tom my BS excuse, something made me, almost told me to, hang up.

As I rolled through the dark steel-colored waves, I realized now what that something was.

It was my father.

Even in death, his soul had never stopped yearning for justice. And it was that unsatisfied yearning, now more than twenty years old, that had finally pulled me, like a sunken anchor and chain pulls at a drifting ship, all the way back home.

Why would somebody do that? I wondered. Kill him? Kill two more people?

What did Hailey have to do with it? Or Dennis Tapley? Had Dennis Tapley done it himself?

I didn't know.

I throttled the engines up.

Yet, I thought.

75

I checked all my charts twice as I motored straight as an arrow to the Bellport Bay Inlet. When I arrived, I slid the boat into Neutral as some booze cruise ferry-sized vessel with a lot of jacked-looking tan men on its deck suddenly appeared.

When it was safely past, I throttled forward again and hooked a right into the Great South Bay.

And then there it was on my left, my destination.

The place where corrupt Suffolk County police chief Dennis Tapley had his own beach house.

Fire Island.

I looked over at the dark scrub pine–covered land strip as I pulled farther south.

Like the beach where Sandhill Point was located back in Southampton, Fire Island was just one of the long chain of thin barrier islands along the southern coast of Long Island known as the Outer Barrier.

But unlike the beach on Southampton, Fire Island was extremely remote. Though it technically could be reached by car along a bridge near Central Islip, most of the narrow thirty-one-mile-long island itself actually banned motor vehicles.

It was about an hour later when I slowed and began to head closer into shore beside a famous Fire Island beach community known as Point O'Woods.

Point O'Woods, where Tapley lived, wasn't as exclusive a summer playground as Southampton or East Hampton, but with its mostly summering Manhattan residents, it was by far the snootiest community on Fire Island.

How Tapley had a beach house in such an expensive community on a cop's salary, I didn't know. But I had a guess or two.

A few minutes later, I put the boat in Neutral and let it drift as I opened the envelope Marvin had given me and smoothed its contents out on the console. Marvin had asked around for me and through the south shore cop grapevine had scored big-time.

I looked down at the blown-up Google satellite map with Tapley's small bayside beach house circled in red.

After I took out a pair of binoculars, it was another fifteen minutes of powering in closer and farther south before I finally oriented myself.

When I spotted the roof of Tapley's house five minutes later, I put down the binocs and opened the cooler I had brought and took out the equipment.

The Digital Receiver Technology (DRT) unit known as a dirtbox that I removed from my bag was a small black box about the size of a trade paperback. Into one of its jacks I inserted an antenna, and into another port, my laptop.

I pointed it at Tapley's house and turned it on and brought up the software on my computer. The dirtbox worked by mimicking a real cell site, so now any mobile phone texts or emails or phone calls that anyone in the Tapley household made would be coming to me.

As I pointed its antenna directly at the Tapley residence, I knew I was flat out entering illegal territory now. It was sketchy enough that we used such tech semiofficially for municipal law enforcement on my drug task force down in Philly.

The fact that I was now using it in my dad's old case could most definitely be held against me in a court of law.

But it didn't matter.

After finding out about my dad, that he might have actually been murdered, I didn't care. I was in it for all the marbles.

I powered on my computer and stared at the screen, waiting for it to light.

I was going to find out what the hell was at the bottom of all this, no matter how dark or how deep it went.

76

I was still sitting there an hour later.

As far as I could tell, Tapley's beach house was empty. I could see in through his back deck's sliders and there hadn't been any movement. And according to my illegal dirtbox, not one cell phone call had come out of it or text or email.

I continued to sit up there in the wheelhouse watching and listening some more. I decided to drink a warm beer by myself as the sun went down. It was a spectacular evening, the sun over Suffolk County red orange, the sky teal.

I wanted to text Viv and ask if she was seeing it, too, but I hadn't brought my cell phone. Viv had taken it with her to throw off any surveillance on me while she and the other bridesmaids went into the city to pick up their dresses.

Just as it got dark, there was a roar off to my right, and a couple of tatted-up muscle head jackasses in a go-fast boat went by, hooting and hollering.

After they left, I powered up and headed back west, and ten minutes later, I powered the outboards down again as I drew in ten miles north of Point O'Woods next to Fire Island's Sailors Haven.

Across from Sayville, Sailors Haven was a state park for boaters with a beach, a protected botanical garden–like forest for tourists, a snack bar, and a visitors' center manned with park rangers during the day.

It was coming on night now, and there was only one vessel along the two docks, a small beat-up sailboat. I pulled in along the other empty dock as far away from it as I could, cut the engine, got out, and tied up.

Instead of fulfilling a desire to do some nocturnal botanical gardening, my presence at the beach park was purely tactical.

Because Point O'Woods' private neighborhood of about a hundred exclusive homes actually exerted its exclusivity none too subtly with a guard booth and a barbed wire–topped fence that separated it from the more blue-collar Ocean Bay Park community on its eastern side, there was no getting in that way. That's why I was here to the west. Sailors Haven Park bordered the western side of Point O'Woods, where there was no fence. It was my way in.

The lone sailboat at the other dock actually grumbled on and pulled out somewhere around eleven. When it left, I started gearing up by pulling on some black nylon hiking pants and a black long-sleeve shirt to keep Fire Island's notorious poison ivy off of me. Then I coated myself with bug spray and pulled on the knapsack I'd brought and exited the boat.

A minute later, I passed the Sailors Haven closed visitors' center and stepped onto a boardwalk path through the park's main attraction, the maritime holly forest.

The boardwalk meandered its way through a thick stand of holly trees and sassafras and pines and oaks and tons of shrubs before it let out on a sandy bike path.

This path, called Fire Island Boulevard, I knew, ran the entire length of the island, and I made a right on it in the dark and started walking. After about ten minutes, I slowed as I started to see some gray-shingled rooftops along the ridge of a dune on my right.

About a football field away, there was a set of stairs heading up from the bike path, and I quickly went up it. Most of the Point O'Woods homes I slipped past looked pretty identical, small salt-weathered wood vacation houses with rusty bikes and wagons and flipped-over kayaks on the sandy lawns in front of them.

I didn't see a soul as I finally came to the bayside cul-de-sac where Tapley's house was. I went off into the pine woods to its right and came around in a wide loop, moving slowly to keep my footsteps as quiet as possible in the snagging underbrush.

On a little rising slope far back in the gnarly vine-covered trees behind Tapley's backyard, I crouched and took out a pre-paid cell I'd brought. Happily, I saw it actually got some service, which could be a little spotty on Fire Island, and I called Tapley's house number that Marvin had written along the bottom of the map.

The phone started ringing inside the house a moment later. It was funny being able to hear it as I crouched there in the dark. Not funny *ha ha* either. More like are-you-sure-you-haven't-lost-your-mind-and-turned-into-an-actual-psycho sort of funny.

It rang again and then again. Tapley didn't seem to have an answering machine.

I hung up the phone and slipped it back into my bag and sat there in the pitch-black woods. On the descending slope to the right, you could see the dark bay through the dwarf pine trees. The lights of boats in the distance skimming by. The lights of fireflies in the marsh cordgrass.

As I sat feeling more and more nervous about what I was going to do, I heard a rumble overhead then a ghostly moan and looked up to see the red blinking eye of a jumbo jet from JFK heading east out over the water for Europe. I watched it, wondering if it wouldn't be better if I was now up there instead.

77

Then there was no more stalling. I reached into my knapsack and took out the balaclava and night-vision goggles I had brought and pulled them on.

The dark forest around me lit up green as I thumbed on the goggles, and I went down the little wooded slope and across the backyard and climbed silently up the stairs onto Tapley's back deck.

When I tried the door, it was not that surprisingly unlocked, and I slid it open and stepped inside into the small living room. I stood there still for a full minute, listening. My nerves in knots, the bottom of my stomach gone.

As I stood there, sweat began pouring down my face. I had a

moment of pure panic, fully realizing just how nuts this was. I suddenly wondered how much time I could get for breaking and entering. And how life in a New York state prison was probably worse than a death sentence for a cop.

But there was only one way left to figure out what had happened.

I closed the sliding door behind me and then turned and headed for the green glow of the stairs. At the top of them and to the left was the master bedroom. I peeked through the open door at the empty unmade bed.

I found the gun safe in its closet ten seconds later.

Yes! I thought as I saw in the greenish light that it was an electronic keypad, one just as Tapley's scorned girlfriend had described in Xavier Kelsey's tape.

I knelt before it and reached into my bag of cop tricks again and pulled out the last and best one of all.

What I removed looked like a large hockey puck inside of a sock. It was actually a heavy-duty, rare-earth magnet that was about a thousand times more powerful than the horseshoe-shaped ones you played with in grammar school science class.

The keypad of most gun safes is connected to a solenoid, a kind of electromagnetic switch that opens and closes the latch. This solenoid is actually the Achilles' heel of such gun safes, because if a very powerful magnet field passes over the solenoid from the outside, it can sometimes trip the latch.

I knew this because I'd seen it done by a crazy veteran Philly narcotics cop who had taken me under his wing when I was a rookie. The drug spots we raided often had gun safes, and the magnet trick was about a billion times simpler than cutting the lock with an acetylene torch.

You had to be careful when you did it, though, I remembered from painful experience. The magnet clacked with surprising force to the safe's metal surface when you brought it near, which was why you needed a sock to help save your fingers from get-ting crushed.

I was raising the magnet in the sock up toward the keypad when I heard something outside, a kind of clatter. I slowly laid the magnet on the carpet and stood and went to the bedroom window.

At first as I looked through the half-open curtains, I thought that I was seeing things, that my stress-gripped mind was play-ing tricks on me.

But it wasn't.

Suffolk County police chief Dennis Tapley was coming up his vacation house's front steps.

78

I stood there frozen in the middle of Tapley's bedroom, next to his messily unmade bed, listening to him open his front door downstairs.

From the window, I had seen he was in his police chief's uniform and was armed with his service weapon, some kind of semiautomatic.

When I packed the night before in preparation for my plan, I had decided to leave my gun behind.

Standing there in the dead silence listening to Tapley loudly toss his jingling keys onto his kitchen counter below, I wondered now if that had been such a great idea.

In fact, as I stood there paralyzed with indecision, I seriously wondered if that decision was about to cost me my life.

This was it, I thought as I heard the bottom step creak under his weight. There was no time to hide, no time to run to the window, no time for anything except maybe to die.

That's why I had no choice but to do what I did next. None whatsoever.

Tapley had just reached the top of the landing when I dived from the bedroom doorway and cracked him in the mouth as hard as I could with a wild haymaker right.

He cried out in shock and pain as we both went tumbling down the stairs in a crazy tangle. At the bottom, I was the first one up, and Tapley had just cleared his gun when I kicked it out of his hand.

"Son of a bitch!" he yelled as he leapt up, trying to tackle me.

In a pirouette that had far more to do with crazed close-to-heart-attack panic than anything else, I dodged just out of his grasp. Over the couch behind us he went with a thump and a crash, and when I turned, I saw that he was picking up his gun.

Already moving, I heard the shot as a chunk of the Sheet-rock I'd just been standing in front of disintegrated at my back. I headed for the only place I could go, back up the stairs. Tapley fired at me again.

"I'm gonna kill your ass!" Tapley screamed as I dived back into the bedroom.

I was heading for the window thinking I'd have to dive out of it when I tripped over my burglar bag and went sprawling.

Then I heard Tapley thumping up the stairs again. I reached out and my hand found something, and I leapt up just as Tapley came through the door.

Tapley had the gun half raised to blow my head off when I swung the heavy magnet in the sock and caught him square and flush in his left ear.

His gun went off again as it flew from his hand. Then he bounced off the doorjamb, and there was a heavy house-shaking thud as he landed on his back on the floor in the hallway.

As I knelt down before him in a panic, I thought maybe I had shattered his skull and killed him. But as I patted at his big head, it seemed intact enough, though blood was now coming from his ear. I watched his chest rise and fall. He wasn't dead. But I'd knocked him out cold.

I didn't have a moment to spare. I ran to the gun safe and clacked on the magnet and slid it and heard it pop the latch.

Inside the safe were shotguns, boxes of ammo, some cell phones in a cigar box. There was a shoebox filled with cash, twenties, fifties, gold coins.

I was kneeling and digging in beside the shotguns when I noticed a pouch in some webbing on the door. It was a large plastic bag with yellow tape along the top with the words *Southampton PD* on it.

I lifted it out, and inside I saw a hoodie. I searched around, and a moment later, I saw another plastic evidence bag with something small inside it tucked in with the hoodie.

I took it out and held it level to my night-vision goggles to see it better.

Sonya Serrano, Tapley's old flame, had been right on the money.

In it were bullets. Two bullets.

The two small, very inconsequential-looking gray bits of mushroomed lead that had taken Noah Sutton's life.

79

Most people after breaking into law enforcement people's homes and knocking them cold before robbing them blind would probably take a breather.

But I was a Rourke, and come hell or high water or even impending arrest for assault on a police officer, wedding party duty still called.

When I got home, I'd barely had time to shower and get dressed into the golf clothes Viv had purchased for me for Tom's formal groomsmen's golf outing.

Viv was still in bed, and I went over to her to say goodbye. I knew I was in trouble because she wouldn't talk to me even after I tried to tickle her pits.

I guess she had her reasons. I had been gone all night long.

"I don't even know what the hell you're doing, Terry," she said as I left.

Closing the door softly behind me, I didn't have time to tell her that I was truly wondering about all of it myself.

"You look...bad," Tom said in angry greeting as I piled into the plush rear of his Cadillac Escalade with Finn and Mickey and Nick.

"Do I? That's funny because I feel just terrific," I said, attempting to lighten things up.

Attempt failed, I thought as I took in Tom's pissed-off-looking glare in the rearview.

I didn't blame him for being upset. My treating his seven-figure wedding as an afterthought must have looked as if I didn't give a shit, I realized. And what really sucked was that I couldn't even tell him that nothing was further from the truth.

Not yet, anyway.

As we pulled out onto Meadow Lane and passed the sandy spot where my dad had first told me about Noah Sutton's murder all those years ago, I kept wondering just how it was that I was going to tell my brothers the truth. That Dad hadn't died in an accident. That he had been murdered.

"Well, you're here," Tom said in the dead silence as we got onto the Montauk Highway.

"For you, brother," I said as I remembered the sound the heavy magnet had made when it connected with Tapley's skull, "I wouldn't have missed it for all the world."

Twenty minutes later, the sun had just come up as we got out of the car and stepped onto the circular drive of the storied Maiden Rock Country Club in East Hampton.

In the elite East Hamptons, the joke was country club golf wasn't a sport, it was a blood sport. A *blue* blood sport.

How Tom had gotten us into Maiden Rock was mind-boggling. It wasn't even the palm greasing so much as connecting with the right connected person. Some people said it was easier to get a round in at Augusta or Pebble Beach.

"Gentlemen, if you would like, there are fresh Bloody Marys in the lounge," the white-shirted clubhouse manager said, ushering us in.

As the others went off to partake, I quickly headed downstairs for the locker room.

I'd been in some nice bathrooms before. Especially back at Sandhill Point, where luxury seemed an obsession. But this one was on another level.

What looked like half a quarry of glowing Alpine white Italian marble slabbed the floors and walls and sink countertops and even the ceiling.

Not only that, on the polished countertops and in little zinc glass niches along the walls of this imported limestone cavern were the most immaculately folded white fluffy towels that I had ever seen in my life. Between them, bowling pin pyramids of spring water bottles were lined at precise intervals like regiments of soldiers at attention.

With all of it softly bathed in the expensive high-drama lighting usually only saved up for Hollywood premieres, it looked more like the main showroom at a Fifth Avenue jewelry store than a locker room bathroom, I thought.

I was washing my hands with one of the exquisitely perfumed hand soaps when the door to the locker room opened.

And into the restroom of the gods walked one of the gods himself. At least in his own mind.

It was Henry Sutton.

The "ye high lord and chancellor" of East Hampton blue-blood society saw me, too, almost immediately, and the door closed with a loud click as he stopped in his tracks with his Locust Valley lock jaw agape.

I could tell right away by the panicked look in his eyes that he knew exactly who I was, too.

Which was pretty ironic.

Because how would he know who I was? Unlike himself, my face never appeared in any society pages.

I squealed off the water and slowly turned as the billionaire's perfect tan seemed to quickly drain from his handsome face.

"Wh-what do you want?" he stammered. "Who...who let you in here?"

I slowly dried off with one of the fluffy towels as I squinted at him. At his shiny golf clothes, at his still slightly frosted male-model hair. He hadn't changed much since I'd seen him at the trial more than twenty years before.

Luckily, I had changed. I was bigger than I was at eighteen. Bigger than Henry now, by two inches and much wider. I had easily twenty pounds on him. I looked at Henry's small girlish hands, his buffed nails. Mine were a bit bigger, the knuckles scraped and scarred from fighting drug dealers on dirty concrete.

When I gauged his expression, it was hard to tell what he was looking more like.

Scared to death.

Or guilty.

I'd shocked the crap out of him. That was for sure. He looked like someone had just tased him.

I knew fear when I smelled it. I could tell right away that he seemed to think I was there to ambush him, to kick his pretty-boy ass for what his family had done to mine.

As I stood there staring at him five feet away, still reeling with exhaustion and craziness from my life-and-death waltz with Tapley on Fire Island, I was definitely tempted to fulfill his incorrect assessment.

I still hadn't put all the pieces together yet about what had exactly happened with my dad, but this son of a bitch was eyeball deep in it all. I could see it in his face.

And even if I was just being paranoid, smashing in his exfoliated face just for the heck of it seemed fair game to me. Because he had destroyed so many of my family's hopes and dreams all those years ago, hadn't he?

I thought about my crazy brother Mickey still working as a cable tech and an electrician's helper on the weekends to make ends meet because this asshole or his brother or maybe his sister took West Point away from him with a single phone call.

Because why? We were the little people was why. We were ants and getting stepped on was what ants were for.

Then again, maybe not, I thought as my hand balled into a fist.

We both turned as the door suddenly opened and a group of golfers came in.

Not just any golfers, I saw.

They were Tom and Mickey and Finn and Nick.

"You!" Tom said as he spotted Henry Sutton.

Then I saw a switch flip in my brother's eyes. The crazy switch.

Henry must have seen it, too, because as my brother ran forward, Henry leapt immediately into one of the toilet stalls and slammed the door.

"Help!" Sutton screamed. "Somebody help me! Security! Police!"

Tom rattled savagely at the stall door, truly as unhinged as I'd ever seen him, which was saying something. The money, the pressure of the wedding, and his revenge scheme on the Hamptons for what it had done to our family had coalesced into a hurricane of rage that he was now finally unleashing in one incredible surge.

We were still holding Tom back from climbing in over the top of the stall and beating the billionaire to death when the security guys showed up.

"What the hell is going on in here?" the biggest of them said.

"I'm Henry Sutton and they're trying to kill me," Henry Sutton said.

Tom suddenly broke into laughter as we let him go.

"Well, I'm Tom Rourke, and he's full of shit," he said. "I didn't touch him."

"Exactly," Finn said. "We came in here and the guy in the stall started having a panic attack or something."

"We were worried about him. We were about to call you," Mickey said.

"As a member of this club, I order you to escort these…these… off the premises," Henry Sutton said as the security guards formed a protective circle around him and brought him out.

"For what? Taking a piss?" Tom said, unzipping at one of the grand urinals. "Please get back on your meds, sir. I hope you get better soon."

The head security guy stayed behind as Henry and the others left. He was a big blond middle-aged guy with a mustache.

"We're not going to have a problem here today, gentlemen, are we?" he said.

I shook my head and stifled a laugh as Tom zipped up and shrugged with the most innocent face I'd ever seen.

"From who? Us?" he said.

80

An hour later, we were chilling at the edge of a stand of white birch when my brother took his cigar out of his mouth and handed it to me, juicy end first.

"Gee, thanks," I said as Tom unsheathed a five-iron from his leather Ping bag.

We were three-quarters up the green of the tenth hole. Finn and I sucked, but Tom and Mickey were really good. It was Tom's second shot on the tenth, which was a long par four. He had crushed his drive off the box and had a 170 and a little to go.

Tom reared back and went for it with his five-iron. I'd only played golf with him a few times in high school, and even back then he had a beautiful swing. The way he kept his lower half quiet and kept his hands back, man, could he shellac it.

Mickey let out a whistle as the ball launched down the fairway like it was going to go into orbit. We all could have been grade-schoolers again as we watched in little-brother silent awe.

"No!" said Finn as it hit fifteen feet up over the pin and jumped and began rolling back and back and…

It went in.

I dropped Tom's stogie as we all went ballistic surrounding Tom out in the middle of the fairway. We slapped the hell out of his back as he tossed his club over his shoulder and fist-pumped.

"May the road rise to meet you and may the wind be always at your back as you eagle the tenth hole at Maiden Rock!" Finn said with our mother's Irish accent as we all broke up again.

The nirvana was still floating around as we headed to the eleventh tee. Just as we approached, a couple of security staff in polo shirts, whom we'd met earlier in the locker room, roared by on a golf cart and then stopped. One of the guys was on his hand radio.

"Hi. Are you Terence Rourke?" the bigger of the two said to me. It was the blond middle-aged guy.

Uh-oh.

"Yes. What's up?" I said warily.

I thought about Henry Sutton. Had that wimp called the cops or something?

"Your wife, Vivian, called at the desk. She needs to talk to you."

Still suspicious, I thought about that for a second. I had left my cell phone in the locker. You weren't allowed to bring them onto the course. Club rules. And Viv was pregnant.

"If you want," he said calmly, "we could give you a ride back."

I looked at him, trying to detect anything in his face. He looked back placidly.

"Okay," I said, walking toward the cart, not wanting to take any chances.

"What's up, Terry?" Tom called over.

"Viv needs me on the phone. I'm not sure," I called back.

We hummed along in the cart through a gap in the trees that separated the greens. The seventh hole we were rolling down was especially beautiful with a pale slate blue lake-sized pond on the left, rolling green hills on the right, and tall stately trees that lined the fairway.

We made it to the sixth hole and were approaching a service road when out from the tall stately trees roared a gray SUV that stopped short in front of us. It was followed by another SUV and then a third. As a cop, I knew unmarked law enforcement cars when I saw them.

"I knew it," I said to the security guy. "You're a lying sack of shit."

I watched as over half a dozen heavily armed SWAT officers in military-style uniforms stormed out of the vehicles along with a K9 officer with a barking black German shepherd.

"Yeah, and it looks like you're under arrest, asshole," the security creep said as two offensive lineman–sized policemen with shaved heads flung me down on the cart path and bit handcuffs into my wrists.

81

I guess my tangle with Tapley wasn't as under the radar as I had initially hoped, I thought as I sat hemmed in tight in the first SUV by two burly SWAT cops.

The absurdity of how over-the-top the arrest had been had almost made me laugh, but now as we rolled along, I was beginning to have some misgivings.

Because I was seriously beginning to wonder where they were taking me. The closest Suffolk County PD headquarters was about an hour south. Would they take me there? Somewhere else?

Were they even Suffolk County cops? I couldn't tell from their gray tactical uniforms. There were no patches or markings. They could have been from East Hampton or anywhere.

There were so many damn police departments in Long Island, it made your head spin.

After thirty minutes, we stopped along an ummarked road, and the driver got out to talk to the cops in the SUV parked in front of us.

"Where are we?" I said to the cop beside me.

But he wouldn't say. He seemed about as talkative as the battering ram strapped to the door beside him. And about as smart. And charming.

We got rolling again, and a quarter of a mile ahead, we pulled into a tree-lined driveway. The place didn't look like a police precinct. It looked like a cheesy office building.

What in the living hell? I thought as they parked and took me out of the truck and into the parking lot.

I looked at the small brown-brick-and-black-glass corporate building. There were no cars in the large lot. Beyond it was a two-lane road, and on the other side of it, a grass field, flat and featureless with some silver power-line transmission towers in it.

We could have been anywhere, I thought, starting to get even more worried.

Didn't the SWAT guys in Chicago or somewhere get in trouble for having some off-site location where they would warehouse suspects? I thought.

They brought me inside the building and into an office suite off the empty lobby and put me in a small room with a table in it. It looked exactly like an interview room in a precinct, I noticed. I swallowed when I saw that there was a large ringbolt in the floor for handcuffing prisoners.

But if this was a precinct, where were the other cops? Where was the desk sergeant?

I thought about my options.

Before I fled Tapley's house, I triple-checked to make sure I hadn't left anything behind.

My alibi was being in the city with my wife and daughter

291

while they were picking up their dresses with the rest of the bridal party, and I had the cell phone movement to prove it. They really had nothing. No witnesses. Nada.

This was speculation, I decided. A total bluff.

I guess Tapley didn't care. Was he doubling down? Intimidating me?

I looked around the anonymous room in the anonymous building in the middle of Anonymousville.

It was starting to work.

I thought about my boss back in Philly. How baffled he would be when he heard about all of this.

But he didn't matter.

I just didn't want Viv and Angelina to worry.

One of the SWAT cops opened the door and poked his head in.

"Hey, your lawyer's here."

What lawyer? I thought as the guy left.

The door opened, and I looked up and saw what I could and couldn't believe at the same time.

It wasn't my lawyer.

It was Hailey Sutton's.

82

I stared at Byron Seager as he came into the tiny room. The white-haired tan fiftysomething dream-team lawyer seemed like he hadn't lost a step in two decades' time. He got right down to business by firmly closing the door and putting a briefcase on the table.

He opened the briefcase, and as he sat, he removed a photograph from it and laid it flat on the table for me to see.

It was a photograph of me and Courtney at her restaurant. We were both laughing.

"This is an old girlfriend, right?" he said. "Cozy. You look smitten. Does your pregnant wife know about this?"

I looked at him, stifling the urge to laugh.

"Something like this could be damaging, no?" Seager said, shrugging the shoulders of his crisp bespoke suit. "Women, especially pregnant women, are sensitive, vulnerable. Pictures certainly are effective, aren't they? There's a mystery to them. You and Ms. Frazier look pretty enthralled with one another. Leaves a lot to the imagination."

I kept looking at him.

"That photo might have me sleeping on the couch for a night," I said. "But other people are going to be sleeping in a stone hotel for a lot longer when all this is said and done, Byron. And call me crazy, I'm thinking you might be one of them."

He put the photo away and raised his palms in a submissive way. "I'd like to apologize for that approach, Mr. Rourke. You're right. It was stupid. As well as rude. I'm an employee, as you know, so sometimes I'm called to perform tasks that I don't recommend. But sometimes my clients insist. What I really want to show you is this."

He took out a Galaxy phone from the inside of his suit jacket and showed me a video of a car, a white Cadillac SUV. It was parked in what looked like the lot of the building I was in. In the video, somebody went to the Caddy's liftgate and opened it. In the trunk was a large leather duffel bag filled with mounds and mounds of hundred-dollar bills.

"This is what is in that bag," Byron said as he scratched something on the back of a blank cream-colored business card with a Montblanc pen.

He passed the card over.

$4,000,000.

He slid the card back across the table and took a Cadillac key fob from his pocket and spun it in his hand.

"You get someone to deliver what you have on my client, and a man comes in here and takes off your cuffs, and you're free and clear in that car. That's the deal."

83

I stared at Byron. He had dark brown eyes and a squared-off forehead that was broad and flat like the face of a sledgehammer.

I looked at him for another good minute.

He stared back cool as a cucumber. He was good at staring.

I finally nodded and leaned back as best as I could in the chair and rolled my stiffening neck.

Finally, I broke the silence.

"You know, I heard a story about this old guy who lived in a rent-controlled apartment in an old hotel in Manhattan," I said. "A builder wanted to knock down the hotel and put up a billion-dollar high-rise, but before he could do that, all the rent controllers had to agree.

"They got everybody out except for this one stubborn old man.

They offered him a nice new place, a penthouse in Midtown. He declined. Then they offered him a nice new place and a million bucks. No dice. You know how much that old guy got in the end?"

Byron held up the four-million-dollar card again with a hopeful look on his face.

I shook my head.

"Not even close, Byron," I said. "Here in my palm, in my grubby little palm, I have hold of the rest of your client's life. Every particle of her, every year, every day, every minute from this day forward now belongs to me. You know it. I know it."

Byron sighed. "So that means?"

"All of it," I said.

"All of what?" he said.

"Of her money," I said. "I want all of her cash and assets. I want her business liquidated. I want all of her stock and *the* Glass House and all of her other property and cars and clothes and furniture sold and all the proceeds compiled together and wired into a numbered Swiss bank account by five o'clock today."

Byron stared at me, a smile playing on his lips.

"That's a tall order, Mr. Rourke. Impossibly tall, actually. Especially considering the time constraint. But the fact that you're willing to negotiate is refreshing. Let's talk."

"Oh, wait," I said. "I forgot one thing. This part is non-negotiable. I also want my father back."

Seager squinted at me, the smile gone.

"I get every penny Hailey Sutton possesses and one Sean Rourke brought back to life. And she gets to stay out of prison for the rest of hers. Seems like a fair trade to me. You type up that contract, Mr. Seager. I'll Montblanc my name right on the dotted line. What do you say? Is it a deal?"

"Okay," Byron said, picking up his card and briefcase. "You can't say I didn't give you a chance, Mr. Rourke. What happens next is all on you."

84

Five minutes passed. Then, without telling me anything, two gray SWAT cops came in (if that's what they really were) and guided me back outside of the undisclosed office building.

They put me back into the rear of the SUV and away we went.

I have to say, I was getting extremely nervous again as we drove along. These people were obviously out of their corrupt minds. The evidence I had gotten my hands on was apparently such a threat that they were willing to do anything.

Anything, I thought, swallowing, as we finally shrieked to a stop.

By the time the door groaned open, I'd already decided that whatever these fools thought they were going to do to me, I wasn't about to go along peacefully. I was going to go kicking and biting.

Then I looked out the open door, and I felt a wave of glorious relief.

I landed hard on my ass after one of the goons unlocked my cuffs and then my seat belt, and I was shoved out onto the edge of the Montauk Highway near my old house in the Hampton Bays.

"Assholes!" I yelled as the corrupt cops peeled out, their rear tires spitting gravel in my face.

Without a cell phone, I began to trudge down the storied course's long road toward Southampton in my golf cleats.

"Hey, mister. You really sliced one, huh?" said a voice from a slowing Mustang full of teens before they sped off.

"I'll say," as I finally crossed the Southampton town line.

I took a shortcut and came out on another road with an old cemetery across the street. The cemetery I walked along soon became a quaint pond with benches around it, and I stopped for a moment to catch my breath.

Sitting there gave me time for some reflection. I wondered why I hadn't been charged. If Tapley wanted me behind bars for breaking into his house and burglarizing it and knocking him out, why wasn't I?

What the hell was he doing? Was he afraid to actually arrest me because he had no evidence? Or because he was afraid of what would be revealed about what he had in his possession?

If that were the case, why have me picked up at all? Especially in such a dramatic and intimidating way? Had he reconsidered? Or was it a bluff? A big scare tactic to set me up for a bribery attempt?

If he wanted to spook me, it was working, I thought as I glanced back at the headstones. I was spooked.

After another ten minutes walking down the lovely street, I came across a little hotel and went in and asked to use a phone. I called Viv, who drove straight over and picked me up. I thought she was going to kick my ass, but when I got into the car, she cried as she embraced me.

I told her everything. What had happened the night before. About the arrest. I thought she'd cream me for all the risks I had taken, but again, she surprised me.

"I'm just glad you're safe. What's going to happen now?" she said.

"I have no idea," I said.

"What do you think is going on?"

"Obviously something very strange," I said as she pulled out of the driveway and headed toward the house.

When we got back, we saw Tom standing at the beach house's front steps.

"Terry, what the hell is up? Everything okay? You got arrested?" he said, handing me my phone.

I looked at Tom. There was no way I was going to explain everything to him this close to his wedding. He had way too much on his plate already.

Heck, I wasn't telling anybody now about what I'd learned. No way, no how. Being Irish and therefore an expert on wakes and weddings, I knew the best policy was always to arrange them just one at a time.

"No, no, man. I'm really sorry. It was a joke. An old friend from school heard I was in town. His brother's a cop. They just played a practical joke on me. That's all."

"By arresting you?"

"It's just a cop thing. We're all nuts. Sorry for worrying you."

"That's complete bullshit," Tom said, shaking his head and smiling. "Honestly, you need a lawyer? I know you're up to something, Terry. Do you need my help?"

"No, no, Tom," I said. "Or at least not yet. Believe me, I'll tell you first thing when and if I do."

"Okay, then, I guess. Everyone's out at the pool if you guys want to join them."

85

For the rest of that day and the morning of the next, I decided to lie completely low with my family.

Not sure what these maniacs were going to try next, I decided that Viv and Angelina and I needed to stay behind the high secure walls of the estate until further notice. I even turned my phone off and placed it in a cigar box wrapped in tinfoil to disconnect it from the cell sites.

After lunch, we all went out on the side lawn for an epic game of tailgate toss.

As the beanbags flew and red Solo cups stacked up, the new Brit side of our family had all the kids in stitches.

It was Toby's and Gordon's revenge for all of us making fun

of them at the softball game. They had acquired a soccer ball from somewhere and were playing a game of monkey in the middle with the entirety of the little cousins, including Angelina, playing the part of the screaming monkeys.

I mean, the kids didn't have a chance. Toby was especially talented. When one of my sister's kids came forward, he spun the ball up his leg somehow and balanced it on his forehead like a trained seal.

In the late afternoon after this hilarity, I was back upstairs in the bedroom after my shower when I relented and turned my phone back on.

"Now, why did you do that, you idiot?" I said to myself as I looked at the screen.

There were twenty texts from Courtney.

What I did next was even more idiotic. I hit the button to call back.

"What the hell happened, Terry? You were arrested yesterday?" she said.

"Not really. I was picked up, but I wasn't booked."

"What? What the hell is going on? Who picked you up?"

"The East Hampton PD, I think."

"You think?"

"They were in tactical stuff and weren't very talkative."

"What? Like a SWAT team? Why would they pick you up?"

I almost laughed. My midnight trip to Tapley's was something I was never telling anyone. Even partners. Even old pals. My mom and dad didn't raise no dummy.

I'd have to make up something to tell her, I thought. Tomorrow.

"It's a long story," I said. "I'll tell you in person. Let's meet tomorrow."

"Terry, now's not the time for being cryptic. This is going off the rails. These people have lost it. This is getting actually dangerous now. You have to be straight with me," Courtney said.

Getting dangerous *now*? I thought. No, this had gotten dangerous the second I laid my hands on Kelsey's files and lifted the cardboard lid off what was looking like one of the biggest cans of worms ever buried.

No, it was actually even before that, I thought.

This had gotten dangerous the second Viv had dropped the RSVP to my brother's wedding in the mail.

"Terry, are you there?" Courtney said. "We need to meet now."

I looked over at my lovely worried wife as she came in with my daughter.

"Tomorrow, Courtney," I said, and I hung up.

86

Catch Me Kenny's was a seaside dive bar in Montauk off West Side Drive across from the Star Island Yacht Club.

Courtney and her boss, Walter Marino, were already there with the assistant district attorney, Katrina Volland, when I arrived at around three thirty Wednesday.

"Hey, guys. Great weather we're having, isn't it?" I said as I sat down at their booth.

"Enough with the jokes," Courtney said. "What the hell happened with the arrest?"

I checked the time on my phone.

"Before we get to that. It should be here by now," I said.

"What should be here by now?" Walter said.

"You'll see," I said as the waitress came over.

"My name's Terry Rourke," I said to her. "The bartender is holding a package for me behind the bar. Could you get it for me, please?"

"Sure," she said, walking off.

She came back thirty seconds later with a large white FedEx box and handed it to me.

"Thanks," I said.

I waited until the waitress left with our drink orders before I ripped the seal and passed the box over the table.

"Oh, my goodness," Courtney said.

"Is this what I think it is?" Volland said.

"The holy grail? The missing hoodie and the missing bullets?" Courtney said. "I mean, what? Hailey's stolen evidence? So that's why they arrested you! Where did you find it?"

"It was sent to me anonymously at the house," I lied. "Maybe one of the people I interviewed had it? Your guess is as good as mine. I can't figure it out."

That was my story and I was sticking to it.

Like glue.

"Does this have anything to do with Chief Tapley?" Marino said, peering at me.

"How so?" I said, trying not to have a heart attack.

"He's missing," Courtney said.

Missing?

"What? What do you mean, missing?" I said.

"We heard from our wiretap that he's been missing since yesterday. Wheaton is going crazy. So is Tapley's wife. They have no idea where he is. They found his empty car parked at the Orient Point Ferry."

"Is that right?" I said.

I wondered about that. I thought about the money in his gun locker. *Was he on the run now?*

"Maybe he thinks you're about to scoop him up, and he got out of Dodge," I said to Marino.

"Maybe," he said.

"But we're finally doing this now?" I said to Courtney. "No more bullshit? No more delays? Hailey is going to be retried?"

"Yes," Volland said. "Even Wheaton can't stop it anymore. There's no way for him to get out of prosecuting now."

After the waitress came back, Courtney lifted her drink.

"To you, Terry. You did it," she said. "Game, set, match."

87

The men of the Rourke clan were all downstairs sitting around the basement sports bar while all the ladies and girls took Emmaline into the village for a spa day. Up on the huge TV screen, the Mets were playing the Yankees.

Nick's and Finn's and Mickey's boys were in the arcade behind us playing Pop-A-Shot basketball and doing dance routines, and from their constant screaming, it sounded like they were going completely freaking nuts. But Nick and Finn and Mickey didn't seem to even notice, let alone mind, so who was I to point it out?

The Mets had the bases loaded in the seventh with one out, but as I watched, the Yankee reliever got a ground ball for a double play.

"Another, peach fuzz?" Nick said, hovering an open bottle of blue-label Johnnie Walker over the glass in front of me.

Even though it was three in the afternoon, I nodded. He poured. I sipped. I shouldn't have, but I did.

I needed a damn drink.

Because I wasn't feeling too hot. I still didn't know what the hell was going on. Tapley was missing. Flat out missing. It was on the news now.

But where had he gone? No one knew. Was he on the lam? Was he coming after me? After my family? Also, Viv had gone back to being pissed at me for some reason. Probably because I could be heading for the slammer if everything came out.

And I hadn't heard back from Courtney or Marino or Volland yet. Was this damn case going to happen or what? Had I done all this crazy stuff for nothing?

I was pondering all these things and more when my phone rang.

It was Courtney.

"Good news," she said.

"I like that kind. What do you have?" I said.

"You near a TV?"

"Yes."

"Turn on Channel 8."

I grabbed the remote.

"Hey!" everybody yelled when I changed the channel.

On Channel 8, there was some kind of press conference, a podium with a woman behind it.

It was my buddy Katrina Volland, the assistant district attorney.

I turned up the volume.

"Thank you, everyone," she said. "I called this press conference on behalf of the Suffolk County District Attorney's Office. We are pleased to announce that due to new evidence received by our office, it is our intention to retry Hailey Sutton for the murder of Noah Sutton. We will not be taking questions at this time. Thank you."

"What? Hailey the witch! Dad's case? Does this mean what I think it means?" Finn said, jumping up.

"You did this," Tom said, turning toward me. "This was what you were doing? Running around all this time? You were trying to get them to open up Dad's case?"

I hadn't told the others what was going on yet. I was going to wait till after the wedding. But this publicity changed everything.

"No," I said, shrugging. "I had nothing to do with it."

They all stared at me in shock as I knocked back my drink in one shot.

"Only kidding," I said, throwing my hands in the air.

"It was all me, Tom. And, yes, that's why I've been running around. Remember you said keep my badge handy? Well, I followed your advice and it worked. Hailey thought she was free and clear. Fat chance. We just nailed that bitch to the floorboards."

"But how?" Mickey said.

So I told them. About how I found the Sutton Slay files, my interviews with the staff, how the chauffeur was coming forward as a witness. Of course, as with Courtney, I lied about the whole stealing-the-evidence thing. What they didn't know there couldn't hurt them.

I also left out the part about our father possibly being murdered. We still had a wedding to attend. The wake could wait until after.

"Oh, you sneaky little son of a bitch," Tom said, hugging me. "What a wedding gift. Just what I wanted. Hailey Sutton in an orange jumpsuit!"

Then we all turned toward Finn, who was over at the sound system when suddenly the strains of Chumbawamba's one-hit wonder—and the Rourke family theme song—filled the room.

"'I get knocked down, but I get up again'!" we sang as we knocked over barstools and shoved at each other, jumping up and down, making more noise than the kids.

"'Ain't ever gonna keep me down'!"

The song wasn't over yet and the kids had joined in and we were all still mosh pitting in the center of the room when the song suddenly stopped.

We all turned to see our wives standing there.

"This is babysitting?" my sister, Erin, said to her husband, Nick.

You could have heard a pin drop as we struggled to think of something to say in response.

"It was all Finn's idea," Tom said, elaborately checking his watch. "Oh, look at the time. I have to call the caterer."

88

"Screw this. What's taking so long? Let's go down to the bar and play some cards," Tom said as we all sat around in Sand-hill Point's auditorium-sized living room, wearing our tuxedos.

The big day had finally arrived.

"I'm down," said Mickey, who was the best man, as he started humming Chumbawamba.

"No, no, no," Finn said. "Mickey, sit your ass down. You have one job, keeping that dummy sober until the reception, okay? No downstairs. No cards. Get serious. No whiskey drink or even lager drink. You also better have the rings or I'm going to kick your ass."

I laughed as I shook my head at my crazy brothers.

We turned as the house manager, Robin, came in wearing a gray caterer's uniform and a Bluetooth hands-free mike in her ear.

"Gentlemen, I believe you are to take your stations," she said.

My brothers and I all looked at each other nervously as we stood and smoothed our lapels.

Because, at long last, it was finally here.

The Thomas Rourke & Emmaline Fullerton beach wedding day had arrived.

We filed out the side entrance onto the sun terrace. On the grass was perhaps the hugest white tent I'd ever seen in my life, with dozens of white tables arranged inside. Beside the tent was an avenue of white rose petals sprinkled onto the grass that we followed toward the now flower-garlanded stairs to the beach.

We finally saw all the people as we reached the top of the staircase. My brothers and I stopped and stood there, smiling like idiots, as a crowd of about 150 people, mostly family dressed to the nines down the bluff on the sand, let out an enormous roar. I could only imagine what the reception would be like once the throng of additional guests arrived.

I shook my head in awe at the storybook setting the wedding planners had created as I followed Tom down the teak steps. I mean, I knew it was going to be over-the-top nuts, but it looked like an emperor was being coronated.

At the base of the stairs, a full twenty-one-member string section from an orchestra was playing some ethereal Handel or Vivaldi melody. They were seated in tuxedos before an enchanted forest that had somehow suddenly grown out of the sand.

We passed by the musicians and entered a fairy forest of a dozen of what appeared to be real cherry blossom trees that formed an aisle between the seated assembly. Their lush overflowing branches reached up and formed a fairy-tale pink umbrella above us as we walked toward the raised wedding bower.

The four-post bower itself looked like it was made of peonies,

311

a pastel wonder arch of softball-sized blossoms in coral and pale plum. Behind it, the endless Atlantic Ocean had pitched in by coloring itself lavender in the setting gold sunlight.

In that incredible champagne-colored light, I looked over at Tom and laughed. My impossibly confident and cocky brother had never looked so nervous in his life.

"Deep breaths, Zeus. Deep breaths," I said.

89

We all shook hands with the priest, some kindly Brit and family friend of the bride, and took up our positions as the music suddenly changed to the wedding march.

The crowd oohed and aahed again as the ladies began processing down the steps. The bridesmaids wore long strapless flowing chiffon dresses that were the same pale plum color of the peonies.

My two girls couldn't have been more beautiful.

Viv looked striking with her hair fashioned in an elaborate updo replete with tiny flowers as she came through the enchanted forest behind Angelina, who was sprinkling rose petals.

Then all eyes were on Emmaline as she came down the steps with her dad. She scrubbed up pretty okay. Her scooped-back princess dress had a tulle skirt with a bodice made of Swarovski crystals. As she glided through the beach fairy forest toward us with her strawberry blond hair and big green eyes behind her birdcage veil, I truly thought Tom was going to pass out.

Then Emmaline's dad handed her over and a look of such sublime happiness passed over my brother's face that I found myself wiping away a tear. I looked out at the ocean behind us and thought about my dad, our lives, life itself.

It actually might have even been more than one tear that rolled down as the violins ceased and the ocean roared and the priest cleared his throat and smiled.

90

We were back up on the lawn in the receiving line awaiting the stream of wedding guests in front of the huge white tent when I received the call.

I had my phone in my pocket, and when it rang, I was going to just leave it, but then I looked up to see Mickey on his, so I said to heck with it.

I took it out and saw that Marvin Heller was calling, so I sort of scooted away to the right and took it.

"Hey, Marvin. Why aren't you here yet? The ceremony just ended. You need to hurry or you're going to miss the reception."

"I'm on my way, Terry, believe me. You have a wife, don't you? Mine takes about ten years to get ready. Anyway, sorry to bother you with the wedding and all, but you really need to hear this."

"Hear what?"

"I just got a call from my boy Stan."

Stan, I knew, was Stanley Lubbock, Marvin's old buddy on the Southampton PD who was a forensics tech.

After I had recovered the stolen evidence from Tapley, I dropped it off at Marvin's house. He immediately sent it down to his buddy Stan to make a backup copy of everything on the down low.

We needed to be safe, I knew, just in case Hailey in her new trial managed to bribe some other bad cop to make it disappear again. Once bitten, twice shy.

"What's up?"

"Hope you're sitting down, my friend," Marvin said. "You got a hit."

"What?"

"You got a hit on the bullets. Stan put what he had into NIBIN."

NIBIN was the National Integrated Ballistic Information Network. It was like a fingerprint database for forensic evidence.

I hadn't even thought of that. I had just wanted a backup forensic file.

"It came back as a hit, and not just a hit as in a match either," Marvin said.

"Slow down. Walk me through it. What are you saying?"

"Remember the wadcutter bullets they found in Noah Sutton's head in July of 1999? Well, another couple of wadcutter bullets were fired from the same exact gun and found in the head of another victim, Julie Rainard, in May of 1999 down in Maryland."

What?

"Another victim? From the same gun?"

"Yes. Two bullets, as well."

"What the hell does that mean? Disenzo whacked someone else with the same gun?"

"I don't know. Because here's where it gets interesting. Are you ready? The victim was a twenty-eight-year-old biotech researcher who worked for a little company called…"

"Shit, no! No!" I said. "Cold Springs Chemical!"

"Shit, yes! Yes!" Marvin said. "Cold Springs Chemical got all these government contracts, and they say Rainard was a whistleblower. Nothing was stolen, and the neighborhood where she got shot while jogging had literally zero crime. People say it seems like it was a hit."

Cold Springs Chemical, I thought.

What had Father Holm said?

I thought it had to do with the family company.

"The same gun?"

"Yep. Same exact gun."

I stood there in shock, my head swimming.

So this meant what? Hailey actually didn't do it? She hired a contract killer? Or the family hired a killer because of the company stuff? But what about Hailey's hoodie? Had I somehow gotten it all wrong? After all this?

"Where are you now, Marvin?"

"Home, getting ready, like I said. What do you want me to do?"

"Hey, Terry, ixnay on the phone already," Finn said. "Here come the guests."

"I'll call you back," I said. "Or talk to you when you get here. I need to think this through."

91

We were on the sundeck steps finishing up the picture-taking when my cell jingled.

I thought it was Marvin again, so I snuck it out for a peek. It was a text message from a number I didn't recognize.

Been following you around. Feel like I actually know you.

I froze.
Who is this? I texted.

Bedroom terrace. Cute kid.

My blood went cold. I glanced up.

I felt numb, faint.

Between the balustrades, there was a long thin cylindrical object pointing down at the gathering.

It was the suppressor at the end of a rifle. A gloved hand rose above it and gave a little wave.

I was about to ask what he wanted me to do when he texted again.

Walk to the front of the house. Contact no one or I'll kill your family.

"Finn," I said, my head swimming. "I'm going to be sick."

"Shut up, Terry. Stop joking."

"I'm not kidding. Cover for me," I said, running down the stairs across the lawn toward the front of the house.

My phone rang the second I was through the porte cochere. I picked it up.

"Now walk out up to the gate," said a man's voice.

"I'm at the end of the driveway."

"Go left."

I did. I walked south down Meadow Lane.

"Do you see all the party buses parked along the road there?"

"Yes."

"Go to the third one on the left. That's the one. The door's open. Get on it."

I walked over to the bus and pushed the half-open door and got on.

It seemed to be empty.

What the hell was this? I thought. *Bad* was the only conclusion my reeling mind could come up with.

Incredibly, incredibly, incredibly bad.

"I'm here."

"Okay. Go to the fridge."

"Yep."

"Inside of it is a red Solo cup."

I opened the fridge. The red cup had a Post-it note on it.

DRINK ME

"Just like *Alice in Wonderland*, right, Terry? And guess who the confused little girl gets to be?"

I lifted it out. It smelled like beer but also slightly medicinal. "What is it?"

"Don't worry. It won't kill you, Terry, but it will knock you out. You want your family safe, you knock yourself out. Now, bottoms up."

I held the cup in my hand, my heart beating in my ears like a grand finale symphony drum. I didn't know what I should do. Go back and somehow try to get the drop on this son of a bitch? Or was there more than one? Would he kill my family anyway?

God help me, I prayed. *I don't know what to do.*

If he wanted us dead, he would have killed us, I finally decided. He wanted me alive. For now at least. I'd do anything to get him away from my family.

"I can see you on candid camera, dumbass, so don't try anything. Now drink it!" he yelled.

I lifted the cup and drank it. It tasted awful.

"Have a seat," he said. "I'll be there directly."

The drug in the drink didn't work quickly. It worked fricking immediately. I could feel a head rush along with a tired feeling. A warm flush came over my face. In a minute, I felt completely doped.

I suddenly felt nauseous as something rushed over me like a tide of black water and I went out.

92

When I came to, I wasn't on the floor anymore. I was sitting back in something. Sort of reclined back. I would have guessed it was a La–Z-Boy except it was almost painfully hard backed.

"You were pretty slick, Terry," said a voice. There was a little bit of a twang in it. Texas maybe, I thought.

I opened my eyes with effort.

I was still in the bus and there was some superfit-looking fifty-ish guy sitting across from me. I saw he was wearing the same gray uniform as the rest of the caterers. When he took off his chef's skullcap, he had a bristled steel-colored high and tight flattop. His muscular face looked like it was doing a push-up when he smiled. He could have been a drill sergeant.

Glancing outside the window behind him, I could tell we weren't parked on Meadow Lane anymore. Instead of a beach road, there was a thick forest beyond the bus's windshield.

When I finally looked down at myself, I saw I was bound at my ankles and wrists in a seat bolted to a rolling triwheeled hand truck. The chair was tilted back forty-five degrees, and there was a strap above my eyes pulled tight so that I couldn't even turn my head left or right. I felt like an upended turtle.

The device was a safety restraint chair, I realized. I knew about them because they were what the Philly prison system used to transport violent prisoners.

Dear God, help me, I thought, trying to move and failing completely.

"You were pretty slick, losing me those few times," the drill sergeant guy said in his Texas twang.

He was chewing gum, and he paused for a second as he blew out a bubble.

"I admire someone who can play the game, even an amateur like you. And tuning up Tapley. I mean, I've seen some cauliflower ears before, but dang! You shattered his eardrum. You deafened that big old boy. Must have some pop in that right hand. Or maybe you hit him with an aluminum baseball bat? Either way shows you're serious about going about your business. I admire that. I tip my hat."

"You know where Tapley is?" I said, my mouth dry.

"Oh, yeah," he said, nodding as he continued to chew his gum. "Same place you're going if you don't start playing ball, son. But again, I admire your spirit. They said you'd take the money, but I knew better. I know a man on a mission when I see one. That's what really separates the men from the boys in the end. These rich folks don't get that. But that's all it is. To go all in. Do or die. Every time. So few of us old-schoolers left, son. You and me, we're a dying breed."

I took in his easy physical confidence, his muscular hands. He wasn't the tallest guy in the world, but he was wide and thickly muscled, and radiated health and vitality. He really did look like a killer, like a Marine. A finely tuned natural-born killer who, when he wasn't running PT, was sharpening knives and oiling machine guns.

A professional, I thought, watching him smile as he blew another bubble.

The best money could buy.

"Can I ask you a question?" I said.

"Fire away."

"How did you take out my father?" I said. "What did you do? Scuba dive over? Crack him over the head? Grab him while his back was turned? Hold him under until his lungs burst?"

"You think I killed your old man?" he said, squinting.

Then he leaned in over me until we were almost nose to nose. I could smell the gum in his mouth, see the flecks of amber in his crazy green eyes.

"You better believe I killed him," he said, smiling. "I motored over to a couple of hundred feet astern of his rusty shit bucket and shot him in his thick Irish skull with a plastic baton round. You know, the kind they use to disperse crowds?"

I swallowed as a tear ran down along my nose.

"Hell of a shot, too. He went over like a duck in a carnival gallery right into the drink. Truly one for the scrapbook. Nothing like a baton round to the noggin to make it look like a slip-and-fall."

He giggled.

"Just business, you know. Nothing personal. Now you know, you stupid little asshole. Happy? Or maybe not so much."

More tears poured down my face silently. I balled my fists, put the sadness somewhere else, and brought my simmering rage right back.

"How about that innocent kid, Julian Sutton's friend? Philip. You toss him off that building?"

"Oh, him," the killer said, grinning some more. "Oh, yeah. He was my first toss-off. You never forget your first, you know? What's funny, when he hit the concrete, I thought I'd hear like a splat, right? Nope. It didn't sound like a person at all. Much louder. And crunchier. You know what young Phil sounded like when he landed? He sounded like a TV set somebody dropped out of a high-rise window. Who knew?"

His phone began to buzz. He chewed his gum as he looked at the message. Then he stood and came around behind me and unlocked the chair's wheels and rolled me toward the rear of the bus.

"Is my family okay?" I said as he locked down the wheels again.

"Shhh. You just wait right here," he said. "I know you're a real unsolved mystery fan, so you're going to like what's coming up next."

The second he closed the bus door behind him, I felt the panic well up. The airtight restraints didn't budge a millimeter as I ripped at them as hard as I could. I tried rattling and rocking at the metal chair to knock it over, but it was impossible. It wouldn't budge.

I was bathed in sweat, my arms and stomach muscles aching from still trying to free myself from the hellish steel chair five minutes later when the door opened.

My eyes flashed about as wide as they could go when I saw who it was.

What in the hell? I thought.

It was over somehow? The guy had left? I was saved?

93

"Courtney?"

"Hi, Terry," Courtney Frazier said, closing the door behind her. "It's not what you think," she said quietly. "I'm not the cavalry."

She walked over and sat across from me. She was wearing a sky blue athletic top with a short white sporty skirt.

Golf clothes? I thought.

She looked very prim and proper all of a sudden. Stuck up, in fact.

What in the hell was this?

"I guess there's a few things you need to know now, Terry," she said.

I looked closely at her. At her anchor babe white-blond hair.

At her pretty eyes that were as blue as her top. I noticed a watch I hadn't seen her wear before. It was a lady's Cartier in stainless steel, shiny and bright against her tanned wrist.

Then I started laughing. I must have still been doped up a little because it wasn't playacting for effect or something. I really cracked up.

"Yeah, I know. It's a surprise," she said.

"I don't…" I said, still giggling. "I don't know what to say. You're in on this?"

"Stay focused, Terry," she said quietly. "Your family's life depends on it."

That took the humor out of it. I blinked hard twice, trying to think clearly, get my emotions in check.

She tented her fingers in her lap.

"It was over, Terry. I had this so taken care of. But you had to do it, didn't you? You did the one thing we were all trying to avoid."

"What did I do?"

She glanced at her expensive watch, started playing with its diamond bezel nervously.

"You put those damn bullets into the NIBIN system," she said. "Now look where you're sitting. Now look what has to happen."

"Enough with the bullshit! What the hell is all this?" I yelled.

Courtney sat up straighter and looked me in the eyes.

"Hailey Sutton had nothing to do with Noah's death," she said.

"Bullshit. Of course she did," I said.

"She was set up, Terry. It was all a setup."

"Oh, maybe she didn't pull the trigger," I said. "But she did it. With Disenzo. You interviewed Ross yourself."

"No, Terry. Ross works with us. His confession was a setup, as well. He'll say whatever he's paid to say. That was a school play just for your benefit."

I remembered the interview room. Watching Courtney with Ross through the one-way mirror.

I closed my eyes.

"No," I said.

"Oh, yes, Terry. When that asshole Father Holm put you on to Cold Springs Chemical, we had to do something to throw you off the scent. That's why we set up the fake arrest of Ross. He was ready to falsely testify, too. We were going to finally resolve the whole thing by finishing the frame job on Hailey that was arranged all those years ago. It was working like clockwork, especially after you found and then gave us the bloody hoodie.

"But you screwed it up at the very last second, didn't you, Terry? You were going to get what you wanted. We were going to get what we wanted. It was a win-win. Then you had to go and snatch defeat from the jaws of victory right at the buzzer."

"So, you're saying what?" I said.

"Henry Sutton killed his brother Noah. Not Hailey. It was Henry all along."

I let that sink in.

"Henry? So, Henry framed Hailey?"

"Yes. Smart, huh?" Courtney said. "Deflecting suspicion away from himself like that. But as it turns out, her lawyer was actually *his* lawyer. So, they could both manipulate the shit out of her. He was only pretending to support her, Terry. He was staying in her six so he could get the knife in deeper."

"But why?" I said. "Because of the company? The fight for the controlling shares?"

"No. It was just a grudge. A deep old family grudge. A Cain and Abel sort of thing. Some families aren't as nice as yours, Terry."

What?

"In his sophomore year of college at Columbia University, Henry brought home a girlfriend, the love of his life, a vivacious and very beautiful young woman he'd met in New York. They'd

327

been living together for a month in his apartment. Her name was Melissa, and she was an aspiring actress, a lively dark-haired beauty from small-town Texas. Everybody was shocked because Henry was so quiet, but the two seemed made for each other.

"Noah reacted to this new addition to the family by seducing her. Though he had slept with half the actresses in Hollywood and could have had pretty much any woman he wanted, on a cruel whim he decided to set his sights on Henry's first love. While Henry was abroad at Oxford, Noah worked on Melissa all semester, had flowers delivered to her classes.

"Henry found out about the affair when he got back. He said he forgave her, and he even tried to win her back for a while. But it was over. Melissa moved back to Texas. Noah had ruined Henry's life just for the hell of it."

I sighed as I recalled my recent PhD-level studies in Sutton family history. I didn't know much about Noah Sutton's brother Henry. There wasn't even a separate folder for him in Xavier Kelsey's files.

"But that's when they were kids in college. Noah was thirty-six when he was murdered," I said, confused.

"Henry never said a word after Noah demolished his only real chance at a happy life. Took it amazingly well. But he was planning. Planning and waiting until the precise moment when Noah found some real and lasting happiness. And it looked like Noah really was happy when he found Hailey. Then when Henry heard Brooke was working to get Noah's shares, he couldn't risk Noah changing his will. He knew it was go time."

"Go time?"

"Henry knew that upon Noah's death, his shares would go to Hailey. If Hailey were convicted, the shares would go to the secondary beneficiary. Only Henry knew who that was."

"Who?" I said.

"The three siblings each got an equal cut of Noah's shares."

"Coup attempt over," I said. "Henry and Nelson would retain

control of the company. I see. Revenge and keeping power. So Henry blew Noah away?"

"Of course not," Courtney said, rolling her eyes. "These are very wealthy people, Terry. They can afford to leave the dirty work to experts."

"I see. That charming guy I just met? That scumbag outside. He did it," I said.

"That he did, Terry. He works for Cold Springs Chemical. He's been the Sutton family fixer for years. But with Noah, he made one mistake. The gun he used had been used on another Sutton matter in Maryland."

"The whistleblowing researcher."

She nodded.

"Should have tossed the gun, huh? Or used a different one," I said.

"In retrospect, of course. It was definitely a screwup. But back then, different municipalities didn't share ballistic reports, so the NIBIN system wasn't a concern to link things up."

"So the family panicked when they heard I was poking into things, fearing that I would somehow find the bullets and have them cross-referenced?"

"Bingo. Cold Springs Chemical is now one of the largest chemical companies in the world. This matter cannot be brought to light. Not even close. There's just way too much money and power involved. It's always about the money, Terry. And money is power, of course."

94

"But what about the other evidence?" I said. "The gun in Hailey's bedroom that the maid saw? And Noah's blood splatter on the hoodie?"

"The gun was briefly planted in the house with the intent for the maid to see it," Courtney said. "And the hoodie was stolen from her closet. The hit man had the hoodie draped on his chest when he did the shooting to catch the splatter. Then it was planted in the neighbor's garbage."

"So, Henry wasn't just content to kill his brother? He wanted Hailey in prison for it, too?" I said.

"Yes. Think of the perfection of it. Framing Hailey for it not only was the cherry on top of paying Noah back, it totally diverted all suspicion off himself at the same time."

"But wait. If he wanted Hailey framed, then why have Tapley steal the evidence? The bullets and the hoodie?"

She stared at me.

"Pay attention, Terry. Henry Sutton had nothing to do with that. That was a twist no one saw coming. No one had any idea what happened to the evidence until you uncovered that it was Tapley."

"Tapley stole the evidence on his own?"

Courtney nodded.

"Turns out he did it for DA Wheaton, his buddy. Wheaton was an up-and-comer in the Suffolk County DA's office at the time of the Sutton trial. He would have been a shoo-in to take the top slot when it came up except there was a better lawyer there. Much better. Sean Rourke."

My eyes went wide.

"Your father was a bit of a drunk, but he was a nice-looking one. Telegenic. Better looking than that gnomish-looking weasel Wheaton, that's for damn sure.

"And he was about to win one of the highest-profile cases of all time. He was on his way to the bigs. That's why Wheaton had Tapley steal the evidence in order to throw a monkey wrench into the works to make your father look like a loser. Which happened. In spades. Losing that case obliterated him."

What complete pieces of shit, I thought. That made sense. That actually made sense.

My father was double-teamed. Sabotaged by his own coworkers, and then murdered by Henry Sutton once he found out that Philip Oster had seen the hit man.

"Not just him," I finally said.

"But then you came along and stole Tapley's ace in the hole," Courtney said. "What the hell did you hit him with, anyway? A lead pipe? You really crushed his ear."

"Wait, Courtney. How the hell do you know all this? About why Tapley did it and about how I took the evidence from him."

"From the horse's mouth."

"From Tapley?" I said. "He told you? You've been talking to Tapley? You know where he is, then? Where is he?"

"Terry," she said, squeezing my wrist. "Don't worry about Tapley. You have far more important things to think about right now."

I couldn't believe it. The whole time I'd been trying to blame Hailey, but I was wrong.

I looked over at Courtney.

There were multiple scumbags on the periphery, multiple factions, all working their own angles.

"You offed Tapley, huh. How about Hailey? Is she still breathing? You kill her, too? Or is she next on the hit list? How many people dead is this worth?"

"Exactly how many it takes," Courtney said. "Don't you get it? Hailey doesn't matter. The only thing that matters now if you want to save your family is you telling us everything there is to tell. This guy doesn't mess around. He will peel you apart, Terry. Real slow. He likes burning people. With chemicals and other weird experimental stuff. Cold Springs' storehouses are at his disposal. That's his real kick. His experiments. Gets off on it. He's sicker than you can even imagine. Just tell everything you know now, and it'll be quick, okay? Even painless. I promise."

She stood then and turned for the door.

"How come you're mixed up in this, Courtney?" I said. "Did Henry Sutton get his claws into you while you were investigating the Suffolk County DA's office? How are you involved?"

"Grow up, would you, you naive asshole," she said, suddenly angry. "How do you think I got involved? Where in any part of the Hamptons that matters does the Family Sutton *not* hold sway? Where did I get the five million for my restaurant, huh? Lifeguarding? My government paycheck?

"Henry Sutton's newest wife was my roommate at Georgetown is how. You know, instead of pissing off people who have literally unlimited amounts of money, you should try doing favors for them instead. It can actually be very rewarding."

"Take off these restraints, Courtney," I said. "You can still get out of this if you cut a deal. It's not too late."

Now it was her turn to crack up.

"I hate to burst your bubble, Terry, but that's not going to happen. You lost again. This time in *completely* straight sets."

"Last chance, Courtney," I said.

But she didn't take it.

Instead, she gave me a nice long look at her perfectly tanned country club legs as she turned and left, closing the door behind her.

95

I sat there. After another minute or two, I heard the sound of Courtney's car as she drove away.

Staring up at the bus ceiling, I suddenly realized if they had been tapping my phone, Marvin was probably in trouble now, too. As well as the forensics cop who had run the NIBIN search.

Was that where we were? I thought as I looked out the window again. Near the Southampton police department to get at the forensics clerk?

It was about five long minutes later into my terrified pondering when there was a sound outside. A crackling sound, tires on gravel.

Was it Courtney coming back? I thought.

When the door flew open a second later, the Texas killer had a roll of already opened duct tape in his muscular hands.

"We have a visitor," the killer said as he taped me up none too gently around my head and mouth. "You say a word, I'll kill them. Then I'll come back here and slit you open from your nuts to your chin. Got it? Then I'll go find your family and we'll really have some fun."

I listened very carefully after he left. I heard the bus door open. Then I heard the approaching car stop right behind the bus. After twenty seconds, there was a knock at the front.

"Open up! Southampton police! Who's in here?"

Yes! The real cops! I thought.

But wait. Where was the killer? I wondered as the sound of gunfire suddenly ripped out.

There was a cymbal crash explosion of shattered glass as the bus's front windshield was blown in. When I heard the pocking sounds of bullets punching through the bus's aluminum, I spasmed in my chair trying to duck, but it was useless.

It wasn't just any kind of gun either. I wasn't exactly a gun expert, but outside the bus from somewhere close came what sounded like the long earsplitting snap, crackle, and pop of a machine gun on automatic.

I closed my eyes, waiting to get hit, as some more return shots were fired from the back of the bus. Then all the firing suddenly stopped.

"10-13! Flanders Road! Officer under fire! Under fire!" I heard a cop yell.

Flanders Road was in the Bays near the police precinct, I knew.

"Terry! Terry! Are you in here?" the cop yelled a moment later.

"Bugh hugh bugh hugh!" I yelled.

The cop who burst in was a big pale white guy with a shaved bald head and a uniform name tag that said *Kelly*.

He undid the hand restraints and started to peel the tape off, then took out a knife and got the blade in between my cheek and the tape and sliced it off instead.

"Where'd he go? The shooter?" was the first thing I said.

"Into the woods."

"Toward the precinct?"

"Yes," Officer Kelly said. "I called it in. We'll catch this son of a bitch. We've been looking for you, Terry."

"How?"

"Oscar Womack, the groundskeeper at the house," Officer Kelly said as he undid my ankle restraints. "He saw you get on the bus."

Good old Oscar, I thought as I leapt up and ran.

"Wait up! What the hell are you doing?" Officer Kelly said as I ran off the bus full speed into the woods.

96

I quickly thought about the situation as I ran through the pines.

If the guy was a pro, he'd know the terrain, I thought.

Where would I head if I needed transport out of here?

I immediately changed my direction, and five or six hot and sweaty minutes later, I came out of the tree line into the gravel lot of the nearby Southampton town dump.

Just in time to see a grumbling dump truck crash out through its gate.

"Dammit!" I yelled as I booked across the lot.

A shocked-looking town worker with a beer gut and a goatee stood gaping in the doorway of a trailer by the shattered fence.

"Police! I need a car!" I said.

"That one!" the man said, pointing at a small beat-up town pickup truck to my left. "Just turn the ignition. It doesn't need a key."

The dump truck was about a mile and a quarter down old Riverhead Road when I caught up to it. It was hauling, doing about seventy on the narrow curving road. Suburban houses began to appear on the side of the streets as we both went through a stop sign without even a tap on the brakes.

"Shit!" I yelled as I watched the killer clip an old-age home short bus as it made a right through a gas station onto Canoe Place. I screeched in through the lot of the gas station right after it, thanking God he hadn't driven through one of the pumps.

It was about a quarter mile down Canoe Road when he bailed. There was a puff of dust as he swayed the truck off the road left into the opposite lane and then into the grass of Mariners Cove, a little marina on the bay. Then there was a thunderous explosion of crunching metal as the fishtailing dump truck came down an embankment and took out a whole row of cars in the parking lot.

I was just in time to see the killer jumping out of the smoking truck as I came roaring in behind him. As I screeched to a stop and leapt out, I watched him shove a guy up on the marina's dock and then jump into a little flat fishing boat.

He'd pushed the boat off the dock and was still pulling at the outboard's rip cord when I leapt from the dock and landed on top of him hard and we both went into the bay.

As we tangled together under the water, I felt him trying to get an elbow around my neck in a choke hold. But as I spasmed, I slipped his grip and caught him good in his throat with an elbow.

As I pushed away from him, I realized that the water we were in was only about six feet deep. We circled like boxers both staring at each other as we started hopping up and down like we were playing Marco Polo when the water is up to your chin.

The approaching sound of a glorious police siren got louder and louder.

"Hear that?" I said. "You're toast, asshole. Texas toast."

I watched him turn and start bobbing up and down, trying to grab at the rim of the fishing boat to pull himself up. But it was just a bit too high.

"Just missed it that time," I taunted him.

He screamed and then came swimming for me. He might have been great at shooting people or throwing them off buildings, but I could see right away he sucked at swimming. I swam back easily farther into the bay. There was no way he was going to catch me. I used to be a lifeguard, after all.

"You can do better than that, Hoss. You're not even trying," I taunted him again.

"What? You don't want to fight me? You afraid, you little coward?" he said, huffing and puffing. "Even after I killed your daddy, you're still afraid, aren't you? I killed your daddy and, oh, it was sooo—"

Before I knew what I was doing, I swam forward and got him around the neck with my own elbow. I screamed as I locked in and pulled back with everything I had.

He reached back at me with his powerful arms but I had him. I knew I had him, and he made a high crazy shriek as I pinched closed his thick windpipe.

"Terry, stop! No! Let go! Get away from him! I got him!" a voice suddenly screamed from the marina dock.

Through my sweating eyes, I saw it was my new good friend Officer Kelly. He had his Glock pointed right at us.

That's when I let up.

But it was the wrong move.

Gun or no gun, the Texas commando seemed to gain a new life as he swung around and cracked me in the mouth with a hard left. Rearing back in the water with my lip bleeding, I suddenly saw in his other hand he had a nasty curved little knife that he had produced from somewhere.

I immediately lunged left as loud pops started coming out of

Officer Kelly's service Glock. I remember seeing spouts from the bullet strikes in the water and then watching as the curved knife went flying.

Then it was just me bobbing up and down while my father's killer rolled back in the salty water bleeding and howling like he was on fire.

EPILOGUE

LAID TO REST

97

Six months had passed since my brother's extremely unforgettable-in-every-way beach wedding. I put on my clicker and got off the Montauk Highway.

But not in Southampton.

I was in Riverhead, and I winced as I suddenly remembered everything that had happened since then.

The worst part, by far, came in the immediate aftermath of everything back at the beach house when I had to tell my family about how Dad was murdered. Telling my mother was especially brutal. It was only the second time I had seen her cry in my life, with my father's burial being the first.

But maybe we'd finally get some closure now, I thought a

few minutes later as I pulled into a parking lot and stared at the ugly gray concrete face of the Cromarty Courthouse for hopefully the last time in my life.

It started to snow very lightly as I got out of the car. I was on my own today since Viv was home with Angelina and the newest Rourke, Sean II.

But it actually wasn't all tears, was it? I thought as I pictured my cute leprechaun of a son.

I smiled as I remembered all the videos of little Seany Viv constantly sent to my mom. The last one had Angelina holding him while "petting" our dog with a spatula, of all things. Even so, by the number of hearts and smiley face emojis Rosemarie constantly sent back, maybe her spirits were getting picked up a little after all.

I crossed the street and spotted the doughnut cart near the courthouse entrance, still there just like last time, and I got a coffee and another chocolate doughnut.

As I stood there enjoying my breakfast of champions, I noticed that there were some reporters standing around. They were mostly locals, though, no national news armada this time.

Which only made sense, I thought as I chewed, when you realized that probably a lot of money was being paid to *not* cover this particular trial.

There was no Xavier Kelsey attending this go-around, which I found bittersweet. Though he was definitely here in spirit, as none of this would have ever seen the light of day without his extensive research, which had inspired me to get to the bottom of all of it.

But, in a way, that's why I was here. After all the media dust had settled, I had contacted Kelsey's publisher and let them in on what had happened and how the famous author had played into everything.

After some negotiations, they had offered a book contract to me to complete the story of the Sutton Slay, and I had accepted.

Which was why I had come up from Philly this morning.

To write the final chapter.

I was still standing there in the courthouse plaza five minutes later licking the chocolate off the waxed paper when my brother Tom arrived behind me with Marvin Heller.

"Hey, you. Missed a spot of chocolate there, Sergeant Sloppy," my big brother said, suddenly licking his thumb and roughly scraping at my cheek with it.

I laughed as I danced back away from him. Then I shuffled left and sucker punched him in his arm hard enough to make him wince.

"Terry, what the hell? Ow!" Tom cried. "Marvin, you see this? Police brutality. And, look, he spilled coffee on my damned suit, too."

"Glad you made it, Terry," Marvin said, ignoring the both of us idiots and shaking my hand like an actual civilized person. "All the way from Philly, wow. How long did it take you?"

"Three and a half hours," I said. "This weather wasn't helping. Whoever heard of snow at the beach? It's unnatural."

"Yeah, *unnatural* is the word of the day," my brother said, blowing into his cupped hands.

"It's still on, right? The big showdown?" I said as we started across the plaza.

"It's on all right," Marvin said. "You showed up at the right time, Terry. There's going to be some fireworks today."

The local media we walked past took some pictures of us this time for a switch. In the camera flash, I noticed that my big brother looked very tense as we walked toward the front door.

"You all right, Tom?" I said, leaning over to him. "You don't have to do this if you don't want to. I can cover for you today. You've been coming for the last two weeks."

"You kidding me?" Tom said, adjusting his silk tie as a court officer ushered us all inside. "I wouldn't miss today for all the world."

98

The hall outside the courtroom on three was crowded as hell, just like last time. As was the inside of it. So much so that we weren't able to see the occupants of the defendant's table as we headed toward our seats near the front.

"Come to order," one of the court officers suddenly called out as the judge—some stringy-looking fiftyish white woman wearing glasses—came in wearing her black robe.

As everybody sat, I finally looked to my right at the defendant's table and saw him.

There he was sitting beside my old pal Byron Seager, Esquire.

Henry Sutton in the flesh.

The billionaire was facing two counts of murder in the first degree this cold January morning. One for ordering the murder of his brother Noah, and one for ordering the murder of my dad.

He was facing another first-degree murder charge in Massachusetts for ordering the killing of Philip Oster as well, but New York State wanted first dibs.

New York State no longer had a death penalty, but Henry Sutton was looking down the barrel at life without parole at the very least.

But even facing judgment, he still looked prissy, I saw. With the frosting of blond still in his hair, he appeared youthful and good-looking and smooth. He was also wearing a just-so silk cardigan that gave him an almost prep school boyish look.

Watching him, I also noticed something else. There were no other Suttons here this time. He was getting exactly zero support on that end. The *Post* said the others in the Sutton family weren't even in the country. They had all fled to the Maldives for a British yacht race and weren't expected back until all of this latest family slime was resolved.

I shook my head. It was hard to believe that the elegant man-child had his own brother murdered as well as my father.

But hopefully not that hard, I thought as I looked over at the jury. Or the prosecution was going to have its work really cut out for it.

Speaking of which, I thought as I watched the prosecutor, Katrina Volland, stand.

Volland, my old partner from my summer investigation, had become the interim district attorney after Wheaton was indicted in the FBI corruption case that had finally dropped.

Wheaton's trial was starting next week. As was Courtney's.

All dogs really did have their day, I thought.

In court.

"Your Honor, we would like to call Mr. Kyle Wilton," prosecutor Volland said.

I looked over as the door to the left of the bench opened and in came the Texan drill sergeant who had killed my dad and had come a hairsbreadth from killing me.

It turned out that Wilton, Henry Sutton's longtime fixer and hit man, had agreed to turn state's evidence. According to the papers, Wilton had admitted to the assassinations of more than a dozen people over the years for Henry and Cold Springs Chemical, and he was now ready to talk about every single one of them.

Because of this, most people were speculating that Wilton was in the market for an assisted prison house "suicide" due to all the money and power involved.

But yet there he stood, I thought as I watched him head for the defendant's table.

He looked fine. If anything, the former Green Beret sergeant, now wearing an orange prison jumpsuit, looked even more jacked than the last time I saw him.

I was looking down at his big cuffed hands to see where one of Officer Kelly's bullets had blown off two of his fingers when pandemonium suddenly broke loose.

In the form of my crazy brother.

Before Marvin or I could blink, Tom, sitting beside us, suddenly leapt to his feet and ran like a shot down the center aisle and vaulted the rail.

Like myself and the rest of the courtroom, the court officers thought Tom was going for Wilton. But my brother fooled us all again.

At the last second, he juked to the right and then dived across the defendant's table and took Henry Sutton out of his seat in a brutal tackle. On the way past, I happily saw Tom was even able to catch Byron Seager in the ear with one of his highly polished wingtips.

Tom managed to get in two really good loud, popping shots to the billionaire asshole's pretty-boy face before three hulking court officers tore him away. As Henry Sutton stood, I could see the blood dripping out of his pin-straight nose and the huge tomato-red knot under his eye.

"Oh, my," Marvin said, smirking. "Looks like Tom there let his emotions get the best of him."

"No," I said as I stood there still in shock. "I think old Henry got the best of Tom there for sure."

Tom was handcuffed, yet smiling his pirate grin, as they frog-marched him past us out of the courtroom.

As I went to follow him out, my big brother turned and shook his head.

"No. Stay and watch, dummy," Tom said. "One of us has to be here at least."

Things calmed down after a lot of gaveling by the judge.

The annoyed-looking lady was clearing her throat, no doubt about to remind us all that the violent assaulting of defendants was legally impermissible, when Byron Seager stood.

"Your Honor, a sidebar, please."

The entire court went into mumble mode and then dead silence as Volland and Seager and the judge conferred.

Even the killer, Kyle Wilton, was staring at them from where he sat waiting in the witness box.

A moment later, the judge whacked her gavel a couple of good hard cracks as Volland and Seager finally sat.

"Ladies and gentlemen, this court has just been advised that the defendant has changed his plea from not guilty to guilty."

A huge collective outcry shot through the courtroom.

"Sentencing date will be determined by the end of the day. Bailiff, take Mr. Sutton into custody. This court is adjourned."

Everyone looked on as Henry Sutton was handcuffed. Then we all looked at each other in wide-eyed shock for a silent beat.

"What in the world?" Marvin said as we both stood slowly. "Did I just hear what I think I just heard?"

I wrapped Marvin in a hug. It was only after I let him go that I realized I was crying.

"We won," I said as I clapped him on the back. "We did it, Marvin. We finally won."

99

Marvin and I were coming out of the packed elevator with the still stunned crowd into the even more packed and buzzing courthouse lobby when I saw her by the metal detectors on her phone.

"Marvin, I'll meet you outside, okay?" I said.

"You really sure you want to go there, Terry?" Marvin said.

"No, but I'm going to do it anyway."

Hailey Sutton looked up from her phone as I arrived in front of her.

She stared at me wide-eyed.

"Mrs. Sutton," I said. "I just wanted to tell you for myself and for my whole family that I'm sorry. I, like a lot of people—

including my father—thought that you had killed your husband. But we were wrong. I'm really sorry about what you were put through."

"You should be," she said, staring at me angrily. "You know what kind of torture this was for my family?"

"I just wanted to apologize for everything. That's about all I can do. Take care now."

"Your father was a real son of a bitch," Hailey Sutton said, folding her arms as I turned. "He dug up all the dirt he could."

I looked at her and nodded.

"The law isn't pretty sometimes. But he was doing his job. You have to admit, you did look pretty guilty. And you were less than forthcoming."

"I wanted to cooperate, but the lawyers…"

We both watched Byron Seager with his phone glued to his ear as he exited the elevator and the courthouse.

"Yep, the lawyers," I agreed.

Hailey was heading for the door after him when she suddenly turned.

"Actually, wait. I'm sorry, too. I guess. About your father, I mean. We're actually the same, aren't we?"

"The same?"

"That son of a bitch Henry in there took away someone you loved, too."

I was just about to follow her out when a door in the hall opened on my left and my brother Tom came out.

"Hey, dummy, I just heard. We actually did it!" he said, smiling ear to ear as we hugged.

"Terry, Terry, Terry," he said as we walked down the hall. "Man, could that have gone better? That weasel Henry Sutton goes down *after* not one but two Rourke knuckle sandwiches! I mean, someone call Hollywood quick. But wait. Why did he change his plea do you think? Does he have something else up his sleeve?"

"No," I said. "I guess he was waiting until the last second to see if Wilton would make it to the stand alive. Since he did, Henry figured why sit there and be humiliated while they aired all the agonizing embarrassing details about Cold Springs Chemical."

"Took one for the team, huh? What a weird family."

It was snowing more heavily as we hit the cold plaza outside.

"I'm so pumped," Tom said. "I have an idea to celebrate."

"Speaking of weird. Here we go," I said, rolling my eyes.

"No, no. You're going to like this, Terry. What I was thinking is, this summer we should rent out a house on the beach. Maybe in Southampton. You know, some sun and surf. Mingle with the rich and powerful. I'm thinking we do it right. Meadow Lane, of course. One of those big white elephants. Get a taste of the high life, you know? Maybe we'll have a family reunion or something. What could possibly go wrong?"

I opened my mouth to say something.

But then I just started laughing instead as the snow fell around us.

"Yeah," Tom said, starting to laugh himself as we walked across the parking lot. "On second thought, staycation this year is probably a better bet."

★ ★ ★ ★ ★